THE CHALET SCHOOL AND THE ISLAND

gr .9

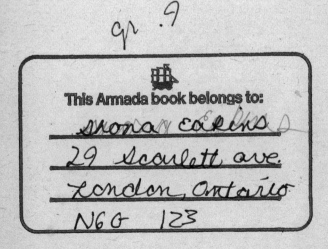

This Armada book belongs to:

Sharon Calrins

29 Scarlett ave.

London, Ontario

N6G 123

THE
CHALET SCHOOL
AND THE ISLAND

ELINOR M. BRENT-DYER

First published in the U.K. in 1950 by
W. & R. Chambers Ltd., London and Edinburgh.
This edition was first published in Armada in 1967 by
Fontana Paperbacks,
14 St. James's Place, London SW1A 1PS.

This impression 1982.

Printed in Great Britain by
Love & Malcomson Ltd., Brighton Road,
Redhill, Surrey.

CHAPTER ONE

A Problem Solved

"JACK, my lamb, what ages you've been! Come along and sit down. I'll ring for tea, and then we can be cosy and talk."

Dr. Jack Maynard grinned as he sat down in the big arm-chair his wife had pulled up for him, and stretched out his legs with a sigh of relief. "That's better! Hurry up with that tea, Jo; I'm ready for it, I can tell you! Where are the kids, by the way?"

"Upstairs in the nursery. I said they might have a tea-party with the dolls' tea-things. Len is to pour out, and they've promised me to be good. I had to do something with them. We can't talk school business with the girls sitting with their ears waggling with curiosity, and I simply can't wait till I know what you've done about Halsden House."

"I can relieve your anxiety on that score, anyhow. It's off! "

"*Off?*—Tea, please, Anna——" Then as Anna, her faithful Tirolean maid, left the room to bring in the tea, Jo Maynard turned to her husband, dismay in her face. "My good man, what *do* you mean? Have they backed out or something?"

"They want to sell. If we'll buy, all well and good. The whole show's ours as soon as we like. If not, we can take our pigs to another market."

"There's something gone wonks with that metaphor, but I can't bother now to work it out. Jack, what on earth are we to do? We've simply *got* to find somewhere for the School, and pronto, too! "

"You're telling me! " her husband returned feelingly. "Jem and Madge and Nell and Hilda and I have been mill-ing round and round till my head feels muzzy. No one wants to spend the money for something we shall have to sell again in six months' or a year's time—at least, I suppose so. Ernest Howell says he doesn't want the place for years, if ever. It's miles too big for him; and if the School ever goes, he rather thinks he'll try to get rid of it in any case. As long as we want it, that's all right. We can have it. So, unless Madge and Jem decide to move the place back to Tirol in a year or two's time, the School will come back here as soon as Plas Howell can be given a clean bill of health."

Jo looked thoughtful. "I say! It's a sticky problem, isn't it? Did Madge say anything about that other place—something or other Castle?"

"No; but Nell Wilson did—any amount! She took the week-end off to go and inspect, and came back dancing mad at having wasted time and petrol over it. There's neither gas nor electricity, and, according to her, the plumbing dates back to the early days of Good Queen Victoria."

"My sainted aunt! How did they ever have the nerve to offer it for a school then?"

"I wouldn't know! Anyhow, it's been turned down, good and plenty."

Anna entered with the tea-tray at that moment, so the pair fell silent while she laid it out on the table before Jo, and then, addressing her mistress, said, "*Bitte meine Frau,* ze children should a walk have after zeir tea, *nicht wahr?*"

Jo nodded. "By all means, Anna. Do you want something from the village?" she added, knowing her handmaiden's ways.

"*Ja, meine Frau.*"

"Okay; you take the family, and go if you like," Jo said easily, as she picked up her teapot. "Have you any money, or do you want some?"

"*Nein, meine Frau.*" Anna bobbed the curtsy that not even the long years in England had taken from her, and withdrew, and Jo filled her husband's cup, handed it to him, and indicated the muffin-dish in the fender.

"Crumpets? And you might pass them to me while you're busy."

They began their tea, and when she had eaten her first

6

crumpet, Jo looked across at her husband and said with a certain wistfulness, "I suppose it's absolutely hopeless at Plas Howell? We simply *must* clear out? Couldn't the School manage in one wing while the men see to the plumbing of the rest?"

Jack grinned at this. "Do use your common sense, Jo! Of course they couldn't! All the drains communicate somewhere or other. And apart from that," he added, as he began on his fourth crumpet, "will you tell me how you propose to squash two hundred girls, a Staff of twenty-seven, *and* all the domestic staff into a third of the space they now occupy?"

"You'll get indigestion if you eat crumpets at that rate," Jo said absently. "No; I suppose it couldn't be done. But what *are* we going to do, then? Halsden House was the only possible place that's turned up so far. Oh, I know we could have bought any one of half a dozen, but we don't want to buy—only rent. Oh, isn't it a *mess*!"

She poured herself out a second cup of tea while she thought things over. The Chalet School, begun by her sister Madge, now Lady Russell, in Tirol when Jo herself was only twelve, had grown and flourished in that lovely part of the world until the Anschluss had driven them away. They had begun again, first in Guernsey, and later in the great mansion Plas Howell, which was three miles away from Howells village, on the outskirts of which her own home now stood. The school had grown once more, and had reached good standing in the educational world. Several Old Girls had returned to teach in one capacity or another. Others, who had married, had sent their own girls to the school they all loved. Her own triplet daughters, now eight years old, were members of the Kindergarten, and looked forward to entering the Junior School next September, when her eldest son Stephen, a sturdy young man of five, would go to the Kindergarten.

Now, it seemed as if all these plans were to be upset. Half-way through the previous term, first one and then another of the members of the school had suffered from a mysterious sore throat accompanied by fever and other unpleasant symptoms. The school was closely connected

7

with the great Sanatorium beyond the Welsh Mountains where many doctors fought against the terrible white man's plague, tuberculosis, so the authorities had taken alarm at once. One cause after another for this throat trouble had been tested, and the result had been that the fiat had gone forth that all the drains must come up for complete overhaul. It would be a lengthy business, and naturally the school could not stay in the mansion while it was being done. Unluckily, it had proved a most difficult problem to know what to do with everyone until, as Jack Maynard said, the place could be given a clean bill of health. No one was anxious to rent a house to a big school for a matter of six or twelve months, though they could have bought easily enough. But then, none of the people concerned had any wish to buy, either. Halsden House had finally seemed like ending their worries, but that morning Lady Russell had sent an S.O.S. to the Heads of the Chalet School and the Maynards. Trouble had cropped up. Jo had been unable to go as Michael, her youngest son, was teething vigorously, and had given them one bad fright by a slight convulsion fit over the last tooth. Her husband had gone, however, and this was the news he had brought back with him.

Jack Maynard passed his cup, and then asked, "How's Michael?"

"Better, I think. I haven't really looked yet, but I rather think the tooth's through at last. At any rate, he howled off and on most of the morning. Then, at two o'clock, he suddenly gave a gulp, stopped his yells and fell asleep. I ran up to look at him just before you came in, and he was sleeping peacefully, and quite cool now, poor little man! He *has* had a time of it, hasn't he?"

"He's been anything but angelic," her husband agreed. "That name of his is a misfit, my dear!"

"I'd like to hear you with a new tooth coming!" she retorted. "I'll bet you'd raise the roof! We'll go up after tea and have a look at him."

"Won't Anna pop him in the pram and take him with the others?"

"No; I told her to leave him alone so long as he was

sleeping. He needs it, poor lamb! He hasn't had a decent night for ages now. There's one mercy: once his teeth are through he always makes up for lost time."

"I rather think someone else needs to make up for lost time, too," he said, with a quick glance at her. Jo was naturally pale, but now she was white with weariness, and there were heavy shadows under the soft black eyes with their long lashes.

She made a face at him. "If it's all right I'll go to bed early to-night, and have a good long night of it. I'll be all right in the morning."

"Well"—he set down his cup, having drained its contents—"I've finished; so if you're ready, we might run up and look at him now."

"Okay! I'm ready. Ring for Anna—or no; don't! She'll be getting the kids ready for their walk. It's a lovely evening," as she glanced out of the french window at the garden glowing in the evening sunshine. "We'll go up and take a peep at Michael, and then I'll clear when we come down."

"That's all right by me. Come along! Oops!" as he took her hands and pulled her out of the chair.

"Mind the table!" Jo shrieked. "Jack, you *are* an ass! You might have overturned the whole thing, and where would my china have been then?"

"On the floor, naturally. Stop yattering, and come along and inspect our youngest! And you might give me a little credit for not wanting to see the crocks in smithereens any more than you do!"

Jo chuckled. "Good enough! Let's go!"

They went upstairs side by side, for the staircase was wide, with shallow steps, easy for small or tired feet, as might be expected in a house as old as Plas Gwyn. Anna had set off already with the children, and Jo stopped at the landing window to wave to them as they danced down the drive. Her husband came to look over her shoulder.

"Nothing much wrong with them now," he said, as the little crowd disappeared through the gate. "Even Charles and Margot are growing as sturdy as the rest."

"Oh, I've never worried much about Charles," Jo said, as she turned to mount the rest of the stairs. "He's more

9

slightly built than the others, but he's remarkably healthy on the whole. I suppose he caught the throat from the girls, for certainly *our* drains are all right."

"Oh yes; passed with a flourish. Now where's this young man of ours?"

They went into the night nursery, a pleasant, very big room, with five little beds set round the walls, and a cot near the door communicating with a small room which belonged to Anna. Jo went across the floor and bent over the cot.

"He's just a little pale," she said in an undertone. "But he's sleeping very sweetly."

"Is he indeed?" the baby's father remarked, as the long lashes quivered, and then lifted, and Michael stared up at his parents with big blue eyes. Suddenly he gave a chuckle, and held out his arms. Jo stooped down and lifted him.

"He's hungry, poor mite! Anna will have left his food ready. Come into the nursery, and he shall have his tea while you tell me the rest of the news." Jo moved across the room, and he followed her.

When she was sitting, busily feeding the boy with cup and spoon, he said, "I don't know what we can do now. None of us wants to buy, of course, but something must be done before Madge and Jem depart——"

"*What?*" Jo dropped her spoon on the floor, and it is safe to say that only instinct made her clutch Michael to keep him from following. "*What* did you say, Jack? Madge and Jem *depart*? Depart *where*, I'd like to know?"

"Oh, the deuce; I didn't mean to tell you till later on."

Jo mechanically picked up the spoon. The next moment it was removed firmly from her hand. "Here! You can't put that thing into the kid's mouth. I'll go and wash it for you."

"All right; but be quick. Michael doesn't like having his meals interrupted. Besides, I simply must——" Jo stopped, for she was talking to the empty air. However, Jack returned a minute later with the clean spoon, just as Michael was putting up his lip, ready to howl. She grabbed the spoon, and stopped the howl. Then she turned to her husband. "Now say that again, please. Sit down, and tell me what you mean by it."

He sat down. "Hey! Don't feed the kid like that! You'll choke him—or give him wind!" he protested, for Jo was shovelling the milky food into her son's mouth. She laughed, and paused, while Michael swallowed his mouthful. Then she went on more quietly:

"I'm sorry. Mamma didn't mean it, old chap; but really, when Papa gives her such horrid shocks! Well, suppose you tell us what all this is in aid of."

Jack had seated himself in Anna's rocking-chair, and he rocked rhythmically backwards and forwards as he told her the very latest news.

"Jem has been elected to go as our representative to that big T.B. conference they're going to hold in Canada, and Madge is going with him. She's taking Josette and Ailie, and leaving the others to us. Marie and André will remain at the Round House, and Rosa will go to help with the kids. She asked me to break the news gently to you, and she's coming to see you to-morrow. Now you know why we simply must get something settled as soon as possible. They sail at the end of April, and will be away about six months. Jem applied for leave of absence for that time. He wants to visit other Sanatoria in Canada and the States, and learn something about their treatment. I don't know if Madge will travel with him. Probably not, as they're taking the two kids. But she's going to stay in Canada as long as he's over there. They're taking Josette because she's been growing rather too quickly and she's never been as strong as they would like since that accident when she was a baby. I said if they liked to leave Ailie with us, we'd have her as well as Sybil and David; but Madge says not. She doesn't want Josette to be on her own, and in any case with our little crowd she thinks you have as much as you can manage. By the way, Primula Mary will be here for the holidays."

"That won't matter. But if Madge is off to Canada, then she can take the McDonald girls with her. Shiena has been agitating to have them for the last year, but there hasn't been anyone to send them with, and I flatly refused to let

11

them go alone. Shiena is very happy out there, but, of course, Andrew is away a good deal, and even with small Morag she gets lonely. There are good schools in Quebec, she says, where Flora and Fauna can go daily. After all, I've had them for four years—they're sixteen next birthday—and Shiena hasn't seen much of them in all that time. So *that's* settled. You'd better ring up and ask Jem to arrange about berths for them."

"If he can get them! Most ships are booked up ages beforehand. Still, he may be lucky on this occasion. You're right about it's being a good idea to send them to Shiena with Madge, though." He paused. Lady Russell had made another suggestion, and he wasn't at all sure how Jo would take it. Meanwhile, she gave Michael the last spoonful, wiped his milky mouth, and sat rocking him gently in her arms. He was still tired, and in two minutes' time the long lashes had dropped, and Jo sat still.

"Is he off?" his father inquired cautiously.

"Nearly, I think. We'll give him a few minutes, and then I'll put him back into his cot." They sat silently, while she watched the small face against her. Then she rose, moving gently, and carried the boy back to his cot. For a minute or two she stood, watching. Master Michael had a nice little trick of rousing up when you put him down, and yelling with the full force of fine lungs. Now, however, he was still worn out with the pain of the troublesome tooth, and he remained fast asleep. Jo heaved a sigh of relief, and then pulled her husband from the room.

"Come away downstairs! He'll be all right now. Besides, I must hear all the ins and outs. This really is news! I thought Madge was stuck to the Round House for keeps. When was she last away for more than a fortnight at a time?"

He laughed as he followed her into the drawing-room, where she began to pile the china on a big lacquer tray that usually stood against the wall. "For turning on a spate of queries, I'd back you against anyone, Jo. The whole idea, so far as I understand it, is that Jem thinks Madge needs a change after all these years. He doesn't want to be parted from her for the time this would mean, and she doesn't want to be parted, either. Then it's a chance to establish Josette's health once for all, and Jem could hardly be responsible for a small girl of eight or nine when he'll be having conferences most of the day. It's a jolly good idea, you know. The clear, dry atmosphere is just what Josette needs."

"Oh, I agree! In one way I'm rather sorry it isn't you that was chosen, for then we could have taken the crowd, and it would have done Margot all the good in the world," Jo replied, as she picked up the muffin dish. She happened to be looking at him as she spoke, and the next moment the dish was in smithereens on the fender as she wailed, "*Jack Maynard!* You *don't* mean the idea is to send Margot with Madge?"

"Just look what you've done! " her husband said, with provoking calm.

"It's *your* fault! Oh, Jack! Don't say you want me to send her all those miles away! She's still poorly and pulled down after that go of throat. How could I let her go away from me just now?"

He stood up and took her hands. "Sit down, Jo, and listen to me."

"I'll sit down and listen; but if you talk till you're black in the face, you won't make me any more ready to agree, and so I warn you! "

However, she sat down, and for nearly an hour, Jack talked and argued. In the end, he was victorious. Jo had agreed that Margot, the youngest of the triplets, and always the most delicate of their children, should go with her Aunt Madge and two young cousins to Canada when they sailed in April. All three little girls had suffered from the septic throat which had run rampant through the school; but Margot had been very ill indeed for a few days, and this trip ought, both her father and uncle thought, to put her right. She would not be lonely, for her cousin Josette was only a year or so older than herself. Jo knew she could trust the child to her sister. But she had never been parted from any of her children before, and it took all Jack's eloquence to coax her to agree.

"Very well," she said at last. "I simply hate the idea; but

if it will do so much for her, I can't be a pig and refuse. She can go. But—but—say as little as you can about it, won't you?"

Her husband clapped her on the back. "You're a plucky girl, Jo. You'll have your reward when the monkey comes home as fit as a fiddle."

"I hope so, I'm sure." Jo spoke ruefully. She had agreed, but she was far from being reconciled to it. In an effort to change the subject, she glanced round. The next moment she had picked up a packet of letters from a bureau, and was holding them out. "Oh, I say! These came after you had gone, and I forgot to give them to you before—what's that?"

Her quick ears had caught murmurs from upstairs which were a warning that Michael was waking up. She dashed out of the room to him, leaving her husband to heave a sigh before he settled down with his letters. She was away some time, for Anna came back with the other children, and she stayed to preside at supper and bed. But when the little flock were all safely bedded down for the night, she delayed only long enough to change her frock before she descended to find Jack at the telephone. "All right!" she heard him yell—he was wildly excited—"I'll wire him pronto, and then let Nell and Hilda know the problem's solved—Yes—Yes—Okay—'Bye!" Then he hung up, and turned to his wife, who was eyeing him severely from the bottom of the stairs. "Jo, the problem is well and truly solved! The Chalet School will remove very shortly——"

"Where?" she interrupted him.

"To an island—in the Irish Sea, off Wales—one of a group—not very large, but big enough. There's a huge old house *with* modern plumbing and electricity all ready for them. The place is St. Briavel's—the island I mean. There are several others, but most of them are only rocks. There's a monastery on one, and a sea-bird sanctuary on another."

"But how on earth have you heard of it?" Jo demanded. "St. Briavel's?—Oh, isn't that where that pal of yours is living?"

"Yes; in the Big House. It's much too big for them—he's married, and there are some kids, but they can't get help.

14

A smaller house has fallen vacant, so he and his family are removing there. I wrote to him last week and told him about our difficulties here. He offers the Big House to us for as long as we want it, and at a really reasonable rent. It's a chance in a thousand, for they're removing as soon as they can, so the school stuff can go whenever they get it packed. The summer term will begin a week or so late, I'm afraid; but at least there'll *be* a summer term!"

Jo was looking very thoughtful. Now she took the letter he handed to her, and going into the drawing-room while he ran upstairs to say good-night to his family, sat down and read it carefully. When he returned at length she was ready for him.

"It does solve the school's problem. You're quite right there! But it's going to mean the children have to be boarders. We can't take the girls away, but I'm not being deprived of all my crew yet. Stephen won't go in September as we'd planned—or not unless the school is back at Plas Howell by then."

"Not a hope, my dear! It'll be all of six months at soonest before they can get those drains into proper shape—more likely to be ten or twelve. They seem to think there's some seepage from farther along, and they'll have to do a hefty bit of digging to find out just where. All right! Stephen can stay and either go to the village school for a year or two, which won't hurt him, or else I'll see if Fair-fields can take him. Only that means weekly boarding, remember."

"He's too little for that. Let him go to the village school. Mrs. Lott has the babies, and she's a nice creature, and they're very happy with her. We'll think of Fairfields in two or three years' time. He's not much more than a baby now."

"Okay! Have it your own way. But I warn you he may pick up all sorts of language."

"I can deal with that! But with Margot in Canada, and the other girls at school on this island, I simply must keep my boys or go crackers!"

"It'll come to that in six or seven years' time, though, Jo."

"I'll have got more used to it by that time," Jo retorted.

"Well, it looks as if there were going to be a good many changes this year; but I'm jolly glad the school's problem has been solved! "

CHAPTER TWO

The School Reaches the Island

THE journey had begun with a buzz of chatter and laughter. As the time went on, however, a good deal of that died, and for the last half-hour there had been silence, broken only by an odd remark. It had been a long bus-ride from Swansea where the majority of the School had assembled, and most of the Juniors and Junior Middles were tired of it now. Many of them had had long train journeys first, for the pupils of the Chalet School came from all over Britain. They, however, had travelled in charge of a mistress through Wales, and would be already at Carnbach, the little country town where they had to meet the ferry which plied back and forth three times daily between the mainland and St. Briavel's.

"There's the sea! " a small voice suddenly exclaimed, and the occupants of the bus turned to look at the gleam of silvery blue far away to which the owner of the voice was pointing.

"Thank goodness! " Gay Lambert, Games Prefect, gave a prodigious yawn. "That should mean that we're not far away now, and I don't mind telling you I'll be thankful to get out and stretch my legs after all these hours of sitting. I feel like a broody hen! "

A chuckle went round the bus.

"It's no worse for you than the rest of us, Gay, my lamb," retorted a tall, bespectacled Senior. "You haven't half the length of leg that *I* have to dispose of! And Janet and Nancy are taller again. I should think they must be tied into knots by this time! "

"I don't know about Janet——" another of their number

16

began, but was interrupted by the Junior who had first spotted the sea.

. "Janet's with us all right; but Aunt Jo told me that the Chesters and the Lucys are being taken straight to the island by their Uncle Nigel—Blossom Willoughby's father, you know—in his yacht."

"Lucky them!" Gay heaved a sigh. "Oh, well, it'll soon be over now. Here we go—and here's the sea," she added, as the bus mounted a rise in the road, and they found themselves running along a carriage-way parallel to golden sands. In front of them lay the houses of a small town, and across the placid bay they could see dark shapes heaving heavy shoulders up against the sunset sky, across which reeled colours more vivid and glorious than any artist could ever squeeze on to his palette.

The girls looked eagerly, and Gay's was not the only sigh of satisfaction that sounded as they gazed at the sight.

"You know," the bespectacled damsel remarked, "I think it'll be rather super to have the sea for a while. The School is decent; but there's no sea anywhere near—no lake, even. To be able to have boating will be a change, and a jolly one."

"*Will* they let us boat, d'you think?" Gay asked thoughtfully.

"Jolly lousy of them if they *don't*!" replied a Senior Middle of about fifteen, thus drawing on her head a sharp rebuke from the dark-haired prefect in charge.

"Annis Lovell! You know perfectly well that's forbidden slang."

"Yes; but we aren't at school yet," Annis retorted impudently. "You can't fine me for slang till we are, Jacynth."

"Oh, *taisez-vous*, idiot!" muttered the girl sitting next her. "You'll only put the prees' backs up, and have them down on you all the time."

Annis subsided, and Jacynth was wise enough to take no further notice of her in public, though she said in an undertone to the people sitting beside her, "Evidently young Annis hasn't come back any more reconciled than she was last term. Keep an eye on her, you people."

"I believe you!" A Senior with an untidy head of hair

17

that had earned for her the nickname of 'Mops' spoke emphatically. "Annis Lovell will bear watching any time of the day—or night either," she added significantly.

"She's a little goat if she starts that game again," Gay said. "You don't think she really will, do you, Kathie?"

Kathie Robertson grinned at her. "I don't *think*—I *know*! Young Annis has come back determined to do something to make them expel her."

"Talk sense! Who's going to *ask* for expulsion? I've known one—and only one—at school here, and I don't want to know another, I can tell you!" This was Ursula Nicholls, the girl with the glasses.

"You don't know Annis! She was holding forth to the rest of her crew in the train from Newcastle, and they were making such a row, I went to squelch them. I heard her say it then." And Kathie quoted: " 'Well, I suppose Aunt Margaret can send me to any school she likes, but she jolly well can't make me *stay* there. My name isn't Annis Jane Lovell if I don't make Bill and the Abbess thankful to get rid of me at any price before this term ends!' "

"What did you do about it?" Gay demanded, wide-eyed.

"Told them to make a little less noise, please, as I could hear every word they said right into my own compartment. I *will* say for her that Annis looked rather dropped on when she heard that. It may be just talk, of course; but I rather think not." Then Kathie changed her tone. "Hello! We seem to be here at last! There's Bill, anyhow!" And she waved her hand to the tall, snowy-headed woman with the startlingly young face who was standing on the little jetty, to which an elderly ferry steamer was moored.

The bus drew up, and Jacynth rose and went to the door to take charge. "Make sure you don't leave anything behind," she said. "Mary-Lou Trelawney, whose umbrella is that in the rack above you?"

"Mine, please." The eleven-year-old addressed climbed up on the seat and rescued the umbrella, looking disgruntled. It had seemed such a good idea to forget all about that wretched umbrella, only Jacynth Hardy always did have eyes like a hawk! Mary-Lou jumped down to follow her chum Clemency Barras, muttering to herself.

Clemency grinned at her. "Silly ass!" she said. "You might have guessed what would happen. Anyhow, Mary-Lou, Auntie Doris paid for the thing, so you jolly well ought to look after it. Don't be such a moke!"

Mary-Lou reddened but said nothing. After all, there was nothing to say.

One by one the girls scrambled out of the bus, cases in hand, and racquets and cricket-bats tucked under the other arm. Gay Lambert and Jacynth Hardy had 'cellos to see to, and Kathie Robertson was carrying a violin case. When the last girl had left the bus, Jacynth left her 'cello in its wooden travelling-case in Gay's charge while she carefully looked round to make sure that nothing had been left behind. Satisfied, she followed the others to where Miss Wilson, one of the Heads of the school, and two or three other mistresses were marshalling the crowd on to the ferry-boat with instructions to find seats and keep quiet.

"All clear, Jacynth?" asked Miss Wilson, with a smile. "Good! Then will you go and help to look after your own bus-load? Here comes the next!" as the second bus swept up to the jetty gate, and another throng of girls began to tumble out.

It took nearly an hour before the last one was aboard and the ferry was well packed by that time.

"It's a good thing it's a calm night," Jacynth observed to Gay, her inseparable friend, as the great gang-plank was slowly wound up, and, with engines throbbing noisily, the clumsy boat began to turn round and steamed slowly across the bay. "We're well loaded."

"If it hadn't been—calm, I mean—I don't suppose we'd have done it in one trip," Gay replied. "Bill takes no chances."

They stopped talking, and gazed over the smooth blue water to the island towards which their course seemed to be set.

"It's on the small side," Jacynth observed presently. "There won't be room for anyone but us there, I should think."

"There's a house there all right. I suppose that's the place

19

for the School," Kathie said. "Oh no; we're changing course, and going north."

"I don't know how you know which way it is!" Gay told her.

"Scots people always do," Jacynth laughed. "I've heard they even talk of a man sitting at the north or south side of his hearth."

Kathie chuckled. "I believe you! I always know," she added, in changed tones. "Don't ask me how I do it, for I can't say. Something inside tells me. Oh! Look, you two! That must be our show!" as a long, green shape slowly appeared from behind the first island. "I can see two or three cottages by the shore. Isn't there a village there?"

Before anyone could answer her, a little bell rang, and they all turned to see Miss Wilson standing on one of the seats, ringing for silence. When she got it, and they were all gazing up at her, she spoke.

"Just a minute, girls! First, I'm glad to see you all again. Welcome back to school. Now I have a few instructions to give you. The Big House, where we shall be for the next term or two, is about a mile from the ferry landing. Naturally, there are no buses, so we shall walk. Miss Linton will be at the landing with her car, and Miss Burnett has Miss Annersley's. They will take your cases, so that you have only your racquets, cricket-bats, and so on to carry. Jacynth and Gay, you must give your 'cellos to them, as well. You can hardly walk a mile lugging those unwieldy things with you. When you leave the ferry-boat, form into line, Gay and Jacynth leading, and march up the road. Miss Linton will go slowly ahead to show you the way—though I think you could scarcely miss it," she added. "One last thing. You may talk, of course, but please talk and laugh quietly. We don't want the people on the island to begin with a bad impression. Now, any questions? No? Very well, then. That will be all." She jumped down, and went to rejoin the little group of mistresses in the stern of the boat, while the girls turned to discuss her remarks.

"Walk? Well, I'm jolly glad to hear that!" Gay said decidedly. "I'm sick of sitting! Oh, look! There are more cottages—and some bigger houses, too. It's quite a place, isn't it?"

"There's the church, at the back of the cottages!" Jacynth pointed. "I suppose we'll go there on Sundays. What will the Catholics do?"

Mary-Lou, standing near, overheard her. "Auntie Jo says there's one island where there's a lot of monks, and one of them will row over on Sundays," she said. "She went with Auntie Madge and Uncle Jack to see the new place. There's a shop in the village where you can buy nearly everything, and she said she thought perhaps Bi—I mean," in some confusion, "Miss Wilson and Miss Annersley—would take parties over to Carnbach sometimes on Saturdays."

"Sounds all right," Gay commented. "All right, infant. Trot off now."

Mary-Lou flushed up, but Clemency gave her no chance to say what she thought of Gay's off-hand manner. She pulled her away to point out yet another island on which a small house could be seen, and in wondering who lived on such a small island, Mary-Lou forgot.

Meanwhile, the ferry was drawing nearer and nearer to the big island, so that they could see another little jetty with some cars standing in the road leading from it, and a little group of people waiting at the landing-stage, who waved as the clumsy vessel slowly wallowed along. The girls waved back eagerly, and Gay suddenly cried that she saw Julie Lucy and Nita Eltringham, two Guernsey girls. Julie was a Middle, and Nita, a Senior, and both very popular people with their own crowd. Then the boat began to turn again, and at last they were moored; the gangway was lowered with much rattling of chains, and the girls, led by Jacynth and Gay, began to file off. They had reached the island at last!

The mistresses waiting by the cars welcomed them with smiles, and, as each couple passed them, took the cases, and set them in the back seats of the two cars. The 'cellos were strapped on to the back of Miss Linton's, and Kathie was invited to hand over her violin, but she refused.

"No, thank you, Miss Linton. It isn't any trouble, really, and you'll be full up to judge by the looks of it."

Pretty Miss Linton laughed. "I could manage your fiddle, Kathie, but if you'd rather carry it, you do. Mary-Lou, give that umbrella to me before anything happens to it. Why wasn't it strapped up with your racquet and bat? Give me your little case, too, Verity-Ann. Oh, you want to take it with you, do you? Very well, then. Doris, I'll have that box."

It took a little time; but at last everything was done, and then, with Miss Linton driving slowly ahead—Miss Burnett had driven off as soon as her car was full—the School formed into a long 'crocodile', and marched off in the direction of the Big House, while the few natives who were down by the jetty goggled at them, and others stared out of windows and doors as they filed past the cottages with their little gardens gay with spring flowers.

The road wound uphill, though not too steeply at first, running between may hedges from which came a heady scent of almond. In the fields were spring cabbages and young beans; then they passed those, and came on sweet pasturage where white-faced red Hereford cattle lifted their heads to stare with soft, startled eyes at the long lines of girls going up the road.

"Isn't the air sweet?" Gay said to Jacynth, sniffing loudly.

Jacynth chuckled. "It's sweet; but that's no reason why you should behave like a bloodhound on the track," she pointed out. "Stop it, Gay! You'll have every one of the kids doing the same. We'd be a charming vision for the natives if we arrived like that! "

Gay broke into giggles. "What a picture! All right; I'll be good." She cast a glance at her friend. "You do keep a stern watch on me, don't you? What with Ruth at home, and you at school, if I don't turn out a model of all I ought to be it'll be a miracle."

"Not it," Jacynth said serenely. "It'll simply mean that you've got so much more than your share of original sin that *no* one could make the slightest impression on you. Hello! We turn in here, evidently. This must be the beginning of the grounds."

Miss Linton's car had swung in at a five-barred gate, and was progressing slowly up a drive that had once been gravelled. Tall holly hedges walled it in on either side, and it was impossible to get a glimpse of what hid behind them, so thick was the holly.

The girls followed the car with eager curiosity to know what their new abode would be like; but they had quite a long walk before they came to a second gate, and found themselves treading on fresh gravel, round a wide bend which—at last! —brought them before the Big House.

It was not in the least like Plas Howell. That had been a Georgian mansion, built in the Palladian style. Jacynth Hardy had once said of it that it looked like a beautiful lady who had grown old gracefully. This was a square-built house, with walls that had been whitewashed from time to time. A climbing rose flung growth of young green across the walls, clambering right up to the slated roof with its serried row of dormer windows. Two steps led up to the deeply recessed door, and on one side were three wide bow windows, while on the other were three sets of french windows. Above them were two rows of flat Georgian windows with small panes, the sashes flung right up, so that the fresh air could sweep through the rooms. The drive ran between two big lawns which had wide flower borders all round, at present full of tulips and wallflowers. To the left, the far side of the lawn was bordered by flowering shrubs, and lilac was already in bloom, with rhododendrons and laburnums giving promise of glories to come. The right-hand lawn seemed to drop to another where two tennis courts, surrounded by more wide flower borders, had already been marked out and netted. Beyond that there seemed to be an orchard, for the rays of the setting sun caught a soft pink mist of blossom. Farther, they could not see. Standing in the open doorway were three people whom everyone wanted to greet—Miss Annersley, Miss Wilson's co-Head; Lady Russell, the founder and owner of the school; and Joey Maynard, who had ceased being a schoolgirl some years before, but for all that was accounted by everyone to be a very vital part of the Chalet School.

The girls broke ranks, and surged up the two steps, to be warded off by a laughing Miss Annersley, who said: "Welcome, everyone, to our new home! I hope you'll all be as happy here as you have been at Plas Howell, and that when we leave, it will be with pleasant memories—and that *you* will leave pleasant memories behind you," she added. "Now, there isn't room just here for the whole bunch of you, so suppose you join up in your forms. Then, beginning with Lower Second B, you can go to your form-rooms, where your form-mistress will tell you which dormitories you are in before she shows you the way—yes, Gay? What is it, dear?"

"Aren't the Kindergarten coming?" Gay asked.

"Yes; but not till the day after to-morrow. We thought it wiser to settle you folk in first. That's why you have come on Tuesday instead of our usual Thursday."

"Oh, I see. I thought it was because we'd had an extra fortnight this Easter."

"No; we shall make that up by breaking up a week later this term, and cutting out our half term week-end. Now will you help to get the girls into their forms, dear? Then we can begin."

In ten minutes' time, they stood on the left-hand lawn in their forms, Lower Second B in front, and Special Sixth at the very back. At a word from Miss Annersley, Miss Carey came and led off the first set, and one by one, they were marched away to their form-rooms where they found many of the familiar furnishings in place. The younger girls were all on the ground floor; but this was not Plas Howell, with its many big sitting-rooms and reception rooms, and two Fifths and all the Sixths were upstairs.

"Well," Gay cried as she looked round the pleasant room which was theirs, "I don't see where the K.G. are to go. I should have said we were chock-a-block with *us*! And what about science and art and dommy sci? Where do we have *those*? Tell me *that*, please, someone! "

Before anyone could reply, the door opened, and a big, pleasant-looking girl of their own age walked in.

"Hello! " she said cheerfully. "I'm Dickie Christy, and they say I'm to be with you. How do you like it?"

"You're—*who*?" Gay demanded, too startled to be polite. "*What* did you say your name was? *Dickie*? But that's a boy's name."

"I know it is," Dickie acknowledged as she perched on a table. "Actually, it's Delicia; but no one ever *calls* me that! I'm always Dickie."

"Come to that, Gay," Kathie put in, "*your* proper name is Gabrielle, but I can see you if we tried to use it! Dickie Christy?" She turned to the newcomer. "Why—this must be your home, then."

"Well, it was," Dickie agreed. "But you know how it is. You can't get help, and there are only five of us, anyhow, Dad, Mother Carey, and my kid sisters and me. Dr. Maynard wrote to tell Dad what a mess your school was in with the drains going bad on you, and how you couldn't get a place for love or money. It so happened that one of the little houses was going just then, so Dad wrote to Dr. Maynard and told him you could come here as we were going to Wistaria House, and you could rent it for as long as you wanted it. So that was that! We moved at the beginning of last week, and your folk came in next day. Dad had fixed it up with Miss Annersley that I was to come and have another year of school—I'm not seventeen, yet."

"But—haven't you been at school?" Gay demanded.

"Oh, of course. But I couldn't very well go when we came here. Before this place came to Dad it belonged to an old cousin, and we lived in Plymouth, and we went to school there, Cherry and I."

"Cherry—one of your sisters?" Ursula asked.

Dickie nodded. "Not a sister, really, I suppose. More a connexion by marriage. Her mother and my father married about six years ago. I was ten, and Cherry was five. Gaynor, who's our youngest, came the next year. She was four last month. But just the same, Cherry and I are sisters, whether we're relations or not! " she finished rather defiantly.

"Isn't she coming, too?" Jacynth asked. "What a pretty name she has! "

"She's a jolly pretty kid, too. No; Cherry's not coming," Dickie replied curtly, and they were silent for a minute or two.

25

Kathie was the first to speak. "Why isn't she coming?" she asked. "She's not—shy, or anything is she? Our kids are imps, but they're quite a decent crowd. Let's see; she'll be eleven now, isn't she? Mary-Lou would look after her. She's a demon, is our Mary-Lou, but she's quite a nice little soul, for all that."

Dickie was silent for a minute or two. "I'd better explain," she said slowly, at last. "Cherry's been ill, poor kid —I.P." Then, as the girls stared, "Infantile paralysis. It's left her very lame. The doctors say she ought to be all right in time, for it wasn't the worst kind of attack and she has responded very well to treatment. But—it's made a change in her. She used to be awfully friendly—just like a puppy, you know. Since then, she's been shy and—queer. Hates meeting strangers, and runs and hides. Dad and Mother Carey wanted her to come with me, of course; but she got so upset at the bare idea that they gave it up." She paused for a moment before she went on, "Look here! You'll have to know! Cherry just hates you being here. She hates having to go back to a little house when we've lived in a big one—though she hasn't been here nearly so long as Gaynor and I have. She was ten months in hospital, poor kid! If you see her, don't try to make friends, for I know she jolly well *won't*! Oh, I know it's idiotic and all that, but the doctor says it's part of the illness. It does change people a bit sometimes. He thinks that as the lameness gets better she'll come all right again. Just for the present, we've got to put up with it."

There was another silence. The girls were not very sure what to say. Dickie herself changed the subject.

"Do you know where you're sleeping?" she asked casually. "You don't?"

"Matey and the Staff are too busy with the kids to worry about us yet," Gay explained.

"Oh, well, that's all right. I can show you myself. At the back there's a kind of offshoot—kitchens, scullery, coalhouse, and washhouse. There are bathrooms built over them, and five rooms above that—they haven't any attics over. Matron has put you people up there—four to a room. I'm there, too. Shall we go up and take a dekko?"

"Might as well," Jacynth agreed, getting up from her chair and picking up her case. "Come on, you folk! You know what it's like on first day. Matey and Co. will be quite pleased if they haven't to run round after us. Show us the way, will you, Dickie? We could settle in before supper, and then lend a hand if we're needed."

CHAPTER THREE

Reminiscences—and a Rebel

By the end of the week the kindergarten had arrived, and when the next Friday evening came, the school, with one exception, had settled down in its new quarters. The babies had been housed in what had once been the coachman's flat, above the stables, which had been turned into the Domestic Science kitchens. A big army hut had been added, and was divided into four rooms where the little ones had lessons.

"And that," Miss Wilson observed, as she surveyed the place shortly after the finishing touches had been given, "makes a separate St. Agnes House again."

"What's even better," Miss Phipps, Head of the Kindergarten, responded, "is that Ivy Norman is coming back to us *at last!* "

"Won't it be like old times?" This was Miss Burnett, the history mistress, who had once been Head Girl of the school as Mary Burnett. She was leaving at the end of the present term to be married in September. "I wish we could have had Miss Stewart and Miss Leslie and Miss Maynard——"

"Don't be an idiot, Mary! " Miss Wilson's eyes danced as she broke in. "Every last one of them is married with troops of kids. How could they possibly come back? Con Stewart has twin boys and a small girl; Kit Leslie is the proud mamma of five boys—I must say I think she might have managed *one* girl by this time! —and Mollie Maynard has beaten everyone else with her seven—even Jo! How,

27

I ask, do you propose they could find time to teach, even if they could come back?"

"And apart from the fact that Mollie is in New Zealand, Con safely back in Singapore, and Kit firmly settled just outside of Sydney," Miss Annersley added, "it wouldn't do *you* much good, even if they did come. Correct me if I am wrong, but didn't you tell us your future home would be in Aberdeenshire?"

"It's simply awful the way people get scattered all over the globe!" Miss Burnett sighed. "Oh, all right! I'm an ass! The mill never grinds with the water that is past—time gone is gone forever—and all that sort of thing. However, we shall have Ivy again, and that's something."

"Why didn't she come back sooner?" Miss Slater, who had joined the school a mere five years or so previously, and had never known Miss Norman, though she had heard about her, wanted to know as they turned back to the Big House.

"Well, when we reopened in Guernsey, she already had an excellent post. Then Mrs. Norman had a seizure, and Ivy had to get a job in a day-school in Worcester where they were living, so that she could be at home as much as possible. Mrs. Norman died early in January this year, and all the younger ones are out in the world now—the sister and the elder boy are married, I believe—so Ivy was more or less alone. She had given up her post at the end of last summer term, as her mother had become more helpless and needed someone constantly with her. When Ivy wrote to tell me," Miss Annersley continued, as they reached the study where she had invited them to come for coffee and cakes, "she said that there was a good deal of business to see to, but when everything was cleared up she would like to come back to us if we'd have her. Of course we said we would. I was always very fond of Ivy Norman, and she is excellent with juniors. Come in, everyone, and find seats somewhere."

"I'm glad we've got her again," Miss Wilson said, as she helped to clear a table for the coffee tray which Olwen, one of their Welsh maids, had just brought in. "What with

Mary and Gillian both leaving to be married, and Beth Carey getting that post at the training college, I was beginning to feel more than a little worried about next term. All those three were with us in Tirol—thank you, Olwen; I'll take that now—and I haven't been looking forward to having a deal with people who know nothing about our peculiar traditions, I can tell you—not after the great Miss Bubb! "

A laugh went round the assembled Staff at this. Two or three years before, Miss Wilson, Miss Annersley, Mlle de Lachenais, Head of the languages department, and Miss Edwards, who taught junior maths, had all been involved in a road accident in which they had been more or less badly injured. As this had happened less than a week before the summer term began, and at a time when there was severe shortage of Staff, Lady Russell had been obliged to accept people who had good enough paper qualifications, and hope that they were otherwise capable of managing. Miss Bubb, coming fresh to the school, and unaware of its peculiarities—among other things, that it was closely connected with the big Sanatorium over the hills—had contrived during the few weeks in which she had been Head pro tem. to upset a good many people very badly. The climax was reached when Gay Lambert had broken out in wild rebellion, running away home when the temporary Head, by way of punishing her for rudeness and insubordination, had refused her permission to go to say good-bye to her step-brother-guardian, who was leaving for China. Miss Bubb had insisted that Gay should not be allowed to return to the school. Lady Russell, guessing that a good deal lay behind Gay's revolt, had refused to listen to the Head, and since Miss Wilson had returned to the school in reply to a frantic letter from Jo, and was able to see to organization if nothing else, she had promptly accepted Miss Bubb's tendered resignation, paid her a term's salary, and got rid of her in short order. Miss Bubb had vanished from everyone's ken, and 'Bill' had no wish to introduce strangers into the school again.

"Don't worry, my dear. Miss Bubb only came because Madame was at her wits' end. We'll be able to do a little more picking and choosing this time," Miss Annersley said, laughing, as she poured out the coffee. "You sit down and enjoy this, and don't worry about new Staff yet."

Miss Norman duly arrived at the beginning of the next week, and was welcomed with open arms by such of her colleagues as had known her in Tirol. For the next few evenings, once work was done, these folk enjoyed such an orgy of reminiscing as made those members of the Staff who had not been with the school in Tirol grumble enviously that they seemed to have had *all* the fun there!

"Oh, it wasn't always fun—not at the time, anyhow," Miss Wilson remarked, from her corner of the big settee. "Sometimes it was most annoying, like the time when Corney Flower, Evvy Lannis, Elsie Carr and Co. got themselves up as Red Indians and had a most uproarious game at Oberammergau. *How* I should have liked to spank them all round! Oberammergau of all places for such a prank!"

"It was far worse when Jo went off after Elisaveta of Belsornia that night when Prince Cosimo kidnapped her— Elisaveta, I mean—and we didn't know for ages where the monkey was," Miss Annersley put in.

"Yes; that was hair-raising enough for anything." 'Bill' turned to Miss Slater to explain. "We had been warned that Cosimo, who was certainly more or less mental, would try it on. He hated King Carol, who was the Crown Prince then, and he hoped to use Elisaveta as a lever to get the Crown Prince to abdicate his title in favour of himself. Jo knew a certain amount—she and Elisaveta were always great chums—and when our Princess meekly went off with Cosimo's jackal under the impression that she was being taken to her father who had been badly hurt, Jo merely waited to make a few arrangements, collected Rufus, her St. Bernard, and set off to rescue Elisaveta."

"And—what happened?" Miss Slater demanded eagerly.

"You must ask Jo for the story when you see her next. She can tell it best."

"Well, tell me one thing. Was it then your hair went white?"

Hilary Burn, the games mistress, and also an Old Girl of the school, grinned. "Oh, Slater, haven't you heard *that* tale? It happened when we—that is Bill, and Joey, and

Frieda, and me, and—oh, a whole crowd of us—were in Spärtz, and got mixed up with the Nazis. Joey and Robin began it, of course, and the rest of us went to the rescue. *That* was a hair-raising adventure if you like! Vater Johann, the parish priest, rescued us from the hooligans by shoving us into a secret passage that led from under the High Altar of the church to a cave near the top of the Sonnalpe. We walked for hours and hours and hours. *Never* shall I forget the awful shock we got when we reached there and turned and looked at Bill! She'd gone into that passage chestnut, and she came out of it as you see her—snow-white!"

"Not really!"

"Well," said Miss Wilson herself, "that was the general effect. As a matter of fact, underneath there were broad streaks of red left, though they didn't show. They're still there, by the way. I've quite a time doing my hair so that I avoid a patchy effect! I only wonder I wasn't demented before we got to the cave! I kept thinking I heard yells and hooting behind us. I was the only mistress with the girls, and had all the responsibility. Besides, I knew all too well what would happen to Vater Johann once those fiends broke into the church. It was an experience I never want repeated."

"I wish Jo and Madame could have come here with us," Miss Norman said, with a change of subject. "I broke my journey at Armiford, and Jo met me there, and we had two gorgeous hours of 'do you remember'! You know, I simply can't believe that she's the mother of six—including those two leggy kids Len and Con! She looks scarcely a day older. Not so thin as she used to be, but she still has her fringe and earphones. Apart from being a little stouter— and that's an improvement—she hasn't changed one atom. Neither," she added thoughtfully, "has her language."

"Oh, I wouldn't say *that*!" Bill said drily. "Her vocabulary has *extended*, anyhow!"

Miss Norman chuckled. "One would expect that of Jo!"

"And you're wrong, you know, Ivy. In some ways Jo has grown up. It happened when they thought Jack Maynard was drowned. I'll never forget that time, either. In some ways it was the most horrible time of all."

"As for Madame," Hilary made haste to change the subject, "she sailed for Canada this week with Dr. Jem. They've taken her second girl, Josette, and Jo's youngest triplet, Margot. Josette had a nasty accident a few years ago—when we had the great Miss Bubb of whom you've now heard so much—and isn't quite so sturdy as the other three. Margot has always been delicate, the only one of Jo's children who is, and they think a few months in Canada will do her all the good in the world."

"Poor old Joey! She never said a word of all that to me. And now, what's become of my pet aversion, Joyce Linton?"

"It's all right; Gill's on duty at tennis," murmured Miss Phipps as she cast a hurried look round for Gillian Linton.

"I always forget she and Joyce are sisters. There's not a scrap of likeness between them. What's become of Joyce?"

"Married and living in Exeter. She has two kiddies—a boy of six, and a girl of five. Yes—really!" as Ivy Norman raised her brows.

"Good heavens! I wouldn't have believed Joyce would be bothered with *one* infant, let alone two! And so close together!"

"Oh, she's improved a great deal. School taught her a lot. Then her husband is a very sensible man—he's a parson by the way—and he keeps her well in hand, I believe. Joyce adores her boy, and, luckily for everyone, her husband thinks the girl is the cat's bathmat! So things are evened up nicely. Little Jocelyn is to come to us as soon as she's eight. But—yes—it *was* rather a shock when Gill told us she had arrived, and we knew Frank was only seventeen months old. There was a lot of good in Joyce, only it was buried under a thick skin of selfishness. Once she sloughed most of that, she was very much nicer," Miss Wilson said. "Gill is to be married from their house, by the way, in August. Jack Maynard is to give her away, and we have a general invitation to the wedding, though how many will go, I couldn't tell you yet. Holidays will have begun for one thing. Hilda and I are going, of course. Will you make another of the party? The Dick Bettanys are putting us up at that huge old place of theirs. It's only for one night for most, though Hilda and I are staying a week with them. You'd better come along, too. I'm sure Joyce would love to see you!" Miss Wilson grinned like a schoolgirl as she made this remark, and Ivy Norman blushed.

"I'm sure she *wouldn't*! I don't suppose Joyce is any fonder of me than I am of her. My chief memory of her is that awful business when I had her and another bunch for extra French, and Joyce plotted with the rest to behave like savages in my lesson. I never have liked teaching elder girls at the best of times, though I've done quite a good deal of it at one time and another. I was very young then, and painfully nervous of them. It was one time," she added reflectively, "when I really did lose my temper most whole-heartedly."

"It did them all the good in the world," Miss Annersley said with decision. "That crowd pulled up after that—all but Thekla von Stift. I suppose that was too much to expect. You can't undo the wrong training of fifteen years in something under six months, which was all she had with us. What has become of her, Slater? I haven't the remotest idea. She did write once to Mlle Lepattre. It was shortly before she died, and Simone told me she had written to Thekla to tell her of Mlle's death. We've heard nothing since, however. Simone said it was an odd letter, partly grateful, partly ashamed, and very short. Thank goodness we've never had another girl like her!"

The story of Thekla von Stift was a painful one to the mistresses who had been at the school so long, for she had been expelled in the end, and in all the years of the school's annals, there had been only one other expulsion. A silence followed Miss Annersley's speech, which was broken by the entrance of the two French mistresses, Mlle de Lachenais, and Mlle Berné, two close friends, and both friends of Ivy Norman's in past years, though they had drifted apart for a time.

"But how comfortable you look, all of you," Mlle de Lachenais remarked, as she went to the window seat. "What do you discuss, then?"

"They've been telling tales of your early years," Miss

Slater explained. "You seem to have had a good many thrills in Tirol."

"Come and tell us what you have been doing." Miss Wilson made room on the settee. "Sit here, Julie. Jeanne seems to favour the window."

Mlle Berné sat down. "We have been—having trouble."

Bill sat up. "What do you mean? Who's being a pest now?"

"That girl in the Lower Fifth who came last term—Annis Lovell."

"Oh, *that* girl! She seems to be out to make a nuisance of herself. What has she been doing now?" Miss Annersley asked plaintively. "She was reported to me this morning for an untidy cubicle. Don't say I have to deal with her again already! I thought I'd given her enough to think over for some time to come. What is it, Julie?"

It was Mlle de Lachenais who replied. "She is impossible —but *impossible*!" she declared, with a quick gesture. "She did not hand in her Latin yesterday, nor her French to-day. I had the Latin this morning, but it is so bad that I have returned it. We met her in the corridor outside Lower Four B door, and I ask why I have not the French." She suddenly relapsed into her own tongue. "Then I say, 'Why have I not the French, Annis?' and she says, 'I hate French! I will not do it!'" Mlle threw out her hands in despair. "What can one do with such a girl? I told her she was rude and I should expect an apology, and she said, 'If you expect an apology from me, you've had it, chum!'"

"*Wha-at!*" Bill was on her feet in one alert movement. "No, Hilda; you stay where you are. *I'm* dealing with this! We've never allowed impudence here, and so Miss Annis will find out. She had to be spoken to for rudeness to Miss Denny last term, and I thought what I said then would have been sufficient. Evidently she needs something even sharper. All right, Jeanne. I'll see to it. She shall apologise to you at Prayers."

"It is not," Mlle said, "that I wish to bring the girl to disgrace; but there were some Juniors standing by. Such an example is bad for them. I told her to be silent, of course——"

Bill paused on her way to the door. "She was rude to you in front of Juniors? Who were they?"

"Len and Con, the little Mary-Lou, and her friend Clem, and Viola Lucy. They were passing, and they heard."

"And the girls in the form-room," added Julie Berné. "Annis spoke clearly, and all in there must have heard."

Bill looked her grimmest. "I see. Well, Miss Annis will find that that sort of thing won't do here. I'll send for her to the library, and settle her for good and all. I *will not* have the girls behaving like untaught little heathens!" On which note she departed.

Jeanne de Lachenais turned to the rest, looking troubled. "I am sorry," she said, in her own language. "What could I do? Rudeness of that kind can hardly be permitted, especially before small children. I do not say any of them would copy it——"

"I'd like to see Jo's face if either of *her* two tried that sort of thing on!" Hilary interrupted. "They wouldn't do it a second time!"

"I don't think Mary-Lou, or Clem, or Vi would do it either." Miss Phipps added her quota. "I shouldn't like to vouch for all those imps in Lower Four B, though. Can anyone tell me why it is that the meekest and mildest of Juniors seems to become a demon incarnate once she reaches the Fourth?"

"I seem to have heard that remark before," Miss Annersley murmured.

"History repeating itself!" Mary Burnett retorted. "I only hope that a good many of the lovely tales we have been repeating for your benefit, Slater, aren't current coin among the girls. They are such little copy-cats at that age, and I don't think we want any repetitions of some of the wilder pranks of Jo, or Corney Flower and Evvy Lannis— Oh, *do* you folk remember that 'orchestral concert' Corney and Evvy got up one summer term? I wasn't there, but I heard all about it from Betty and Peggy when they came home for the holidays. They almost made me laugh till I wept!"

"I *did*—laugh till I wept," Miss Annersley said reminiscently. "We shan't have *that* over again, anyhow. We haven't any millionaire's child here now." She glanced across at Hilary. "Hilary, do *you* remember when Corney got really going with her saxophone?"

Hilary doubled up at the memory. "Do I not! Still," she added, as she sat up again, "that was funny and harmless, which cheek like young Annis's isn't."

"Oh dear!" Mary wailed. "I hope Bill can squash her properly. I'm all for a quiet life, and I've excitement enough ahead of me in the comparatively near future without having to spend the entire term sitting on a razor-edge of uncertainty as to *who* is going to do *what* next!"

"There's the gong for dinner! I'm hungry!" Hilary Burn jumped up from the pouffe on which she had been squatting while she hemstitched a teacloth for Mary's wedding present. "Julie, may I have the honour of taking you down?" She crooked her elbow invitingly.

Mlle Berné laughed as she took her proffered arm. "You do not grow up, Hilairie."

"Give me a chance! I'm Staff room baby yet—and I mean to stay it!" Hilary retorted. "Even Gill is a year older than I am! Come along, folk!"

The school had its supper at the same time, and Annis Lovell, sitting at Lower Fifth table in company with a dozen girls of her own age, looked flushed and angry. The elder girls noted that Bill was looking her grimmest, and wondered who was in trouble now. She had sat down in her place beside Miss Annersley with a quick murmured sentence to that lady, and Miss Annersley's pleasant smile had changed to a sharp frown. The two Heads had a quick conversation in fluent Italian before they turned to join in the general chatter of the rest of the mistresses, and the girls felt that something had happened. Still, they were not prepared for what occurred when they had finished. Miss Annersley struck her little table-bell, and the hum of chatter all over the room ceased at once. Everyone turned to look up to the High table as they called it, where the Head was standing, looking down the big room. They would have risen, too, but a slight movement of her hand kept them in their seats.

"Annis Lovell," she said, "please come up here."

Annis hesitated. Then she rose and went to stand before the long table set across the room. Miss Annersley looked at her sternly.

"I understand that you have been impudent to Mlle de Lachenais."

Annis said nothing. What she had intended to say was frozen on her tongue as she met the blue-grey eyes, usually so kindly, but now like pieces of steel. Instead, she went crimson, and despite herself, her long lashes dropped over her eyes. Miss Annersley gave her two minutes by the mantelpiece clock before she spoke again.

"I see you understand me. We do not allow that sort of thing here, and I must ask you to apologise to Mlle at once, and promise her you will never again be so rude to her."

It was impossible for Annis to go any redder, but her eyes flashed under their dark lashes, and her lips set in a straight line. She stood there, making no effort to speak. The Head gave her another minute or two before she spoke again.

"Annis, I told you to apologise to Mlle at once. Do you mean to obey me? I warn you, it will be better for you to do as you are told."

No reply: but the hot colour still scorched Annis's face.

"Very well." The Head's voice was so icy, that a few people who had guilty consciences shook in their shoes. "Go to my study and wait there till I come. Matron, will you please take her."

Matron, small, wiry, a beloved tyrant with both girls and Staff, rose at once, and marched Annis from the room while the Head said Grace and then dismissed the girls to their evening ploys before she went to wrestle with the rebel.

Next morning, Annis's place at table was vacant, and it soon became known that she had still refused to do the Head's bidding, and was to remain in solitude until she chose to give up her anti-social behaviour.

"Silly young ass!" was the comment of a good many of her peers.

"She's asked for it!" said others.

Two or three of her own form wondered how long she

would keep it up; and Kathie Robertson, discussing the school's latest sensation in a select meeting of prefects, demanded maddeningly: "What did I tell you?"

CHAPTER FOUR

Cherry

"ALL I can say is I wish the little ape would hurry up and apologise! Everyone seems on the watch for cheek from us these days. You can scarcely open your lips to a Staff at present, and it's jolly unfair. *We* don't go round saucing people like Annis Lovell."

"D'you mean *people* like Annis Lovell, or *saucing* like Annis Lovell?"

"You know what I mean!" Nita Eltringham flung herself down in her chair with a frown. "Do use your wits, Peggy! As if it mattered what one said to a mook like that!"

Peggy Bettany chuckled, but quickly grew serious. "I know. All right, Nita; sorry I ragged. All the same, I don't see what *we* can do about it."

"We can't do a thing as long as she's in solitude," another Fifth Former joined in. "She mayn't speak to us, and we mayn't speak to her. What *can* we do?"

"Nothing as things are!" Anita snapped the words out. She was form prefect for Lower Fifth A, and she felt the cloud under which the form was resting, thanks to Annis Lovell, very deeply.

More than a week had passed since that eventful evening when the young lady had refused to apologise to Mlle for her rudeness, and she was still in solitude, which meant that she had her meals by herself at a small table; sat at a desk in the farthest corner of the form-room; slept in San since there was no one there at present; and was not allowed to join in the games, but had to take her exercise by means of solitary walks with either a mistress or a prefect in charge of her. The punishment, a stiff one, was very rarely given. When it was, it brought most recalcitrants to their senses in short order. Annis, however, only stiffened her upper lip, and remained obstinate. More people than Nita Eltringham were beginning to worry about her, and wish she would give in. There were no sympathisers for her over this affair. Lower Four B had not hesitated to give *their* version of the story to all and sundry, and the general opinion of the school was that she deserved all she got.

"It's so jolly rotten! " wailed Bride Bettany. "I just went to ask Bill if we might have a picnic on the shore some day, and she said: 'You'd better wait till your form *deserves* a privilege before you ask for one.' It isn't *us*: *we* can't be blamed for what a goat like Annis does! I wish she'd never come here! "

A tall, boyish-looking girl with a head of cropped, wavy hair, and steady grey eyes, who was straddling a chair, her arms folded along its back and her chin resting on them, spoke up. "She's a gump all right. Perhaps," she added brilliantly, "the Staff are afraid her cheek'll be catching if they don't squash us pronto."

"Talk sense! As if it could be! Really, Tom! " Nita said irritably.

Tom nodded. "I know. But after all, the poor things are grown up. You never know how grown-ups will take things, do you? All the same, I wish Annis would see sense and see it pronto. I'm sick of this! "

"You're not any sicker than the rest of us," Bride told her. "Do you realise that though the Sixths and the other Fifths have been over to Carnbach, it's never even been suggested that *we* should go? It's Mummy's birthday next week, and I haven't a thing for her, and you know how much you can buy down in the village! "

"Better go and ask Bill or the Abbess if you can go yourself," Tom suggested.

Bride jumped up. "I jolly well will! After all, they can't eat me—only say 'No' if they feel that way. Mind out of the way, Rosalie! " And she whirled out of the room before anyone could stop her.

"What possessed you to say that, Tom?" Nita demanded.

Tom grinned unrepentantly. "Because it's time someone did something about it, or the whole term's going to be spoilt. If I know anything of Bride, she'll let off steam now she's worked up, and perhaps she'll make Bill or whoever she catches see a little sense about us."

"More likely make them madder than ever with us," Nita said gloomily. "Oh, well, I suppose *talking* won't make it any better. Anyhow, we're supposed to be outside, so we'd better go. Otherwise, someone will be dropping on us for that, too. Come on, you people!" And she led the way out to the garden, where they were presently busy with various ploys.

Meanwhile Bride, boiling at the injustice of it all, had gone her way to the study, where she found Miss Annersley sitting working at her desk. She looked up as Bride entered in answer to her call, and smiled.

"Well, Bride? What is it child?"

Bride bobbed her curtsy. "Please, Miss Annersley, it's Mummy's birthday next week and I haven't a thing for it. May I go over to Carnbach on Saturday and get something?"

"Why didn't you do your shopping when you were over before?" the Head asked.

"But we haven't been. All the Sixths and other Fifths have been, but not us," Bride said, her grievances well to the fore.

"You haven't?" Miss Annersley opened a drawer, took out a notebook, and opened it. "How was that, I wonder? You were supposed to go yesterday afternoon with Miss Linton. What happened?"

"No one ever told us," Bride said aggrievedly, "and we didn't go."

The Head considered. "Oh, I remember! We decided to send you yesterday as it was a more or less free afternoon for you—only needlework and prep. Then Mrs. Christy from Wistaria House told us that Wednesday is early closing day in Carnbach, so we left it. You folk are going this afternoon, and Herr Laubach will take your art after tea for once. So *that's* all right, isn't it? Here, wait a moment

40

and I'll write a notice for you to put up on the notice-board in your form-room." She scribbled busily for a moment or two. Then she handed the slip to Bride. "Run along and put it up. There's the bell for the end of break, so you must hurry. Your last lesson this morning will finish ten minutes earlier to give you time to run upstairs and change before Mittagessen. You must all be at the gates by two o'clock to meet Miss Linton who will be your escort. If anyone wants money from Bank, she may go to Miss Edwards before she goes to change. You will find her," the Head glanced at the big time-table sheet pinned up beside the window, "in Upper Second. Now be off!"

Bride thanked Miss Annersley, curtsied, and departed to find her form sitting very properly in their desks, waiting for the arrival of Miss Burnett and the history lesson. She waved her slip triumphantly at them.

"Miss Annersley says we are going to-day," she said. "Last lesson ends at half-past twelve so we can change. If you want money from Bank, go to Teddy in Upper Second first." She pinned the slip to the notice-board and sat down in her place two seconds before Miss Burnett arrived.

The atmosphere of Lower Fifth A had changed before then, and she was welcomed by rows of beaming faces—only one excepted. Annis, sitting at her lonely desk in the corner, had risen perforce with the others, but a black scowl was on her brow, and she barely opened her lips to join the polite "Good morning, Miss Burnett" with which the rest greeted the mistress. Miss Burnett replied amiably, and they sat down and the lesson began.

They were doing European history this year, and the lesson on the French colonisation of Canada was an interesting one. Miss Burnett knew her subject well, and most of the girls had read one or more novels on the subject, for the school library, collected over a period of years, was well stocked. Lessons of this kind at the Chalet School frequently became discussions, for the authorities were anxious for the elder girls to learn to reason for themselves, and this lesson was no exception to the general rule. They were dealing with the doings of the Comte de Frontenac, and the establishment of French rule along the St. Lawrence.

Half the form had already revelled in *Shadows on the Rock* which gives such a vivid picture of life in Quebec at that time, and the other half was waiting anxiously for it. Miss Burnett explained the political situation in France, which had so much to do with the failure of the French Government to back up Frontenac as they should have done, and the girls took a few notes before they were free to ask what questions they pleased. Only Annis sat silent in her corner, apparently paying little attention to what was going on. She was very quiet, and Miss Burnett, glancing across at her, thought she looked white and weary. Perhaps it was for this reason that, when the bell rang for the end of the lesson and she had gathered up her books and left them, she hurried to the study and suggested that Annis should be allowed to go with the others.

"I know she doesn't deserve it," she urged, "but she's looking poorly, and probably the trip across the water would do her good. We don't want the little idiot to be ill, however bad she's been. Ask Matey!"

Matron, sent for, gave it as her opinion that it was a good idea. "Send a sensible prefect with her," she advised. "No reason why she should be with the others. Jacynth or someone like that could look after her quite well, and the change might do her good and help her to change what she's pleased to call her mind about apologising!"

Miss Annersley consulted the timetable again, and discovered that three prefects were free—Jacynth Hardy, Nancy Canton, and Kathie Robertson. "I'll send Jacynth and Kathie with her," she decided. "Nancy is a nice girl, but she's feather-headed, and it would be very boring for just one of them alone." She sent for Jacynth and Kathie, told them her wishes, and finally had Annis sent to the study.

The girl came in, bobbed reluctantly, and stood just within the room.

Miss Annersley looked keenly at her, noted the white cheeks and heavy eyes, and softened despite her own sense of justice.

"Come here, Annis," she said quietly.

Annis slouched up to the desk and stood playing with her fingers, her eyes cast down and a sullen expression on her face.

"Are you not well?" the Head asked gently.

"I'm all right," Annis mumbled, still not looking up.

"I think you look as if you had a headache. A good blow on the water will help that, probably. Jacynth and Kathie are going over to Carnbach this afternoon when the rest of your form go, and will take you with them." She paused, but Annis had nothing to say. Then she went on: "Annis, my dear, have you nothing to say to me?"

Annis remained silent. By this time she had worked herself into a belief that she was being thoroughly ill-used; that everyone hated her, and she hated everyone; and that nothing on this earth should ever make her apologise either to Mlle or anyone else. At the same time, she was aware of a feeling of relief at the thought that she was to get away from this place, even if it was in charge of two gaolers, and for only an hour or two. But Miss Annersley was speaking again, and something in the deep, beautiful voice which was one of the Head's great assets forced her to listen in spite of herself.

"Annis, I know you are very unhappy. Why won't you put an end to this silly rebellion, apologise to Mlle, and end it. I know you will not find her unforgiving. Come, dear! Give it up, and be one of the Chalet School again, and enjoy all the pleasures we are finding here."

Annis shook her head, shutting her eyes to force back the tears that had unexpectedly welled up at this appeal. She could hardly have spoken just then, even if she had wished. Miss Annersley guessed as much, and, wise in her own generation, said no more about it. Perhaps the afternoon away from school surroundings would help her words to take effect.

"You must go back to your form now," she said. "Go and change when the others do, but wait for Jacynth or Kathie to fetch you from your form-room. Wait! " as Annis turned to leave the room. "Who is with you now?"

43

"Miss Wilson for geography," Annis replied, in the same sulky tone.

"Explain you have been with me, and ask her to excuse you. Run along!"

Annis went, and the Head, leaning back in her chair, mused over the situation for a few minutes. "I wish we had Joey here!" she thought. "She can generally manage the most obstinate girl. Poor, silly child! How I wish she would give in and end this deadlock!"

Meanwhile, Annis had gone back to her form-room, where she delivered the Head's message to Miss Wilson, and then went to her seat. She was forced to work in this lesson. Even she, hardy as she was, dared do no less. Luckily for her, her interview, and the docking of ten minutes at the end of the lesson, prevented the mistress from inspecting her work, and when they were dismissed, she put her books away and went upstairs with the others to change into a fresh frock and prepare for the trip. It was more than half-way through May now, and though the sun shone brightly there was a fresh breeze, so the girls had to wear their coats on the water. They were all ready in due course, and while Annis remained in the schoolroom in obedience to Miss Annersley, the rest filed off down the drive to the gate where they were met by pretty Miss Linton, who marched them off briskly down the road to the ferry.

The big clumsy boat had been tied up at the landing since midday, and now the gangway was down, and already two or three people were on board. The seventeen big girls, very neat and fresh-looking in their cream coats over brown-and-white checked gingham frocks, with flame-coloured ties, and large white hats with a twist of flame-coloured silk round the crowns, went on board, and settled themselves in the bows, where an elderly lady was sitting, a large empty basket at her feet. A little farther back on the same seat was a strange pair—a man and a little girl. The man wore grey flannel slacks that had seen very much better days, and a blue shirt open at the neck. His thick hair was blown by the wind, and a short beard covered his chin. He looked at them with twinkling blue eyes as they went past, but said nothing. The little girl was a picture, with black curls framing an almost perfect little face, delicately featured, and with the lovely tinting of a tea-rose. She was clad in a short blue frock and a thick cherry-coloured jersey. A pair of small crutches stood beside her, and the girls saw that her legs were in irons. She scowled at them as they took their places, and there was no one to tell them that this was the new girl, Dickie Christy's small adopted sister, Cherry. Dickie had asked the Sixth to say nothing about her, and the school at large knew no more than that there were little sisters at home who did not come to the school. They assumed that they were babies, since some of them had seen Gaynor, and thought no more about it.

Miss Linton knew who the child was, of course, but she said nothing, and the girls, pleased to be with a favourite mistress, clustered round her, chattering gaily about their own concerns. Then Jacynth and Kathie came with Annis beside them, and Cherry's grey eyes opened widely as she saw that though they certainly belonged to the school, since they wore the same uniform, yet they made no effort to join the slightly noisy crowd in the bows, but remained near the wheel-house. Her long illness had sharpened her faculties, and she saw that the youngest of the three was clearly miserable. No smile came to her lips, and she stared sullenly across the dancing water to the mainland without a word. The other two spoke to her occasionally, but she either did not reply, or else spoke just a word or two. Cherry's curiosity was aroused. What could be wrong? Then her guardian called her attention to the flight of the gulls, and she gave the matter no more thought.

Meanwhile, the man, who was no other than Mr. Bellever, the warden of the sea-bird sanctuary on St. Brandon Mawr, another of the islands, had produced a parcel of herrings which he broke in pieces, flinging them out over the side as the ferry ploughed its way across to Carnbach, and calling to Cherry to notice how the birds dived for the pieces. The Chalet School contingent were interested, and fell silent also, watching and listening to what he said, though they had no idea who he was.

He pointed out the great black-backed gull which scattered the rest of the flock for a moment, for the black-backed gull is a cannibal as well as a fish-eater. Three or four small birds with long, black, hook-tipped bills, smooth black heads, and black wings and back and tail suddenly appeared, and he called to Cherry to notice that the under parts were snow-white.

"Shear-waters," he said. "They come out at nights, mostly, on land. In the daytime, though, you often see them on the water."

"Do they have nests on the cliffs like the gulls?" Cherry asked.

"No; they're like the puffins—nest in holes in the earth. Look, Cherry! See that chap careering over the surface of the sea? Watch how his wings seem almost to cut the waves. Those are shear-waters. There's a whole colony of 'em on Brandon Mawr. You should hear 'em at night when they come out! Hair-raising, the noise they make!"

"I know the gull's noise now," Cherry said eagerly. "It's rather like a cat mewing. Is the shear-water's noise like that?"

"Anything but! It's—it's like the wailing of lost souls."

"How horrible!" she shuddered. "I shouldn't like to hear that at all!"

"Maybe not. Well, I won't ask you to listen to-day, any-how. Just a run across to the island to show you the layout of it. If we're lucky, you'll see an oyster-catcher or so on the rocks. They're gaudy fellows, with their carmine legs and reddish-orange bills. When you get near enough—if you can, that is—you see that their eyes are bright scarlet."

"What is the rest of them like?" Cherry asked eagerly.

"Plumage black and white; and the legs are long—rather like stilts. They've got a queer, rather musical cry, 'Tu-lup! Tu-lup!'" He imitated the strange cry, and even Annis was attracted from her miserable self.

Cherry listened intently. "Oh, I like that! I'll remember that! Shall we hear them this afternoon?"

He laughed. "I'm afraid not. The oyster-catcher will be sleeping, so unless we disturb him, he'll have that orange bill of his tucked under his wing. We may not even see him, you know. He's a very shy fellow, and as wary as an old fox. Still, we'll hope for the best."

By this time, Gillian Linton had guessed who he was, and her eyes widened. She glanced at the girls, and noticed that they were listening fascinated to his talk. Not that he bothered about them. He had got permission from little Mrs. Christy to bring her girl away to Brandon Mawr for the afternoon, and he was concentrating on entertaining her. He had made friends with the Christys when he had come to ask leave to visit a part of the outer cliffs where puffins nested, and had been attracted to Cherry, not solely because of her beauty, nor even through pity for her lameness, but because, in her shyness and wariness, she reminded him of many of the sea-birds which were his chief interest in life.

Miss Linton could hardly tell her party then and there who he was, but she was glad to see that they were interested. There was quiet among them for the rest of the trip until the ferry reached the mainland and the gangway rattled down, and they were marching across it. One or two of the girls glanced back as they turned along the road leading to the main shopping centre of the little town, to see the man swing Cherry up on his shoulder, tuck her crutches under his arm, and run lightly down to the shore to where a rowing-boat was tied to a ring in a rock.

"Did you see that?" cried Molly McNab, who was noted for being a regular Mrs. Malaprop. "He must be a real Goth, the way he lifted that kid and raced along carrying her! "

Peals of laughter greeted this remark, and Bride, walking just ahead of Molly, turned to remark: "If you mean *Goliath*, I'd say so! A Goth is someone who doesn't know a beautiful thing when he sees it! "

"Oh, well, you all know what I mean," Molly retorted, being a good-humoured young person who was rarely put out at anything. "Miss Linton, wasn't he interesting when he was talking about the birds?"

"Very," the mistress agreed. "I wonder if any of you girls have any idea who he is?"

"Not the foggiest," Bride replied. "Is he someone well known?"

"Very well known. You've heard him on the wireless often—at least, I hope you have. That's Kester Bellever, the naturalist. I've seen a photo of him somewhere, and I recognized him when he began to talk."

"Who's the kid, Miss Linton?" Tom Gay asked. "Is she his? She's not much like him."

"Oh no! That's Dickie Christy's—well, it's rather difficult to say what the relationship is," Miss Linton returned. "Dickie's father married the little girl's mother, who was a widow with just this daughter, Cherry. I believe Dickie regards her as a sister, though."

"What happened to lame her?" Bride asked, as they turned up a narrow alleyway. "Was it an accident, or was she born that way?"

"Neither. She had an attack of infantile paralysis, and it left her like that. Some of you may have heard that the late President Roosevelt suffered in the same way. But fortunately, Cherry is improving, and I know the doctors think that in time she will outgrow her lameness and be strong and fit again. Meantime, she won't come to school, and does lessons at home."

"Poor little soul!" Nita Eltringham said. "Why won't she come with Dickie? I'm sure our kids would be good to her, and she must be awfully lonely at home, though Dickie does go for the week-ends."

"I understand that the illness left her very shy. They would like her to come, but it's no use trying to force her. If some of you girls—or, better still, some of the people of her own age like Mary-Lou and Verity-Ann and that crowd —could make friends with her first she might change her mind. Perhaps you'll have a chance now that you've crossed in the ferry together," Miss Linton said. She had no idea that Dickie had enforced silence about Cherry on her own peers; nor, of course, what Cherry's views on the arrival of the school were.

"I'll have a word with young Vi," said Nita, referring to her small cousin, Viola Lucy. "What a lovely kid she is—a real picture kid!"

"Yes, she's very pretty," Miss Linton agreed. "Now which of you want chocolate? Here's a sweetshop—the best in the place, I may tell you."

Several people wanted sweets, so they thronged in, and for the next hour or so were all so busy with their shopping, that they forgot Cherry Christy and Kester Bellever.

Meanwhile, Jacynth and Kathie, having received their orders from Miss Annersley, avoided the shops for the moment, and set off with their sulky charge along the shore. They were in time to see Kester Bellever put Cherry safely in the little boat floating on the tiny ruffled waves; then he dropped one of her crutches into the water where the receding tide began to bear it quickly away. Cherry uttered a cry of dismay at the sight.

"Oh, Mr. Bellever! My crutch!"

"All right," he said, quickly kicking off his sandals, and rolling his slacks up above his knees. "I'll get it. Sit still, Cherry!"

Someone else was before him. None of the girls wore stockings, once the warm weather had begun, and Annis was out of her sandals even faster than he, plunged straight into the water, with a gasp for its coldness, and made after the crutch.

"Annis! Come back!" shouted Jacynth, preparing to follow her with Kathie as a good second.

Kester Bellever checked them at once. "All right! She can't get more than knee-deep for a good hundred yards. It doesn't begin shelving till then. Ah! She's got it! Good kid! Cherry, I'm sorry. Don't know what made me so clumsy. But all's well, for here comes your crutch."

Annis had splashed the back of her coat, but she had the crutch safely and the sulky look had left her face as she brought it to the side of the boat.

"Here it is," she said, handing it over. "It's a bit wet, but that's all. It'll soon dry." She looked doubtfully at the prefects then. "I forgot I'd to stay with you," she said.

"It's all right," Jacynth answered quickly. "You were quite right to go, Annis." She gave Cherry a smile. "You wouldn't have liked to lose it, would you, Cherry? What a pretty name you have!"

Cherry looked up at her. The scowl which had come when she saw the uniform first had faded, and she gave the tall, rather grave-looking prefect a beaming smile as she said: "Not just now, I wouldn't. I wouldn't mind losing them both if I could do without them, though. But I can't! "

"You will some day," Mr. Bellever said cheerfully. "I say, young woman, you've splashed your coat a bit. What's your skirt like?"

"It's just wet at the edge. It'll soon dry," Annis replied. She was looking at Cherry with a queer expression on her face, but she said no more. She rejoined Jacynth and Kathie on the sand, and waited while Mr. Bellever said a few more words to them while he untied the knot which kept his boat safe. Then, with a good shove off, he sprang in, took up the oars, and soon had the tiny craft well out in the bay. The girls waved to Cherry, who, forgetting her grudge against the school which had taken her home and her beloved Dickie, waved back. When the boat was just a dark shadow on the water, the girls went on, for Jacynth had orders to see that Annis had a good walk before they went into the town.

"Which way are they going?" Kathie asked, shading her eyes with her hand. "Oh, he's turning round the corner of the island over there. I wonder who he is? You know who the kid is though, don't you, Jass?"

Jacynth nodded, and glanced at Annis, Dickie's warning in her mind.

That young person had been shaken out of her sulks by what had happened. "Who is she, Kathie?" she asked eagerly.

Kathie replied without thought. "She's Dickie Christy's young sister, I expect," she said. "Didn't Dickie say her kid sister was called Cherry and she was lame through some illness? This'll be the one. Poor little soul! It's rotten luck, isn't it?"

Jacynth gave it up. "It's bad, but you know Dickie told us the doctors had said she'd recover in time," she said. "As for the man—Mops, don't you *really* know who he is? He's Kester Bellever the naturalist. I read an article in a magazine by him, and his photo was at the top. I knew his bird sanctuary was somewhere about here. I didn't think it was so near, though." Then she turned to Annis. "Look here, Annis, Dickie asked us not to talk of Cherry. The poor kid's shy because of her lameness and hates meeting strangers. Keep it under your hat who she is, won't you?"

Annis nodded. "Oh, rather! Are you sure she'll get all right again? It's foul——" She stopped and reddened. "I mean—it's hard luck, as Kathie says. She's just a little kid."

"She's eleven, I believe. Well, we seem to be coming to a cliff, and as I don't feel like wading, I propose we go back and do our shopping. Is your skirt still wet, Annis?"

"No, nearly dry now," Annis said, after feeling it.

"All right. Then we'll turn back. I want a new C string for my 'cello and Gay asked me to get her some rosin. What do you want, Kathie?"

"Nothing particularly. I only came for the trip," Kathie said, with a grin. "Annis, what about your wants?"

"I want a book if I can get one. I had some birthday money the other day. Do you think Kester Bellever has written any?"

"We'll go to the bookshop and ask. But I should think they'd be on the dear side. Books like that are generally twelve and six to fifteen shillings, I believe," Jacynth said.

"I've got ten shillings—and a shilling of my pocket-money."

"Well, we'll try, anyhow. Come on!"

They all met at the six o'clock ferry, where the Fifth had various purchases to show. Jacynth had got the 'cello string and the rosin, and Annis had succeeded in buying *Sea Parrot* by Kester Bellever for eight and six. Jacynth and Kathie had given her the best tea they could manage, and the girl who left the ferry-boat at St. Briavel's was a very different one from the girl who had gone on to it that afternoon. Cherry and her friend were not there, and when Annis said something to the prefects about it, they decided that Mr. Bellever would probably row her all the way home.

The good of the expedition was proved when Annis, having made herself tidy, went to the study to say abruptly to Miss Annersley, "I'll tell Mlle de Lachenais I'm sorry I was rude, Miss Annersley."

The Head nodded. "Very well, dear. You'll find her in the Staff room, I expect. And then hurry down or you'll miss all your drawing."

CHAPTER FIVE

'Impertinent Questions'

THE trouble with Annis being over for the present, at any rate, the school settled down to a little peace. Cricket and tennis had begun, and while the weather was fine, Saturday afternoons were devoted to picnics. They soon knew the island with its many coves on the western side, and in the village people began to nod and smile to them when they walked down to buy their sweets and stamps at the little post office. Then the weather changed. A strong west wind brought with it rain, and the girls were confined to the house except for a brisk walk in raincoats and wellingtons once a day. This continued for a week, and cricket and tennis were at a standstill. By the time that Saturday had arrived, they were all thoroughly tired of it, and the Juniors, at any rate, were ripe for trouble, which was never far to seek where they were concerned.

During the Easter holidays, Jo Maynard had been moved to teach her own small girls as well as Mary-Lou Trelawney and Verity-Ann Carey, who both lived near at hand, the old game of 'Impertinent Questions'. Most folk know it. Two packs of cards are needed, one being dealt round to the players, and the other spread out, face downwards, in the middle of the table. The dealer draws a card at random, asking a question before she turns it up. Then the players look for its mate in their hands, and whoever has it claims it, *and* the question! However, she can ask the next, so things generally even themselves up.

On one occasion, it had even proved useful in solving a minor mystery. Three days previously, a pane of glass in the conservatory at Plas Gwyn had been broken, how, no one knew. Jo had not troubled to ask the children, for the day of the accident had been fiercely stormy, and she knew they had never been outside all day. It was, therefore, with no ulterior motive that she asked laughingly when it came to her turn: "Who broke the conservatory pane?"

To her utter amazement Margot cried: "Me, Mamma! But—but it wasn't really! The ball fell out of the window, and bounced up and broke the g-glass! I n-never m-meant it to b-break the glass! Ya-ah-a-ah! " And she broke down and howled.

After the first shock, Jo sat back and eyed her youngest daughter with a quizzical look in her black eyes. "I'd no idea *you* were more or less responsible, and I only asked the question because it was the first thing that came into my head," she remarked. "Stop that yelling, Margot, and tell me the whole story, please."

Margot contrived to check her sobs, and Jo found out that the children had been playing 'Catchies', a forbidden thing since the day Stephen had sent a ball clean through the nursery window. On this occasion the window had been open, and the ball had gone through, bounced up from the path, and landed on top of the conservatory, smashing the pane, and then vanishing.

"And we've never found it *yet*," Len said, "though we've looked. You never asked about it, Mamma, and Margot wouldn't tell so *we* couldn't."

"No; I see that," Jo agreed. "All right, Margot. It was an accident, though it was one that shouldn't have happened. You're a silly little girl not to have come and told me at once. It would have meant bed, I know. You *must* learn to be obedient. However, I don't suppose you've been very happy these last three days, so I think you've punished yourself sufficiently, and we'll say no more. Run along to the bathroom and wash your face, and another time, come straight to me and own up."

When the wet days kept them indoors, Mary-Lou and Verity-Ann recalled the game, and for three evenings Lower Third B had a very good time asking each other the most pointed questions, such as, "Who doesn't brush her

53

hair at bedtime?"—"Who has a hole in her stocking this minute?" and the like. It was good fun, and as there was no malice in it, no one's feelings were hurt, and their common-room resounded with shrieks of mirth. The authorities, thankful to have them so harmlessly and happily occupied, mentioned that a *little* less noise might be better, and left it at that. Saturday, however, was a different matter.

The day began badly with three of them being summoned from mending by Matron to remake their beds. There was no real excuse for them. All were girls of eleven, and knew very well what to do. Matron did not scruple to give her unvarnished opinion of them and by the time they got downstairs again to their mending, all three were seething with wrath. To make matters worse, when the half-past ten bell rang, the hated mending was still not finished, and that meant that before they did anything else after Mittagessen, as the school called the midday meal, they must return to their form-room and finish.

Kathie Robertson had been on duty with them, and as she had plans of her own for the afternoon, she was none too pleased at having to shelve them until the trio had darned their stockings and sewn on buttons.

"Little nuisances, all of you," she grumbled at them. "Now sit down and get to work, and don't waste my time any more than you can help."

This was adding insult to injury. Mary-Lou, Phil Craven, and Ruth Barnes all sat down in their seats with sulky faces and set to work, hatred of Kathie rising in their hearts. Mary-Lou was quickly finished, since she had only two buttons to sew on, and was dismissed to the common-room; but Phil and Ruth were slow, and Phil had not only a heel to darn, but the buttons to sew on the cuffs of two blouses as well. It was nearly three o'clock before she had ended her task, and Kathie might be excused for her final remark of, "See if you can't take more care of your things after this. At your age, such untidiness is disgraceful!" before she sent Phil away, and retired with all speed to join her chums.

Phil was a young lady who loved hugging a grievance, and she had an outsize in grievances this time. She slouched along the passage to the common-room, feeling at odds with all the world. Arrived there, she found some of her clan busy with jigsaw puzzles; others reading; still others doing nothing but gaze mournfully out of the windows at the rain which was falling with a heavy, steady drip-drip-drip on the sodden garden, and plainly intending to keep it up for the whole day.

Mary-Lou was busy with Verity-Ann and Viola Lucy at an elderly jigsaw which was a favourite with the small fry because of its picture of gay little Dutch girls playing 'Ring-a-ring-a-rosy', though it was rather hard to do since several pieces were missing. She looked up as Phil entered.

"Finished?" she asked. "Wasn't Kathie in a bait? I do think some of those prefects are the limit! She needn't have gone on at us like that! We got it from Matey this morning."

"I s'pose," Viola said, her small head cocked on one side, "that Kathie was mad 'cos she had to sit with you."

"You think you know everything, don't you, Vi Lucy?" Phil snarled.

"No, I don't." Vi spoke with dignity. "If you'd taken the trouble to make your bed *properly* at first, Matey wouldn't have yanked you out, and then you'd have got your mending done this morning."

"Oh, mind your own business, you little dope!" Phil retorted rudely.

"Dope yourself!" Vi flashed back.

Lesley Malcolm, their form prefect, spoke warningly. "If you use slang like that and anyone hears you, you'll get a double fine."

"Well, she said it first!" Viola said aggrievedly.

"I know; but you needn't have said it too," was Lesley's response to this. "And do shut up squabbling! We don't want to have a mistress sitting with us like the small kids, do we?"

It was a timely reminder. The policy of the Chalet School was to give the girls as much freedom as possible and trust them not to abuse it. It usually worked well, but to-day tempers were on hair-triggers. If only it had been fine, Miss Linton, their form-mistress, had promised to take them for a picnic to the Mermaidens' Rocks at the south-west tip of the island. It was one place they had not yet seen, and they had been very eager for it. Now the rain had come; the picnic was off; and they were thoroughly disgruntled.

"I'll tell you what!" Mary-Lou jumped up from the jig-saw. "Let's all play something we can play together. This old puzzle isn't going to make. I believe there's *more* pieces missing. Let's give it up, Vi and Verity-Ann, and get the others and play something."

"Well—what?" Vi demanded.

"Oh—well—what about charades?"

"That's an evening game," someone standing near said.

"That's no reason why we can't play it now if we like," Mary-Lou retorted.

"Besides, it's three o'clock. No one's going to give us dress-up things now. We'll have tea in an hour," Doris Hill pointed out.

"Well, *you* think of something, then!"

An evil genius made Doris hit on 'Impertinent Questions'! However, nobody was very much interested in what she was doing at the moment, so they pulled out the big drop-leaves table, set it up, and out of the twenty-three, thirteen crowded round it. Mary-Lou was dealer by dint of shrieking "Bags me to deal first!" at the full pitch of her lungs before anyone else had thought about it, and while Vi and Doris spread the second pack over the table, she dealt the other round. There was a moment's pause while they sorted out their cards. Then she drew one from the heap.

"Who is afraid of mice?" she demanded, before turning it up.

Lesley owned to it, and took her turn at drawing. Miss Linton, popping her head in as she went past, was relieved to find that most of the form were enjoying the latest craze, and withdrew to hurry on to the Staff room to join her colleagues, who were amusing themselves with needlework, letter-writing, and novels. Later, she was to be sorry she had not stayed. Not being a prophetess, however, she could not foresee what was to come of that apparently harmless game.

The usual stock questions were asked and owned to with screams of laughter, and the first game came to an end without any trouble. At that point, a Fifth Former came to say that Matron wanted three of them for fittings for new school frocks. Verity-Ann, Angela Carter, and Iris Wells ran off, and the remaining ten settled down to another game, with Viola as dealer this time.

"It's more fun with fewer, really," Ruth Barnes observed, as she picked up her five cards and surveyed them. "Couldn't we have two more packs? It 'ud give us more cards."

"Well, we couldn't, 'cos two people would get the card you turned up," Mary-Lou said quickly. "You couldn't have two people drawing at once."

"No, I s'pose you couldn't," Ruth agreed. "Get cracking, Vi."

Vi drew the card, and demanded: "Who can't do Latin?"

"Me!" Anne Carter showed its mate. "It's true too. I hate Latin. My turn now. I'll ask—Oh—I know. Who lost Golly?"

Golly was the form mascot. They had been careless more than once in leaving him lying about out of school hours, and Miss Linton had threatened to take him from them if they could not remember to put him away at the end of the day. He had been missing at the beginning of the week, and they had thought that she had fulfilled her threat; but when, greatly daring, Vi and Doris had gone together to ask her for him, she had told them she had not seen him since the Friday. Since then, the little girls had hunted for him spasmodically, but so far he had not been found.

The answer came to Gwen Davis, who protested loudly before she went on to demand: "Who sucks her pencils?"

"Me," said Mary-Lou, with a grin, as she thought of the badly-chewed stumps in her pencil-box. "Who makes faces in church?"

"I've got it." This was Vi in scandalised tones. "I *never* would do such a thing, Mary-Lou, and you know it." Then, in rather different tones: "Who mixes salt with sugar?"

"I've got it." Phil, who had joined in because she could

57

think of nothing better to do, produced the ace of hearts. "Well, I don't; but it's quite an idea."

"Don't you do it," Vi said quickly. "You'll only get into an awful row if you do, and you've had two to-day already, Phil."

Phil scowled at her. Then she drew her card and asked: "Who cheats at sums?"

Now the other questions had been asked in fun. No one imagined that Vi would make faces in church, or that Gwen had had anything to do with the disappearance of Golly. But there was no fun in this. Phil's tone was full of malice, and the worst of it was that they all knew what she was hinting at. As a very new girl, Ruth Barnes had looked at the answers to her sums when she had done them. She had had a governess previously, and had been taught to work in that way. If her own answers were wrong, then she had been expected to work the sums again until she got them right. By accident she had been given an arithmetic book which had the answers at the back, and had done as she had been taught. Of course as soon as the thing was explained to her by Miss Edwards, she had been very contrite, and had never done such a thing again. Besides which, 'Teddy', as the girls called her, had taken away the book and provided Ruth with the usual pupils' copy. 'Teddy' had explained the whole thing carefully to the form, for Ruth had had no intention of cheating, and had been badly upset by the remarks of some of her form-mates. No one had ever referred to it until now, when Phil vented her ill-temper in this way.

There was an instant uproar, Ruth proclaiming that she *didn't* cheat and Phil was a pig to say it; Mary-Lou and Vi turning on Phil and angrily asking what she meant by asking such a beastly question; and Phil herself coolly remarking: "I didn't say she did. I only *asked* the question. If the cap fits she can wear it!"

"It was a *foul* question to ask!" Mary-Lou stormed, her pink cheeks going red, and her blue eyes flashing. "Only a *pig* would ask such a thing, and you *are* a pig, Phil Craven! Don't mind, Ruthie! *We* know it's not true. She's a lot more likely to cheat herself!"

"I *never* did—I *never* meant it as cheating," wept Ruth, who had dissolved into tears by this time. "*Teddy* knew I didn't. I've never looked up another answer since, and I've had my sums wrong heaps of times!"

Vi Lucy turned on Phil, too. "You're a horrid little *poop*, Phil Craven, and anyhow, Teddy said we weren't to mention it again, so you've broken her rule as well as being beastly rotten to poor Ruth!"

A little alarmed at the tempest she had roused, but still too angry to care much, Phil retorted: "I *didn't* mention it! Asking a question like that at a game isn't mentioning it! Anyhow, she wouldn't have fired up like that if she hadn't done it. Of course Teddy took her word—she's Teddy's pet!" That was outrageously untrue, for Miss Edwards made no favourites, and if she had, would have been most unlikely to pitch on Ruth Barnes, whose work frequently made her feel inclined to tear her hair.

"Blatherskites!" This was Lesley Malcolm. "Teddy doesn't make pets! She doesn't like any of us very well, *I* think! Look how she goes for us in form!"

"*You* think!" Phil sneered. "You don't know how!"

"She knows as well as you, Phil Craven—and a lot better!" someone put in. "But you're so beastly cocky about your own sums! And you can't write a composition any better'n a K.G. kid, anyhow!"

Phil suddenly saw red. Her temper, always irritable, and none too good that day in any case, boiled over. She made no verbal reply; but she flung herself on the speaker—Gwen Davies—and slapped her face with all her force. It was enough. In less time than it takes to tell, the entire form was embroiled in a free-for-all, even those who had not been playing being drawn into it when they were fallen over, accidentally kicked by the combatants, or sat on by people who had been pushed on to them. Such a noise as the party made could hardly fail to draw someone in authority to the scene, for Ruth wept loudly; Mary-Lou was shrieking insults at Phil what time she tried to tug that young woman's short hair; and Phil herself was treating one of Mary-Lou's fair pigtails as if it were a bell-rope.

59

Other people were involved in different ways, and the air fairly sizzled with their remarks to each other.

Then the door opened suddenly, and two people, apparently trying to claw the frocks off each other's backs, looked up to see Miss Annersley standing there regarding the mêlée with a look that grew grimmer and grimmer!

Anne Carter and Mary Leigh let go of each other and hurriedly slunk to the nearest seats while hissing to such as were near them: "Cave! The Head! "

Mary-Lou was the first to hear. She took her fingers abruptly off Phil's hair and turned, even as Phil, with a yell of triumph, flung herself on her. Beneath the unexpected weight, both little girls went down, and those beside them, turning to look, also saw the Head and stopped dead in whatever they were doing. Silence fell, broken only by Ruth's sobs, a silence that could be felt, so that that young lady uncovered her face, saw Miss Annersley, gave a terrific gulp, and sat quiet, her face still wet with tears.

The Head came slowly into the room and shut the door behind her, also shutting out a motley throng which had been drawn to the scene by the noise. She stood there, looking round in deadly silence, and one by one, heads drooped, and hot colour flamed in the cheeks of most people. What *had* they been doing? And what, oh, *what* would be their punishment?

Miss Annersley seemed in no hurry to speak. She continued to stand in silence, looking from one to another with steely eyes that took in the overturned chairs and small tables; the pieces of jigsaw puzzles lying on the floor; the books lying beside them, their leaves crumpled and, in some cases, torn; the playing-cards adding to the disorder. And her pupils sat or stood with their hearts in their mouths and every ounce of pluck or defiance oozing out of their shoes. Then she spoke:

"Make this room tidy—and do it quietly, please."

Quickly, and as silently as small girls can, the late warriors hastened to do her bidding. Chairs were set upright, and tables restored to their legs. Books were picked up and the leaves smoothed. Mary-Lou and Vi gathered up the playing-cards and sorted them with trembling fingers. Phil

Craven helped Ruth Barnes to gather together the pieces of a jigsaw under their feet. In short order the room was as primly neat as if it had never been used, and then the girls stood still, waiting tremblingly to hear their doom. But she was not ready for that yet.

"Now you may go, three at a time, and make yourselves fit to be seen," she said. "Wait!" She turned and opened the door. Not an onlooker remained. They had caught the expression on her face as she closed the door, and had scuttled off to their own quarters at top speed. She turned back to the culprits. "Now you may go. Viola Lucy, Mary-Louise Trelawney, and Doris Hill first, please. When you come back I will send the next three. Phillida Craven, stand still! Ruth Barnes, where is your handkerchief?"

"I've l-lost it," gasped Ruth, who had been rubbing a dirty hand across her eyes.

The Head made no remark. She simply took out her clean one and handed it to Ruth in silence, while Mary-Lou, Vi, and Doris vanished, to return as soon as possible very clean, and very tidy as to hair, though their frocks still showed signs of the manhandling they had had. The Head waved them to chairs at the far side of the room, and despatched the next three. Half-way through the performance, the three Matron had called off returned, and the scene on which they came so staggered them that at first they could only stammer when the Head asked where they had been.

Verity-Ann managed to recover herself, however, and explained they had been with Matron, whereupon they were sent to the Junior Middles common-room with instructions to stay there till they were told what to do.

Three by three the others went out, untidy and dirty. Three by three they returned, clean and as neat as could be expected. When Gwen Davies came in and shut the door behind her, and had gone to the chair left for her, the Head made the rounds, examining each girl for injuries. There were bruises and bumps, and some people had sore heads from vigorous hair-pulling, but no other casualties. The Head sent Lesley Malcolm for Matron and the first-aid box, and the damage was seen to swiftly and still silently.

And that was almost the very worst of it. If only Miss Annersley had spoken to them, it wouldn't have seemed so awful. But this deathly silence affected them more horribly than the sharpest scolding could have done. A good many people were on the verge of tears by the time Matron put the bottle of Pond's back into the box, shut it with a snap, and departed with it to her own quarters. No one dared to cry, of course. They were not very sure what appalling punishment might descend on them if they did. So they sat there while the Head walked to the fireplace and stood there, looking at them with eyes that they had never seen so hard before.

At long last she spoke. "Now," she said gravely, "I do not wish to hear any of the reasons for your behaviour this afternoon. Let it be enough for the present that you have disgraced yourselves, your form, and your parents. To-morrow, when you have all had time to think over to-day's events, I will see you and hear what excuse, if any, you have for such conduct. At present, you will all go up to your dormitories and go to bed for the rest of the day. You may not speak to anyone except Matron or a mistress. Any girl disobeying this order will be punished accordingly to-morrow." She paused, and the vagueness of her threat appalled their souls. Then she went on: "You may get up at the usual hour to-morrow, and join the school for Frühstück, but you may not speak to anyone until I give you leave. Do you all understand?"

A low murmur round the room told her that they did.

"Very well," she said. "Now, stand! Form into line! Up to your dormitories—*march*! Phillida Craven! No pushing!"

Phil had tripped, but she was too much over-awed to say so. She marched meekly away with the others and they all went to bed, to spend a long, long evening, hearing laughter and music floating up the stairs as the rest of the school danced and played games after tea, which, for them, consisted of mugs of milk and bread and butter. Supper was the same thing, and lights out came directly after supper. Matron never said a word to them as she went the rounds with her trays, and after what the Head had said, no one dared speak even in a whisper. It was a *dreadful* evening! More pillows than one were wet with tears before, tired out with all that had happened, they fell asleep.

The next morning, the same silence was imposed, and by the time that they were summoned to the Head's study to hear their doom, there was no fight left in even Phil Craven. Miss Annersley put a few trenchant questions, and soon got to the bottom of the story. Then she delivered her verdict. For the rest of the term they were to be treated like the Kindergarten, and would have either a mistress or prefect with them in any free time. They would not be allowed to go anywhere by themselves, and they would not go over to Carnbach until after half-term. They would be fined to pay for the damage they had done to the books and jigsaws, and no one would be allowed to use Bank for a fortnight. Finally, they would lose all their conduct marks for the next week.

By the time she had finished, at least half of them were weeping saltily, and the other half were hard put to it not to follow suit. Then she told Phil, Mary-Lou, Vi, and Ruth to stay behind, and dismissed the rest, completely subdued for some days to come. Ruth was speedily disposed of, for she was only told that no one so much as thought she would cheat, and she was a very silly little girl to let the nonsense of another silly little girl upset her to such a pitch. Then she, too, was dismissed. Mary-Lou and Vi were sharply scolded for the really shocking language they had used, and told that if such a thing occurred again, they would have their mouths soaped out. Finally, when the door had closed on them, the Head dealt with Phil. Phil never told anyone what was said to her, but she left the study weeping like a waterspout, and had to be left at home when the rest went to church. But it is on record that after that she really did try to overcome her quick temper. And it is certain that as long as she remained at the Chalet School, Ruth heard no more about her early mistake with the arithmetic book.

"But the horridest part of it all," mourned Mary-Lou, towards the end of the week when most of them were beginning to recover, "is that we mayn't play Impertinent Questions again at school, and it *is* such a lovely game! "

CHAPTER SIX

Joey Arrives

DICKIE CHRISTY was walking along the high road on her way to school. It was Monday, and she had gone home at the week-end as usual, to find her stepmother struggling with the beginnings of influenza, Cherry in the sulks, and Gaynor as full of naughtiness as she could be. Being Dickie, she had taken hold at once, and coerced, coaxed, and scolded her family into reasonable behaviour. Mother Carey she had ordered off to bed at once, and since she was feeling really ill, Mrs. Christy had meekly obeyed her dominant stepdaughter and gone, and there Dickie had kept her for the whole week-end. There she still was, and there she was likely to remain, since Dr. Parry had been summoned, and had ordered it.

Gaynor's sinfulness had been checked by a threat of bed, too, until she could make up her mind to be good. Gaynor hated bed as a punishment. She would far rather have had a spanking. She had looked at her big sister with thoughtful blue eyes, realised that Dickie meant every word she said, and decided that if it was a choice between doing as she was told and being sent to bed for the whole day on a lovely sunny day, it was wiser to be obedient.

Cherry's sulks were a much more difficult matter. Wisely, Dickie left her to herself, while she tackled the cooking, and then, having finished and seen that the kitchen was spotlessly clean, collected the big basket of mending, and went into the pretty garden, where Gaynor was digging at 'mine darden' with small regard for the pathetic plants which resented being disturbed so ruthlessly. Gaynor was hot and dirty, but she was not getting into mischief. Dickie heaved a sigh of relief, propped her *Romoe and Juliet* up in front of her so that she could learn the speech set for homework, and darned steadily. Cherry, in another chair set in the farthest corner of the garden, gloomed with equal steadiness.

For half an hour, Dickie took no further notice of her. Then she raised her voice: "Cherry! "

Two minutes passed. Then Cherry answered sulkily: "Well?"

"Come over here and listen to the latest at school. I can't yell right across the garden, and I've got a really good story for you."

"I don't want to hear it, thank you."

Dickie remained imperturbable. "Oh, very well; I'll tell Gaynor. Gaynor, leave those wretched flowers alone, pet, and come and I'll tell you a story."

Gaynor was tiring of her digging. She dropped her spade and came to squat at Dickie's feet. Dickie told the sad tale of the Junior's fight, and her small sister chuckled loudly over it. Cherry couldn't help hearing a word or two, and inwardly she was longing to know the whole tale; but she was nursing a full-sized grievance, and determined to let her family know it. The day before she had teased Gaynor till that small person wept, and their mother had scolded her sharply. Commander Christy had entered on the scene, made inquiries, and then informed Cherry that as she had been so tiresome, there would be no going to St. Brandon Mawr for her next day. He had rung up Kester Bellever to that effect, wherefore, man-sized sulks from Cherry ever since.

Dickie finished the story, and then seeing her small sister's eyelids drooping, picked her up, carried her into the house, and left her to have a nap on the dining-room sofa. She had gone back to her mending and prep and by teatime had darned all her father's socks and a pair of Mother Carey's stockings, mended a bad tear in one of Gaynor's frocks, and put buttons on two or three other garments. She put her work away, got tea ready, carried a tray to Mother Carey, who was very feverish and aching, and called to Cherry to take Gaynor along to the little cloakroom and wash her. Cherry, still suffering from the

65

C

hump, had snarled: "Do it yourself!" and Dickie had decided that perhaps she had better. At tea, which they had
by themselves, as the Commander had gone over to Carnbach on business, Cherry had persevered in her sulks, so
that Dickie and Gaynor had had all the chatter to themselves. Dickie had washed the dishes, run upstairs to sponge
her stepmother's hot face and hands, and then come back
to the mending and her New Testament until Gaynor's
early bed-time. Cherry had departed at eight as usual, still
sullen, and Dickie, with an empty mending-basket, had prepared supper, and when it was over, and Mother Carey
attended to for the night, had gone thankfully to her own
room. It had been a trying afternoon and evening.

Cherry had wakened in no better mood, and Mother
Carey was still very poorly, so Sunday had been almost as
hard. Luckily the Commander was at home, and he took
Cherry and Gaynor to church in the morning, and spent
the afternoon with them. By bedtime that night, Cherry had
suddenly melted into repentance, and cried out all her woes
on Dickie's shoulder.

"All the same," thought the girl as she hurried along
the road, "I wish she would come to school. I'm certain
she'd be better if she did. She gets lonely and bored with
just Gaynor; and Mother Carey has far too much to do
between the pair of them!"

She turned in at the gates at this point, and found Gay
and Jacynth awaiting her impatiently.

"Why on earth are you walking?" demanded Gay.

"Bike's got a bad puncture so I had to," Dickie returned.
"What's up with you two? You look all excited about
something."

"I should just think we are! What d'you think? Mrs.
Maynard's coming on Thursday for a long week-end! Bill
told us at Frühstück this morning."

"You'll see her at last," added Jacynth rather more
quietly. "You'd have known her weeks ago if we'd been at
Plas Howell still. She always has a party for the new girls."

"If the school had still been at Plas Howell, I'd not have
been at it," Dickie retorted, as they sauntered up the drive.
"I thought you folk understood that. I can be spared from

66

home for the week—and anyhow. I'm close at hand if I'm wanted for anything. But I jolly well couldn't be spared for a whole term. As it is, I've got a note from Dad asking if I can go home after afternoon school for the next few days. Mother Carey is pretty rotten, and Gaynor has been behaving like a little demon."

"Oh, I say! That's bad luck! " sympathised Gay. "What's wrong, Dickie?"

"Flu, I think. Dad saw Doc when he came; but it looks like flu to me."

"Hope you don't catch it," Jacynth said.

"Not much likelihood. I've never had it yet—touch wood! Your head'll do, Gay! —so I don't think I'm likely to have it now."

"Touch your own head! " Gay protested. "It's as wooden as mine! "

"Stop ragging, you two! " Jacynth intervened. "I thought we'd had enough of that last week! Anyhow. you're a pree, Gay, and prees don't scrap like small kids."

Gay grinned at her. "Alack the day! All right; I'll be an angel. Dickie, I hope your stepmother will be all right by the end of the week. We've got a tremendous treat coming off then. On Thursday night, Kester Bellever is coming to give us a talk on sea-birds; and on Saturday he's asked us seniors to go over to St. Brandon Mawr to have a look at the sanctuary if it's fine. The Middles and the kids are going at other times. It'll be swell, won't it?"

"For goodness' sake, Gay, *don't* use that ghastly expression! " Jacynth protested. "It's forbidden to the kids, and ought to be to us. Anyhow, I loathe it. For pity's sake be careful! "

Gay looked rather ashamed of herself. "I forgot in my delight. O-kay, Granny! I won't use it again if I can help it."

"See you don't! " returned her friend austerely.

Gay had been an imp from her earliest years, and got into endless trouble at school until the more serious-minded Jacynth had arrived, and they had chummed up. Jacynth had lost her only relation, the aunt who had brought her up. The news had come when she was already ill with German measles, and the shock had affected her badly. Tender-hearted Gay had promptly insisted on 'adopting' her, and as Jo Maynard, who had told her the sad news, had also promised her a home at Plas Gwyn, she was not so lonely as she would have been. Most holidays were spent with Gay at her stepbrother's home in the north, and Jacynth, under her quiet exterior, had a passionate love and grati-tude for the girl who had helped her, as well as for Jo Maynard who gave her the 'mothering' she lacked when they met. Hence Gay kept out of trouble, thanks to Jacynth.

The pair had taken Dickie into the outer circle of their friendship, and Dickie, who had made few lasting friends, thanks to her various removals, hoped that this would prove a real friendship. Now she looked at them with her blue eyes full of gravity.

"I'd love to go with you. Cherry's been over to Brandon Mawr a good many times; but being at school has rather done it for me. If Mother Carey is all right, I can go, I'm sure. If she isn't, I'll just have to hope for a visit later on."

"Anyway, you'll see our Jo," Gay said, as they reached the house. "You pop off to the Head—it's Bill, by the way. Miss Annersley's had to go to Plas Howell to see how they're getting on with the drains—and then come along to our form-room. You've just got time if you scram now."

Dickie nodded and vanished down the hall to seek Miss Wilson while the other two went to join the rest of their form. Bill was sympathetic about Mother Carey, but she looked rather sober over the influenza.

"If you don't feel well, Dickie, I'm afraid you mustn't turn up at school," she said. "We don't want flu this term if we can help it."

Dickie repeated what she had said to Gay and Jacynth, without the remark about touching wood, needless to state, and 'Bill's' face relaxed.

"Very well, dear. I hope it will be for a day or two only. If you find you can't manage all your prep, come to me, and I'll see what we can do about it. Now you must go. The bell will ring in a few minutes, and I want to finish this letter first."

"Yes, Miss Wilson. Thank you very much." Dickie

bobbed her curtsy and departed, and Bill returned to her letter.

The next two days passed quietly enough. Dickie went home each afternoon to take charge, and Cherry, properly ashamed of her sulks of the week-end, was at her most angelic, and looked after Gaynor without teasing her. Mother Carey's temperature went down, thanks to freedom from worry as well as to the care she received, and by Wednesday she was sitting up in her room with the promise of being downstairs by the end of the week. So Dickie joined in the excitement at Jo Maynard's visit, and looked hopefully forward to being able to go with the others on the Saturday.

Thursday began as usual. The Sixth had history first with Miss Burnett, and then French with Mlle de Lachenais. After break they went to Miss Wilson for two hours' chemistry, the half-dozen or so who did not take it having extra history, and extra Latin. Dickie went to science; Gay and Jacynth did not. Kathie Robertson also took science, and so did Ursula Nicholls, who was keen, but by no means brilliant.

Miss Wilson set them a brief test in practical work, and then devoted her time to wandering round among them to keep an eye on what they were doing.

Half-way through the test, an appalling smell of burning arose, and Bill, at the other side of the lab, came flying to Kathie Robertson, who was standing up, crushing her short thick mop between her hands.

"What are you doing, Kathie?" the mistress demanded.

"I—I singed my hair," Kathie explained, looking sheepish.

"What on earth were you doing to do that?" the irate mistress asked.

Ursula, next to Kathie, spoke up. "It was my fault, Miss Wilson. I thought my bunsen wasn't going properly, so I asked Kathie to look at it, and she did, and she caught her hair in her own," she said lamely.

"So I see. Take your hands away and let me see," Bill commanded.

Kathie dropped her hands, and fragments of burnt hair

69

showered on to the floor. Bill stared at her, and gasped.

"Really, Kathie! And where is your gauze?" she demanded.

"I forgot to use it. I'm sorry, Miss Wilson."

"At your age! Really, you might be Lower Fourth! Your hair will have to be properly cut, for you can't go about looking like that! In future you are to wear something over your hair when you do practical work. As for you, Ursula, if anything goes wrong with your apparatus, *I* am the person to ask; not another girl. Put the gauze on your work, Kathie, and go on. Wait! Have you hurt yourself at all?"

"No, Miss Wilson."

"Let me see your hands."

Kathie spread out her hands, but she had been so quick that they were not even slightly scorched. Miss Wilson dismissed her to go on with her work, and turned to Ursula, who had contrived to get the jet of her bunsen choked in some mysterious way. Bill was busy digging it clear when the door opened, and a tall, slim figure appeared in the doorway. Everyone was busy with her work, no one being anxious to attract Bill's attention at the moment, so no one noticed until Dickie, lifting her head from her apparatus to jot down a few notes happened to glance across at the door. The gasp of amazement she gave drew the attention of Nancy Canton, working next to her. Nancy looked up, and dropped her pencil with a cry of "Mrs. Maynard!" which ended work for everyone. Bill set down the bunsen, and hurried down the room with outstretched hands to greet Jo.

"Joey! We didn't expect you till much later. How have you managed it?"

"Jack drove Miss Annersley and me to Carnbach," Jo explained. "It's a glorious road most of the way, so he let Seraphina out. We did eighty m.p.h. at one part. I didn't mind, being accustomed to him; but Miss Annersley rather held her breath. I saw her doing it in the mirror! May I speak to everyone, or am I interrupting something important?—Kathie Robertson! What in heaven's name have you been doing to your hair? You look worse than Grizel

70

did when her curls got caught by the flames in the hotel at Salzburg! You do look a young sight! "

Kathie turned puce, and a chuckle went round the room.

"She frizzled her hair in the bunsen," someone explained.

Jo grinned, and turned to Bill. "Remember when Evvy Lanis singed off her eyebrows and eyelashes with an explosion?" she asked.

Bill nodded. "I do indeed. Talk of one's heart leaping into one's throat! I thought mine had gone through the top of my head! Well, it's very nice to see you, Joey; but these people have work to do. Say what you want to say, and then—*out*! "

"You were always short with me," Jo complained as she looked round. "Well, everyone, it's good to see you all again. We've missed you horribly at Howells. Nancy Canton, you've *grown again*! When do you mean to stop?"

Nancy, a six-footer, turned scarlet as she replied: "I only wish I knew! How long are you staying, Joey? Have you seen your own pair?"

"First thing, naturally. What did you expect? I'm staying till next Thursday. Anna will look after the boys, and I need a holiday."

"Haven't you brought Michael?" Janet Scott asked.

"Not even him. He's almost a year now, and can do without me. He's very fit, and Mrs. Trelawney agreed to take charge of him for the week."

"How is Margot getting on?" Ursula asked shyly.

"Very well indeed. My sister says she's putting on weight, and is looking splendid. So is Josette. And Ailie is sprouting up. Canada seems to be suiting all of them finely." She stopped speaking, as her roving glance fell on Dickie. Then she went forward. "I'm certain you're Dickie Christy! You wrote to me two years ago, didn't you, about one of my books. I'm so glad to meet you at last. How do you like school, Dickie?"

"Very much, thank you," stammered Dickie, rather taken aback by this very public notice.

"Good! Though I'd certainly have taken a running jump backwards if you'd said anything else. Well, I can see I'm not awfully welcome at the moment, so I'll depart. I'll see you all later on. Bye-bye!" She waved her hand at them, and departed laughing. Miss Wilson followed her through the door, and for a minute or two the girls were left alone.

"Isn't she super?" demanded Kathie, who was not noticeably upset by her accident. "Did you really write to her about her books, Dickie?"

"Well, I did," Dickie confessed. Then, "Cave! Here's Bill!"

The girls stopped talking, and turned their attention to their experiments, and work was resumed.

Meanwhile, Jo had gone back to the house, where she ran upstairs to seek Matron. She found that lady busily engaged in turning out the medicine cupboard, and nearly caused a catastrophe as she leapt forward, caught the wiry little figure in her arms, and gave her a hug.

"Matey! It's wizard to see you again! Oh, *how* I've missed you all! If the school ever goes back to Tirol Jack must get another job out there, for I should go crackers without you! I'd no idea how much I depended on you!"

"I'll thank you not to half strangle me when I've got the castor-oil in one hand and the liniment in the other," Matron retorted, putting the bottles safely down on the table. "Come to the window and let me look at you, Jo."

Jo followed her to the window, and stood still to submit to a close scrutiny. Matron scanned the clear-cut face with its creamy pallor and broad black fringe of hair in silence. Then she spoke.

"You're looking tired. What's the matter? You'd better take a course of my tonic while you're here, I think."

Jo made a grimace. "Have a heart! Matey, you couldn't possibly ruin my holiday by making me take that ghastly stuff! I remember it all too well. I've had some bad nights with Michael's teeth. However, he seems to have got all the worrying ones through for the moment, and Jack said I could leave him quite safely for a week or even a fortnight."

"Come to me after Mittagessen," Matron said, with a

nod. "Yes, Jo; I mean it. You want a rest, but you also need a tonic. Now don't argue! I know what's good for you!"

The mother of six went pink, and said meekly: "No, Matey. All right; I'll come. Don't let my kids know, though," she added in horror-struck tones.

"Do be sensible, Jo! As if I should! Well, there's not quite an hour to Mittagessen, so you'd better go and take a chair out in the rose-garden. I'm busy, and can't be bothered with you at present."

The words were sharp, but the look in the grey eyes under the nurse's cap belied both them and her tones, and Jo grinned. She needed no one to tell her that after all the years she still remained Matey's darling.

"No one loves me just now! Bill has just turfed me out of the lab. I think I'll go along to the Sixth and see if I'm more popular there."

Matron glanced at her copy of the timetable. "It's Mlle, so I don't suppose she'll mind. Very well; off with you, you monkey!"

"Matey! What a way to speak to me, and me a respectable wife and mother!"

Matron knew her Jo. "You may be all you say. You'll never be anything to me but the worst nuisance of a girl I ever had dealings with. Now be off with you, and worry someone else for a change!"

"Okey-doke! Oh, and don't try to improve my language! I know it gets worse every year, but I'm me, and I can't change to please anyone."

Matron said no more, but waved her off; and, greatly refreshed by the encounter, Jo strolled away to seek the Sixth. She peeped in at several doors, to find that she was looking into dormitories. Then she turned a corner, heard voices proceeding from the far end of the short passage, and shot down it to tap humbly at the door and wait for admittance. A pleasant voice said, "Entrez!" and Jo opened the door, and reached her goal at last. Mlle de Lachenais was here, and various members of the Sixth that she had missed in the lab.

"May I come in?" she asked, in her meekest tones, though her black eyes were dancing under their long lashes.

Little Mlle jumped up from her seat. "But Jo! When did you come? How have you come so soon?" she cried in her own language.

Jo told her tale in fluent French that was a legacy from her own years at the Chalet School, and after a little more chatter, they turned to the girls who were waiting for their turn eagerly.

"Hello, everyone!" The visitor had reverted to her mother-tongue. "Well, you all look blooming, I must say! This place seems to suit you. Mlle!" She turned to that lady after a glance at her watch. "It's only ten minutes till bell-time. Can't we talk when I've only just arrived?"

Mlle beamed. "Mais oui, ma chérie! Moi, je parle aussi."

Jo sat down on top of an empty desk. "This is wizard! Gay, you look as bonny and as naughty as ever. Frances, how are the kids at home? Quite well, Jacynth, my lamb? Jean Mackay, you've bobbed your hair!"

Jean, a Scots girl from Aberdeen, laughed. "It was that or put it up. That would have been an awful pest. It's so short naturally, I'd never have been able to keep it decent. So Mother said I'd better have it cut." She pulled out a strand of the thick brown hair that curled riotously over her head, and added: "It was done at the beginning of the hols, and the next time I had it washed, it turned into a Bubbles crop like Gay's! Still, it's pounds easier to keep tidy."

"It suits you," Jo said, her head cocked on one side. She turned to the two last members of the form. "Joan Wentworth, *you've* taken to glasses! What's wrong with your eyes?"

"Overstrain," Joan, a tall, quiet girl, explained. "I've got to wear them for reading and working for the present, anyhow."

"Hard luck! Still, it will save you a lot of bother later on, I expect." She smiled at the last member of the form, Eiluned Vaughn, a Welsh girl who came from near Howell village. "Eiluned, I saw your mother last week, and told her I was coming, so she gave me a parcel for you. Come to me after Mittagessen and I'll give it to you. Now tell me all the news, everyone!"

The tongues wagged busily for the few minutes left before the bell rang for the end of morning school, and by the time Mlle had to call them to order for dismissal, Jo, as she herself said, had been brought well up to date with all the news. She had heard about the Juniors' battle, and chuckled over it whole-heartedly. She knew about Dickie's little lame sister, and their picnics, and other fun. Then she jumped to her feet as the bell went.

"There's the bell! I must go but I'll see you all later. Meantime, just to give you something to be excited about, I'm going to tell you that to-morrow some things are coming for the school which will give you an extra thrill. Now I'm off!" And she shot from the room, regardless of the protests that followed her flight.

CHAPTER SEVEN

Kester Bellever's Lecture

THE talk was to take place after Abendessen, as the school called the evening meal. The Kindergarten went to bed at their usual hour of seven o'clock—Jo's girls with them, much to their own disgust, for, as Con argued: "Next term we'll be Juniors and Juniors don't go till eight." However, it was no use, Jo merely bidding her daughters keep to rules without argument, though she agreed that it *was* hard lines when the Juniors were to be allowed to sit up to listen, since it would be over by half-past eight or thereabouts.

The lecture was to be illustrated with slides Mr. Bellever had made, and Commander Christy was working the school's lantern, which was run off the electric power plant that happened to be in an out-house just behind the big army hut used for the Kindergarten. He had been busy all day fixing it up, and the small folk had been greatly intrigued until Miss Phipps had arrived and hustled them off, giving the patient man a chance to get on with the job in peace. He had finished by half-past three, and gone home,

but now he returned, bringing with him Cherry. Jo, strolling
in leisurely fashion up the big hut, where the sliding doors
which normally divided it into four rooms had been rolled
back to accommodate the school at large, saw the lovely
little face beside the lantern and smiled involuntarily. She
was considerably startled when Cherry replied with a deep
scowl. That young person had only come because she was
given no chance to do otherwise. At half-past six her stepfather had ordered her to get her hat and come with him
as he wished her to see the slides. Cherry adored him; but
she was also slightly in awe of him. When he spoke with a
certain note in his voice, she obeyed without demur. So it
chanced that she was present; but she had no notion of
making friends with anyone, or regarding the school with
anything but enmity.

Jo sauntered on to her seat amongst the Staff, replying
to greetings which reached her from every side. She had
spent the afternoon with Miss Norman, who happened to
be free, bringing the news for each of them up to date, so
most of the girls were seeing her for the first time since the
end of the previous term. It was almost a royal progress
to her chair. Then she sat down between Mary Burnett and
Grizel Cochrane, both of whom had been at school with
her, while Gillian Linton, another old school-mate, and
Hilary Burn, who had become a pupil the term after Jo
herself had left, were next. Jo settled herself, and glanced
at them. Then she gave a little private grin.

"Well," she remarked, "here I am! But I ought to be
sitting between the two brides-to-be, you know—the old
married woman; Mary and Gill, prospective wives; Hilary
and Grizel, spinsters!"

"Joey! *Will* you hold your tongue?" demanded Miss
Burnett, deep crimson at this. "The girls will hear you!"

"Well, aren't you a bride-to-be? Or have you given your
nice doctor-man the noble order of the mitten?" Jo queried.
"Everyone knows you're leaving to be married, along with
Gillian. Why be so shy about it?"

"You just hold your tongue, Joey," Gillian said quietly.
"If you don't, I'll make Peter include you in that series of
cartoons he's doing for *The Ship of Britain*—you know the

ones? 'Woman in her various spheres.' I'll tell him to do you as 'Woman, the married writer'. Then see how you like *that*!"

"Blackmail!" retorted Jo. "Oh, very well, since you're both so sensitive. However, Gill, I'll put *you* into my next book—as the villainess."

Gillian collapsed. "I'll never speak to you again if you do such a thing! Oh, Jo! Stop teasing, for heaven's sake! You're a regular gadfly!" Jo chuckled to herself; but she let the topic drop, and for the next few minutes the five sat chatting amiably about past times.

Miss Norman, sitting at the other side of the room with Miss Edwards, glanced across at the group, and smiled to herself.

"Jo and Mary haven't changed much," she thought. "Jo is rounder, but she still has the same wicked look that she used to have when she was up to something. Mary hasn't altered since she was eighteen, I believe—good old Faithful! Gillian looks a little older, but then she's had so much responsibility, what with her mother dying and leaving her as guardian to Joyce, and then having to handle all the business for both of them! As for Hilary, she's an infant still, for all her diploma and added years." Her eyes settled on Grizel Cochrane, head of the music. Miss Norman's own face grew more serious. "Grizel's the one who has changed. She can't be more than two years older than Jo, but she looks at least five. What's wrong with her, I wonder, that she always has such a discontented expression? She has plenty of money as well as her salary, so it can't be that. I've never heard that there was any man in the offing, so I don't think it's that, either. Does she want to compose music and finds she can't? She is certainly most dissatisfied with life if her face is anything to judge by!"

"Ivy! I've asked you before! A penny for them!" Miss Edwards broke in on her meditations.

"Oh, sorry! I was just thinking how very little most of our old girls must have changed if that lot over there are anything to go by," Miss Norman explained. "Grizel is the only one who seems to have done much in the way of ageing. She's still very pretty, but she looks so discontented, and it spoils her. Do you know what's wrong with her?"

"Just what it always was, I think. She was made to go in for music very thoroughly without being really musical. So long as her father lived she had to do as he wished or lose her allowance. When he died, she felt it was too late to take up anything else. So she's just gone on, mainly, I think, because it was the easiest thing to do. But it isn't what she really wanted, and though she's an excellent teacher, and the girls do really well with her, I always feel it's more because they daren't do anything else but work for her."

"Do you know what it was she wanted to do?" Ivy Norman asked.

"I've always had an idea she wanted to take up games and P.T."

"H'm! That's a pity! She must be at least thirty now, and that's rather too old to begin that."

"I know. It's a great pity that Mr. Cochrane didn't let her go in for it years ago, but I believe he utterly refused; threatened to cut off supplies, and Grizel hadn't enough of her own to do it without help. So there it is. All the same, she's an ass to let it spoil her life as she does. It isn't all of us by any manner of means who can attain her greatest wish. Grizel teaches well because she won't do a thing if she can't make a success of it; but I'm sorry for her pupils! She's got a nasty tongue on occasion!"

"She always had." Miss Norman stopped. Then she went on: "Do you know, my dear, I've been looking round, and I've come to the conclusion that it isn't many schools that can show such a good-looking Staff as we have here."

Miss Edwards laughed, and the chatter drifted to other subjects.

Meantime, Jo and her friends, having exhausted past times for the nonce, were talking about the present school.

"What's the new girl like? I saw her this morning in the lab, and thought she looked rather a decent kid."

"Dickie Christy is a very nice girl," Mary Burnett said primly.

Jo grinned at her. "Poor old thing! Where does it hurt you most?"

"What on earth are you talking about?"

The sudden rising of the school as the Heads with Kester Bellever in tow entered prevented Jo from replying, so they had to thrash it out later on. At present, the school glanced curiously at the bearded man who sat down in the chair indicated by Miss Annersley, while she moved to stand in front of the screen.

She gave the girls the command to sit by a slight motion of her hand. Then she said: "Mr. Bellever, whose name is, I know, well known to all you elder girls, at any rate, has come to give us his talk about the sea-birds of Great Britain. We are all looking forward to it, and I feel sure that when he has finished we shall all know a great deal more about them than we do at present. I, for one, certainly shall! Now, you don't want any speeches, so I'll just ask him to begin. Mr. Bellever!"

Kester Bellever stood up, and came to stand at one side of the screen while the Head took her seat. Jacynth switched off the lights as the lantern went on, then returned to her place in the back row of seats between Gay Lambert and Dickie, and the lecture began.

Mr. Bellever looked at his audience with rather a shy smile. "I've talked to all sorts of people," he said, "but never to a school before; so if I talk over your heads, do tell me—and at the end, please ask me any questions you like, won't you? I'll answer them if I can."

He paused, and Jo turned her head swiftly, in time to catch the answering smiles of the girls. She declared later that she had never before seen such a brilliant display of teeth.

"I only wonder he didn't cut and run!" she said feelingly. "The entire lot grinning like that looked like a crowd of hungry cannibals greeting the latest aspirant for the cooking-pot!"

"You grinned yourself!" Hilary told her indignantly.

Then the lecture began, and the girls listened, enthralled.

He began with that jester among sea-birds, the puffin, with its huge parrot-like beak, its black and white uniform, and its reddish orange feet. He described it, told how it nests in burrows where it lays one egg only, and where the

79

chick remains till it is quite a big, fat bird. He illustrated all he said with delightful slides, showing puffins in crowds and single birds; adult puffins, and fat, downy babies; puffins on the cliff, and puffins on the water. Then he left the sea-parrot, as it is often called, and went on to a much less well-known bird, the shear-water. He told them that it is another burrower, with sharp bill, and wings cut at an acute angle, so that when the shear-water skims the sea, they seem to *shear* the waves. Next he described its clumsy body with the legs set so far back that on land it can only shuffle clumsily about, and the bird must have a good take-off before it can launch itself in the air. But he explained that the burrow of the shear-water is a clean affair on the whole, while that of the puffin reeks of stinking fish. Those girls who had been on the ferry when he had pointed out one to Cherry remembered what he had said then, and were thrilled with his pictures of the little bird. From there, he proceeded to the guillemots, storm petrels—Mother Carey's chickens to the sailor—with their soot-black coats and dazzlingly white rumps; then to the oyster-catchers, razorbills, choughs, and so to the murderers and pirates of the bird world, the black-backed greater and lesser gulls, the herring gulls, the buzzards and falcons and ravens which prey on the lesser birds, and account for countless shear-waters and puffins during the season. There were many others he named, but there was not time for him to go into much detail about all. The throng listened entranced by the spell of his clear, quiet voice, and when he suddenly said, "Well, that's all for now. Shall we have any questions?" there was an "Oo-ooh!" of dismay from the younger girls.

Jacynth, warned beforehand, slipped out of her place and switched on the lights again, while the school clapped loudly and long until Miss Annersley half-rose in her seat to glance back, when the applause died away, and there was a brief silence. Jo, realising that the girls were shy of beginning questions, calmly stood up and asked hers.

"Mr. Bellever, you've told us about a great many birds, but you never mentioned eagles. Is it true that the eagle is extinct so far as the British Isles are concerned?"

"Well—yes, and no," he replied. "At one time it seemed

as if they were; but of late years occasional pairs have been seen on the Welsh cliffs. The golden eagle, of course, still nests in Scotland and the wilder parts of western Ireland, and has always done so."

The questions began to come after that; and Mary-Lou Trelawney was considered by her own clan to have covered them all with glory when she jumped up to ask: "Please, which is the biggest of the sea-birds—not the eagles and buzzards, I mean, but the rest?"

He smiled at the round, rosy face as he answered: "The gannets, of which I want to tell you in detail some day, have a wing-spread of almost four feet. And then there are some of the wild geese who have as much."

"Don't gannets live in colonies?" Gay Lambert asked, from the back of the room. "I think I've read about them somewhere."

"Gannetries," he said. "Yes; they flock together in thousands, and the gannetries round Britain are all known and numbered. The gannet is protected, you know. I'll tell you one thing," he went on. "Where you have gannets, you frequently get grey seals. Not that the grey seal is an unusual visitor. I've seen them basking in the sun on the rocks to the west of Brandon Mawr before to-day. And they can be seen all along the Hebrides, too, and in the Orkneys and Shetlands."

"I've seen them there—in the Hebrides, I mean," observed Clemency Barras, Mary-Lou's great chum, abruptly. "Dad painted a picture of them for me. I love their big, soft eyes."

He looked at her with interest. "You know the Hebrides? Then you ought to know a good deal about the birds there, too. Did you say your father had painted a picture of the seals? I'd like to see it some time."

"It's in my cubey. If Matron will let me, I'll get it," Clemency said.

Miss Annersley leaned forward and murmured something to him, and he looked at Clemency with even greater interest. She sat down, flushing hotly. That was the worst of being the daughter of a well-known artist! Clem guessed

81

that Miss Annersley had told him that her father was Adrian Barras.

There was a pause. Then Jacynth rose in all her dignity as Head Girl and called for three cheers for Mr. Bellever, whose lecture they had all enjoyed so much. They were given with all the force of the girls' lungs, and three more followed when he said, again with that touch of shyness: "Thank you all very much. It has been a great pleasure to show you the slides. I hope to see some of you on Saturday on Brandon Mawr; and the rest must come later on. Then you can see for yourselves the things I have been describing to you this evening."

After that, the three Junior mistresses took their charges off to bed while the rest of the school streamed out into the garden, which was still bathed in evening sunshine. Miss Annersley beckoned to Jo to join her, and introduced her to Mr. Bellever.

"Mrs. Maynard?" he said, looking at her with puzzled eyes. "But—surely we have met before. I remember you quite well."

Jo shook her head. "Sorry, but I'm certain we haven't met. I should have remembered it, and I know I've never seen you—except in a photo at the head of an article of yours on gannets that I read some time ago in a magazine."

"That's it!" he exclaimed, while the Head left them to speak to Commander Christy. "Of course! You're Jack Maynard's wife! You have triplet girls, and you write books for girls."

"That's me," Jo agreed, with a cheerful disregard of grammar. "Where did you know Jack?"

"It was years ago, in hospital. He was in with a nasty head injury, and I was having sundry pieces of shell removed from my anatomy. I saw your photo with the little girls—what are their names?"

"Len, Con and Margot," Jo replied briskly. "Len and Con are here with the school, but Margot isn't quite so sturdy as the others, so when my sister and her husband had to go to Canada for a conference, they took her with them for the sake of the change, which seems to be working wonders from what they say in their letters."

"That's splendid," he said. "And what about your husband? Is he all right now? I was moved to another hospital before he left. I've often wondered how he got on."

"Jack's all right now. He had a sticky time at first, but it's over, and he's as fit as he ever was. We've got three boys as well as the girls now," Jo said, changing the subject abruptly. She could never bear to think of those awful months when first they had feared Jack was dead, and then that he would never fully recover from his hurt.

"More triplets?" Mr. Bellever asked, with a grin.

"Heavens, no! Singletons, thank you! Steve is five, Charles was four last week, and Michael will be a year old next month. The girls are eight."

"You've done yourselves proud, haven't you? Six is quite a family."

"Oh, I expect there'll be two or three more before we're finished," Jo replied absently. "Mr. Bellever, am I included as a Senior for the party on Saturday? I'd love to see your birds and seals."

"Oh, rather! Please do come. It's rather a bare spot," he went on apologetically. "I have the mere necessities of life, with all the gear I want for bird watching, and normally I don't want any more."

"Don't worry! We'll bring our eats with us. You may expect to see us complete with bag of buns in one hand and a mug in the other," Jo assured him solemnly. "Thanks awfully! I'll come, then. Hello! Here comes young Clem with her picture, and a covey of autograph books following, so I'll leave you to it." She moved away with a sweet disregard of his exclamation of dismay at the prospect, and proceeded to hunt up Commander Christy to demand if she might call on his wife next day.

"Yes; she'd like it," he said laconically. Then he pulled forward Cherry, who was glued to his side, though Dickie had tried to prise her away to introduce her to some of the younger girls of her own age. "This is our second girl, Cherry—another of your fans, Mrs. Maynard. Dick tells me you've spoken to her already. Cherry, here's Josephine M. Bettany. You've always wanted to meet her, haven't you?"

The scowl faded from Cherry's lovely little face. "Oh, I do so want to tell you how much Dickie and I love your stories! " she said breathlessly. "We think they're all simply marvellous—especially *Tessa in Tirol*. Was there *really* a school there, or did you make it up?"

Jo sat down on a nearby garden seat, and drew Cherry down beside her. "Let's sit, shall we? My dear kid, this *is* the school," she said, with a comprehensive wave of her hand round the groups of girls and mistresses laughing and chattering on the lawn. "We began in Tirol, you know, and I was at the place myself for nearly six gorgeous years. Did no one ever tell you about us during that time?"

Cherry went red. Dickie had tried to interest her in the school, but had been shut up every time she had mentioned it until at last she had dropped the subject altogether where Cherry was concerned. That young woman was blankly ignorant of the school's past in consequence.

"I didn't know," she said meekly.

"Well, it's so. Why, some of the present Staff were at school with me and a good many of the older ones had the joy—*or* otherwise! —of teaching me." Jo heaved an elderly sigh. "That was years ago, of course. What wizard times we did have then! "

"How?" Cherry demanded.

"You've read a good deal of it in my books," Jo informed her. "When you come to the school, some of the others will tell you a lot of the rest, I don't doubt. I know that a good many of our Tirol adventures have become school tradition."

"Is it really true that you spent a whole night on an Alp, drinking milk that tasted of onions and wood smoke, and sleeping on hay?"

Jo gave an involuntary wriggle. "*And* got it all down our necks! I can feel it yet when I think of it! What a set of abject little sights we must have looked when we got down to Briesau next morning! Talk of straws in the hair! The maddest lunatics could have had nothing on *us*! "

Cherry said nothing, but she thought hard. If this was the sort of thing that could happen at Chalet School, it mightn't be too bad. Perhaps she would change her mind about coming. The school was to be at St. Briavel's for at least another term, she knew. She might agree to going in September. It wouldn't be so hard if she got to know one or two of the other girls. If only they wouldn't stare at her legs in the irons!

Meanwhile, Jo was looking round. So was someone else. There was a flurry of pigtails, and a Junior Middle came racing to fling herself on the tall dark lady and exclaim: "Oh, Auntie Jo! Wasn't it a *wizard* lecture? Did you like it? I did—awfully! "

"It was," Jo agreed. "Here, Mary-Lou, do you know Dickie Christy's young sister—at least, I suppose that's what you call it?" she added doubtfully to Cherry, who was looking rather alarmed.

"Ye-es," she agreed, in frightened tones. "We're adopted sisters, anyway."

"I rather thought it would be something like that. Well, this is Mary-Lou Trelawney, an adoptee of my own. I'm her adopted aunt, as you may see. She asked the question about big birds—do you remember? Well done, Mary-Lou, by the way. I was glad you were keen enough to ask it. And now you go and fetch Verity-Ann, and Vi Lucy, and the rest of your tribe and look after Cherry. She'll be coming to school sooner or later, I expect, and she may as well get some idea of what she's coming to before she arrives. Let her down lightly, I implore you! Keep the worst of your sinful ways quiet just yet, won't you?"

"Oh, Auntie Jo! " Mary-Lou had a fit of the giggles. "We never do anything frightfully bad—nothing worse than *you* ever did, anyhow! "

"I'm none too sure of that," quoth Jo darkly. "Do as I tell you and bring the others, like a good kid! Scram! "

Mary-Lou scampered off with another giggle, and returned in a minute with four or five other small girls, and Jo gave them a smiling nod, and got up and left them to make friends in their own way. She had already heard from Miss Annersley and Miss Wilson about the difficulties with Cherry, and had butted in in her own inimitable way. She could not be sure of it yet, of course, but she was to learn later on that, where everyone else had failed, she had succeeded, so far as the coming to school was concerned. Mary-Lou and her chums were a set of jolly youngsters, prepared to take life as they found it. They accepted Cherry's troubles without remark, and no one 'stared' at her legs, though Vi Lucy hoped sympathetically that it wouldn't be long before she would be rid of the irons.

"It means you can't play games or dance, or things like that, you see," she said. "I do call it horrid luck, Cherry. But when you come, we'll give you a hand when you want it till the irons are off. When do you *think* you'll be coming?"

This matter-of-fact way of taking it was a great comfort to Cherry, who fell in with it at once, and went home with half her dislike of the school already gone, and in a fair way to rid herself of the other half before very long. After all, it *had* been jolly difficult to keep their big house nice, and it was much easier in Wistaria House. If it hadn't been the School, it might have been someone or something very much worse. Later on, when she managed to say something about it to Mary-Lou and Co. they quickly provided half a dozen worse ideas for the Big House, and by the time she had heard that it might have been turned into a school for horrid children who needed proper care, or an Old People's Home, or a lunatic asylum—"It's got such high walls, you see," said Verity-Ann Carey, whose idea this was—or part of a Government office, she was quite ready to agree that the Chalet School was far and away the best thing that could have happened to it. That was a week or two later, however, by which time she was coming over two or three times a week to be with the others in their free time. On this present evening, she had half an hour's pleasant chatter with the little band. And how delightful it was to be able to exchange ideas with people of her own age, only Cherry herself, who had been a gregarious young person until her illness, could have told you, though Dickie might have guessed at it.

When her stepfather came to call her to come home, she was eagerly taking her share in the twittering talk of the crowd, and he was startled and delighted when shy Cherry burst out with: "Oh, Daddy! When Mummy is well again, do you think I could have Mary-Lou and Verity-Ann, and Doris, and Ruth, and Lesley to tea in the garden one Saturday?"

"I'm sure you may," he said. "We'll ask Miss Annersley and fix up for a Saturday soon."

So Cherry went off beaming, and her new friends were beaming, too. As Lesley said when they were getting ready for bed, St. Briavel's was quite a decent place for a school, but you did miss your Saturday afternoon parties!

CHAPTER EIGHT

A Gift for the School

NEXT morning, most of the school prepared for an ordinary day of work and games. They knew no reason why they should feel any excitement. The Sixth, on the other hand, got up with a feeling of expectancy. What had Joey meant by her hint the day before? Those who had heard it had passed the word on under strict promise of secrecy to their scientific members, and the whole of the top forms in the school came down to Frühstück in a state of subdued excitement. Gay tried hard to catch Mrs. Maynard's eye during the meal; but Jo remained blandly obtuse, carried on a cheerful conversation with the other people at her table, and seemed oblivious to any member of the Sixth.

"Oh, isn't she maddening!" wailed Gay, when they assembled in their common-room before first bell. "*What* are the things coming that will make us all hop with gladness?"

"*That* wasn't what I told you Jo said," Jacynth scolded. "She said they would give us an extra thrill."

At this point it may be best to state that although in public, and when speaking directly to her, the Sixths always talked of 'Mrs. Maynard', they called her 'Jo' in private and among themselves. Jo herself guessed it, and chuckled over it. The familiarity by no means upset her, since she very rarely stood on her dignity, though she could be icy enough when it suited her, as one or two people could have told you.

To return to the Sixth and their latest excitement.

"What do you think she meant?" long-legged Nancy Canton asked, balancing on the edge of a table.

"A new set of books for the library?" suggested Kathie, who looked more respectable since Matron had cut her hair even all round, and she had been persuaded by the rest to band it with a snood of black velvet ribbon.

"Oh, I think it's something much more startling than that," Gay said thoughtfully. "I wonder if she's coming to stay at St. Briavel's for the rest of the term?"

"Not very likely! Where could we put her? Besides, it would mean bringing the boys, too, and though we might manage to squeeze her in, we couldn't do anything about the kids," Kathie pointed out. "Even if she had Michael with her, there'd still be the other two to park somewhere."

"Oh, I didn't mean here at the Big House, but in the island."

"Just exactly where? There isn't a house to be had, and I doubt if you could find rooms anywhere—not with three lively kids like hers." This was Ursula. "Do you think she might have tents?"

"Oh, she couldn't! Not with a baby and a kid like Charles. He's not too strong, is he?" Nancy asked seriously. "Supposing it rained?"

"I wish we could have them at Wistaria House," Dickie put in. She had always been a 'fan' of Jo's. Now that she had met that lady in the flesh she was so even more. "We couldn't, of course. It's a small house, and we've only the one spare room, and that's no bigger than the slip she's sleeping in here. It couldn't be done, I'm afraid."

"You're wrong, all of you. I didn't even dream of such ideas," Gay told them, with a superior air. "Besides, if she came, I'm certain she'd insist on Dr. Jack being here, too, for the week-ends, if nothing else."

"Well, then, what on earth *did* you mean?" Jacynth demanded.

"Why, I thought she'd bring a gaggle of caravans——"

"A *what* of caravans?" came in a startled chorus.

"Gaggle! " Gay smiled sweetly on them all. " 'Gaggle'— collective noun usually applied to a gathering of geese. Not that I mean anything personal to Jo," she hastened to add. "What a lot of Jennies you are to-day! "

"She's picked up a new dialect! " Kathie remarked. "Explain yourself, Gay, my love; and pronto, too, or you'll be put out of the door. I know you're trying to insult us; but what insult exactly *are* you employing?"

Gay's eyes danced. "My good girl, you seem to have forgotten all your English grammar! "

"She's crackers! " Ursula said despairingly.

Jacynth looked up from the notice she was writing. "She's only calling us asses," she said. "Gay Lambert, if you don't come down off this grammatical high horse of yours, I'll address you as 'Gabrielle' for the rest of the day—and so will the others! "

"Rather! " came an enthusiastic chorus. "Come on, Gay! Finish what you were saying about the caravans! "

"And use plain English," Kathie added. "Otherwise, it's 'Gabrielle' for you, my lass, till tomorrow morning! "

"Oh, you couldn't be so mingy! " wailed Gay, who hated her proper name, and had contrived to prevent most of the junior members of the school from even suspecting that she bore anything so exotic. "All right, then! My idea was that Jo and Dr. Jack might be bringing two or three caravans over and encamping somewhere in the grounds. It would be safe enough for Charles and Michael then, and they would be quite comfy, for of course they'd have all their meals up here."

"It's an idea," Kathie said thoughtfully, "but I don't think it's that, all the same. We'd be thrilled all right, but it wouldn't be 'something for the school', and that, according to you folk, is what Jo said. If it isn't books, though, I can't think what it could be."

"I've got it! " Nancy jumped up in her excitement. "It's a cinematograph lantern that will show movies, as we haven't a cinema near. Our lantern only takes slides."

The rest went into peals of laughter. "Not from Jo it

won't be," Jacynth declared. "She might think of a good many things, but I'll bet she wouldn't think of that. Besides, it would cost heavens knows what! "

"Then I haven't a guess left in me! " Nancy replied.

"Perhaps the Head will say something at Prayers," suggested Ursula. "Anyhow," she added, "if she does that, we'll know soon. There goes the bell! Get your hymn-books, folks, and come on, or Bill will come to an empty form-room, and *won't* she be pleased then! "

This was a timely warning. They caught up their hymn-books, and filed decorously to their form-room, those prefects on duty going off to police the downstairs passages and see that the others went silently according to rules. The second bell rang as the last Junior Middle came racing down from a hurried scramble over her bed, and the three duty prefects hurried upstairs to take their seats before Miss Wilson arrived for register, as she did two minutes later. After register, the bell rang once more for Prayers, so they had to march down to the tin hut without being able to try tentative questions on the mistress. Jo attended, but she was standing with the Staff, and when the Catholic members of the school rolled back the intervening door and turned to face the platform at the top of the room, she strolled out after a murmured word to Miss Wilson, and a strictly private grin at such of the Sixth as were within reach. *She* knew how they were all feeling!

Miss Annersley gave out one or two notices about new plants for the gardens which the girls were looking after themselves, since the Plas Howell men must stay where they were to care for the grounds there, and a gardener was not to be had in the island. Then she uttered a stern warning about possessions left lying around before she signalled to Grizel Cochrane for the march, and they had to march out to their form-room, no one being a penny the wiser as yet.

Jo kept aloof for the whole of the morning. At eleven o'clock she strolled down to call at Wistaria House, and returned at noon to demand her daughters, and carry them off somewhere—where, no one knew. Neither she nor they appeared at the midday meal.

"Oh, isn't Jo being *ghastly*! " Nancy Canton wailed when,

the meal over, they got their deck chairs and went to the garden for the half-hour's rest wisely ordained for them by the Powers. "She must know that we're all nearly passing out from curiosity, and yet she acts like this!"

"That, from all accounts, is just like her," Jacynth replied. "Set my chair up, someone! I must go and see what that imp, Mary-Lou, is after. She and young Clem seem to be having a barney over something."

She stalked off, to find that Clem was firmly pointing out that if Mary-Lou tried to sit in *that* chair, it would collapse, as the front rail was cracked, and Mary-Lou was arguing that it wouldn't if she sat down carefully and didn't move about; and anyway it was a boiling hot day, and she couldn't be fagged to trail up to the shed for another.

Jacynth told Clemency to sit down at once, and ordered Mary-Lou off to the shed for another chair after she had examined the cause of the argument, and agreed with Clem. Mary-Lou went off sulkily, and the Head Girl waited till she had returned with a sound chair and sat down and opened her copy of *The Secret Garden*, before she went over to the clump of beeches under which the three Sixths had settled themselves.

Just before the bell rang for afternoon school, the Heads appeared together, and everyone sat up with interest. What was going to happen now? The Sixths rather thought they knew.

"Girls!" Miss Annersley's voice rang out over the great lawn. "There will be no school this afternoon. Instead, go and get your swimming things and towels, and then line up in forms by the entrance gates, Sixth Forms leading. The following girls will go to the kitchen door for picnic baskets." She read out a list of two girls from each form except the Kindergarten forms. "You must all wear your hats."

Most of the girls only realised that they were to have a picnic instead of the needlework, art, games, and silent reading or preparation which were the general order of the day. The Sixth looked at each other meaningly. *Now* they were to know Jo's secret, and surely it must have something to do with the shore.

"Could it—oh, *do* you think it could possibly be—*boats*?

Or *a* boat?" This was Gay as she raced across the grass, lugging her chair with her.

"*A* boat, perhaps. *Boats* would be as dear as a ciné lantern," Kathie replied. "Oh, I hope it is! I love boating. We do a lot in the hols at home. *Would* it be super! The school used to have its own boats on the Tiern See in the Tirol days, didn't it? I've often wished Plas Howell was near enough to a decent stretch of water for boating. It was the one thing we didn't have there."

"Would it be rowing or sailing, do you think?" someone else asked.

They had reached the shed where the chairs were kept by this time, and the three prefects on duty for the day were busy taking the chairs from the girls and piling them up neatly.

"It'll be rowing, I expect," Jacynth replied, as she placed Mary-Lou's chair on top of the pile. "None of us knows anything about sailing, I imagine."

"Oh, are we going in boats?" Mary-Lou demanded eagerly, having pricked up her ears at this.

"I couldn't tell you because I don't know," Jacynth told her. "Run along and get ready, or you'll be late."

"Little pitchers! " murmured Frances Coleman, earning for herself a glare as Mary-Lou left the shed.

"It's our own fault," Jacynth returned placidly. "No more talk, folk."

The Sixth held their tongues, so no one heard anything more, though Mary-Lou had whispered what she thought to be her news to Vi Lucy and Doris Hill, whom she met with their chairs just outside.

The chairs in their place, Jacynth, Kathie, and Frances hastened to join the others. By ten-past two, everyone was standing in the drive, her towel and swimming things in one hand, while the girls chosen to carry the picnic-baskets headed each form. The younger mistresses were similarly laden, and Matron appeared, carrying the portable first-aid case without which she never accompanied the school on an expedition.

Miss Annersley and Miss Wilson came last, and walked slowly down the long lines, making sure that every girl was wearing a shady panama hat, for the sun was blazing down, so heads must be protected, as well as eyes shielded from the glare that would come off the sea.

"All right!" Miss Annersley said at last. "Now you may set off. We're going to Kittiwake Cove, so turn down by the field, Jacynth. Don't go too quickly, either, you people. Remember that some of us have short legs!"

There was a laugh at this before the leaders, Jacynth and Gay, led the way through the gates at a steady pace, while the Staff ranged up at the side to act as whippers-in for the smaller folk. These young persons were very thrilled at the prospect. Kittiwake Cove had a beautiful sandy beach which shelved only very slightly for some distance, so that it was safe for bathing and paddling. High cliffs were kitti-wakes and herring gulls nested rose above it, but there was a cleft at the eastern side of the cove, through which a rocky, but fairly easy path led down to the shore. The girls had had one picnic there already, and were quite prepared to enjoy another. At one time it must have been a landing-place for the fishing-cobles, for there were the remains of a little stone jetty with rings driven into the stones for tying up the boats; but in a south-west gale, it got the full force of the storms, so a landing-place had been built on the north-east side of the island, and this allowed to fall gradu-ally into decay. It was little more than a mile from the Big House, and when they arrived there, they could lie on the sun-warmed sands and rest. The cove was almost semi-circular, so that even during the full blaze of the after-noon hours there was shade in one part. From every point of view it was an ideal place for a school picnic. To-day, when they arrived there, the tide would be an hour from high water, and the girls could bathe in perfect safety.

The school strolled along the narrow bridle-path which led through a field to the pebbly road that ran from St. Briavel's village to the western point of the island, where those terrible dangers to seafarers, the Mermaidens, ran from the island in a series of rocky ridges, half uncovered at low tide, and out of sight at high tide. The island was well out of the ordinary traffic route; but on stormy or foggy nights many a good ship had piled up on the Mermaidens, to become a total wreck, the cruel granite edges ripping timbers and steel plates alike. Even at neap-tides, rings of white surf circled restlessly at their bases, warning of the dangers that lay hidden.

From the Cliff Road, the school turned to a little sandy track. Then they were scrambling down the rocky cleft by which they reached Kittiwake Cove. When they turned the rock wall that rose up on either hand, they found Jo and her daughters awaiting them. Len and Con were dancing up and down in wild excitement, and Jo's cheeks were pink and her eyes sparkling as she said quickly: "Stop! All you people turn your backs till the rest get here! Go on—I mean it! "

"What's all this in aid of?" protested Gay, nevertheless doing as she was told. "What are you up to, Mrs. Maynard?"

"You'll see in a minute or two." Jo spoke calmly, but two or three of the elder girls were quick to hear a note of excitement in her voice. The school ended the pilgrimage down to the sand, all obediently turning their backs and staring at the high cliffs, once they were there. When even Miss Denny, who helped with the German and Italian classes, and who was decidedly the oldest member of the Staff, had reached the goal, Jo cried, in a triumphant voice: "Now turn round and look at the sea, everybody! "

Everyone turned round, and there was a moment's silence as they stared at the sea, silvery-blue in the heat of the sun, with ripples making fairy laughter as they broke softly on the golden sand in tiny ruffles of white foam. Then a long-drawn "A-ah! " broke from everyone. There, tied in a long line to each other, the nearest boat fastened to the ring in the jetty, were five rowing-boats!

With cries of delight, the entire school surged forward to the edge of the water and gazed at them, while the air was filled with a babble of excitement.

"*Five*, Joey?" Miss Wilson demanded, being, as usual, the first to recover from the surprise. "You said 'A boat or two' when you wrote. How on earth have you managed to be so lavish as to produce *five*?"

94

"Oh, it isn't all me!" Jo was quite satisfied with the result of her effort. "School! Listen to me a moment! *School!*"

Jo possessed a lovely voice for both singing and speaking; but when she chose she could produce a bellow that would have been envied by an old-time skipper on the bridge of a four-master trying to round Cape Horn in one of its worst storms. The startled school stopped making a noise, and turned to hear what she had to say to them.

"I want to tell you," she said briskly when she had their undivided attention, "that Dr. Jack and I have contributed only one of these boats. Madame," she referred to her sister, who was always called so by the girls, "and Dr. Jem have given you one. Twenty-three of the old girls have subscribed to give you the third. The fourth comes from Mr. and Mrs. Lucy, Mr. and Mrs. Ozanne, and Dr. and Mrs. Chester. The fifth has been given by Gwensi Howell and her brother, the owner of Plas Howell."

Excitable Gay sprang forward. "Three cheers for everyone who has given us the boats!" she cried. "Come on, everyone! Real rousers, please!"

The cheers set the gulls squawking and mewing, and went on until Miss Annersley clapped her hands loudly for silence.

"I'm sure you want me to thank all the kind people who have given us such a wonderful gift," she said. "Mrs. Maynard!" She turned to her ex-pupil, ready to say a few pleasant words of thanks. She was brought up short by a wicked and unmistakable wink from Jo, who, standing with her back to the girls, felt she could do it with perfect impunity. The Head shut her mouth suddenly, and her little speech slipped her memory. "Er—er—thank you," she said feebly, at last.

Miss Wilson, Matron, and Miss Denny, who were just behind the Head, gave splutters, instantly smothered; but the girls had seen them, and wondered what it all meant. Jo gave them no time to wonder. She ran down to the little jetty and stooped over the first boat, hauling on the rope to bring it close. Then she climbed from one to the other until she was standing safely in the last, where she called for the prefects of St. Thérèse de Lisieux, the oldest

House in the school. Jacynth, Gay, Bride Bettany, and Nita Eltringham stood forward.

"This belongs to your House," Jo said. She sat down in the thwarts, shipped one pair of oars on the rowlocks and rowed in. "Here you are! Please take delivery of her—and hurry up about it! By the way," she added casually, "I'm sure you can all swim. How many of you can row?"

"I can!" Bride cried. "So can Nita." She paused, and looked doubtfully at Jacynth and Gay. "What about you two?"

"Well! We can—after a fashion," Gay grinned. "We're not what you'd call experts, but we can get her along—in time, that is."

"Right! Come on, then, and move her off. Even if you did upset her—which I doubt—you'd only be waist-deep at the moment, anyhow. Come on!"

"One moment, Jo!" Hilary Burn ran to them. "You four, row down to the shore first, please. I've something to say about tides and currents before you begin to do any definite rowing. Bride, you and Nita had better take the oars, and Jacynth and Gay can use the rudder. In you get!"

One by one, the girls dropped down from the jetty into the boat, Jo steadying her while they did so. When Bride and Nita were ready with the oars she scrambled up the rock, and then knelt to push them off. They went well out over the silky surface of the water, Bride and Nita at once handling their oars in workmanlike style as they pulled away from the jetty, and then swung in to the shore.

In the meantime, Jo had handed over the St. Agnes' boat to Kathie and Frances, Tom Gay, and Anne Webster, who declared that they could all row and proved their statement promptly.

St. Clare's came next, and was claimed by Nancy and Ursula, neither of whom knew anything about boats. Luckily, Barbara Smith and Lesley Pitt had both lived by the sea all their lives, and they were able to row her over to join the others.

"Now St. Scholastika!" Jo called; and Janet Scott and a short, plump girl, Joan Sandys by name, came to claim her with Audrey Simpson and Elfie Woodward. Audrey was

.he only one of them who knew anything about rowing, so Miss Burnett, the house-mistress, joined them, and soon had them beached beside the others.

The girls looked at the fifth boat. There were only the four Houses in the school. For whom was she intended?

Jo stood up in her, swaying easily to her swaying movement. "Years ago," she said solemnly, "a Staff House was started. That was in Tirol, and I know it's never been begun again. I propose it should begin now. This boat is for St. Hild's, the Staff House. As Miss Burn, who would normally take charge of her, is already occupied, I think Miss Linton and Miss Cochrane, both of whom I know from old days are experts, had better take charge of her for the moment. Here you are, you two! Who'll come with you to steer?"

"Miss Wilson, if she will," said Gillian.

"With all the pleasure in life!" Miss Wilson came forward, dropped neatly into the boat, and sat down in the stern, taking the rudder-lines with accustomed skill. "Push us off, Jo!"

"Or be our passenger," suggested Gillian. "You ought, seeing it's you we have to thank for this. Don't argue, Joey! We're none of us *daft*!"

Jo sat down meekly in the stern, and was rowed smartly across to join the others, who were surrounded by that time by the rest of the school. They had discarded sandals and plimsolls, and were in the water round the boats, examining them, chattering and laughing, and generally making such a noise that there was some excuse for Miss Annersley's murmured remark to Mlle de Lachenais: "I should think they can be heard all over the island, and right across to Carnbach!" as they went to mingle with the excited throng.

As they were meant for sea work, they were rather broad, clinker-built boats of the three oar variety. The lower timbers had been painted white and round the upper ones ran a broad band in the colour of the House to which she belonged—blue for St. Thérèse; crimson for St. Agnes the Martyr; green for St. Clare; and deep, buttercup yellow for St. Scholastika. The oars were painted to match, and at present there were cushions in House colours for the seats, though these would be discarded when the crews got down to real work. The House name was painted on each boat in gilded letters. Altogether, they were very pretty, as well as safe, owing to their breadth of beam. The girls felt that they really had nothing more left to ask, for the present, anyhow.

Miss Burn delivered a short lecture on the necessity for not rowing too far out, because of the current which raced round the island from the Mermaidens and flowed across to the mainland. Then she suggested that all those who had any idea of rowing should be allowed a short turn in sets of five—four to row, and one to handle the rudder-lines. After that, she herself, and those mistresses who were accustomed to boats, would take out batches of the novices, and give them their first lesson in handling the oars. As for the small girls, the mistresses good-naturedly volunteered to take it in turns to row them about.

"Not Len and Con," Jo said. "They've had a good long row, for we came round from Carnbach in St. Thérèse this morning."

"How did you manage to get the whole five here, Auntie Jo?" her niece, Bride, demanded. "You surely didn't row the lot over one by one?"

"Talk sense! Of course I didn't! We were attached to a motor-boat, and towed round. I should have been dead if I'd done what you suggest!"

"They're quite as pretty as the boats we had on the Tiern See," Bride's elder cousin, Sybil, remarked. "Don't you think so, Peggy?"

Peggy Bettany nodded. "Yes; but I'd no idea *you* would remember them, Sybs. You were only an infant then."

"Yes; but I was out in those boats day after day!" Sybil retorted. "We had one of our own when we lived down by the lake during the summer, and Auntie Jo and Mummy used to take us out every day. It's wizard having a chance to be on the water again after all these years!"

"Well," said their aunt, "if we go back to Tirol some day, you ought to be able to handle a boat. Otherwise you have a good long walk before you if you want to get from one side to the other—unless it's frozen and you can skate across," she added.

"You *do* seem to have had all the fun!" Sybil said enviously.

"Oh yes; we'd plenty of fun. But you have quite as much in ways we couldn't. Listen! There's Gay yelling for you. Scram!"

Sybil flashed a grin at her aunt as she turned to race across the sand to where Gay was calling to her to come with them and learn how to use the steering-lines.

That was a glorious picnic. The boats were in constant use until five o'clock and her own longing made Miss Annersley insist on tea. They went on again after tea, and by the time Matron declared that it was bedtime for the Kindergarten people, everyone had been out in them. There would be blistered palms for a good many folk next day, and Kathie exclaimed disgustedly that her freckles were thicker than ever; still, they thought it a small price to pay for all the pleasure they had had.

"Where are we keeping them, Auntie Jo?" Peggy Bettany asked, as she helped to unpack her small cousin Con from her bathing knickers. "Stand still, Con! You wriggle like an eel! Maeve is an angel compared with you!"

"You tickle so!" complained Con, struggling free at last. "Where's my clothes? Hi! Len! That's my vest!" And she fell on her sister.

"You get dressed and don't scrap," Jo said severely. "As for the boats, Peggy, I'm afraid you can't keep them here. Everyone says that when the gales blow from the southwest the cove isn't safe. The motor-boat is coming round to fetch them, and we've bought a boathouse near the village. In a way, it's better for you to row about there. You miss the Mermaidens' current, and it's safer. But I wanted you to have them at once, and I heard there was a trip from Cardiff over at Carnbach to-day. Some of them would probably want to come over to the islands if they could get boats, and the village and its shore would be the most likely place for them to park. So we brought you here. But as a general rule, you'll do your boating in the Sound."

"Well, anyhow," Peggy said, with a sigh of complete

satisfaction as she turned to help someone else, "it's been a super picnic, and those boats are just the finishing touch! It was a wizard idea, Auntie, and you're a genius to have thought of it! "

CHAPTER NINE

Bird Sanctuary

"It's weird, isn't it, how things always seem to happen when Jo's anywhere round! " Gay said, as those of the Sixth Forms who were not on duty with preparation and mending settled down in their common-room to attend to their own belongings. "I asked Daisy Venables about it once," she added, as she set to work to darn a hole in a cardigan, "and she said Jo had always been the same—she seems to *attract* adventures."

"What a libel! *I'll* talk to Daisy when I see her! " Jo's voice observed from the doorway. "And who gave you leave to refer to me as 'Jo', young woman?"

Gay went scarlet, and for once looked thoroughly taken aback. Jo came in briskly, and shut the door behind her. She had brought her work-bag and proceeded to seat herself in a chair near the window, pulling out some small stockings which she looked over before she went on placidly: "Oh, I always guessed you folk did it, so you needn't look quite so floored, Gay. Only I shouldn't yell like that when the door's open. You never know who may be passing and overhear you."

"It's not our fault really," Jacynth said, looking up from her Latin. "We always used to hear Daisy and Robin and the others call you that. And the Bettany girls, and the Lucys, and so on speak of you as 'Auntie Jo', so it came more or less naturally to us to do it. You aren't really annoyed, are you?"

Jo finished considering one of Con's stockings, and heaved a deep sigh. "I offered to do my family's mending this morning to give Matey a lift. I don't know that I'd have done it if I'd realised quite what I was in for! No, Jacynth; I see how it happened, and I don't really mind so long as you don't let any of the kids hear you doing it. After all, I *am* the mother of six, so I suppose I ought to try to be more dignified. I don't know that the prospect enthralls me, either. What do you say, Dickie? Would you like to be all dignified and grave?" She smiled across at Dickie, who had been given leave to slip into Wistaria House the night before to collect some of the never-ending mending there, since she would not be going home this week-end. Mother Carey was a good deal better, and Mrs. Pugh had offered to come every day and stay all day for the present, so Dickie's mind was at ease.

She looked up from a bad three-cornered tear in a frock of Gaynor's and grinned. "I should loathe it just now. I don't know what I may come to by the time I'm *your* age, though, Mrs. Maynard. I expect I'll have to be pretty careful if I teach as I want to."

"Oh, is that your idea? Gay and Jacynth are going in for music, I know—you're quite certain, aren't you, Jacynth?"

Jacynth nodded. "Yes, Mrs. Maynard. I sat for the Karl Anserl scholarship last week. If I get it, it means three years at the Royal College of Music, and then two at the Conservatoire in Paris. And Gay will do the same," she added, "so we ought to be together for another four years."

"I hope you will get it," Jo said. "I'm sure dear old Vater Bar would have loved you to be his first scholarship winner."

A shade of shyness came into her face as she spoke. Vater Bar, as she had always called good old Herr Anserl who had been head of the school's music for many years, even coming with them to England when the school left Tirol, had died early in the previous year. He had had no relatives and had left everything he had to found this scholarship for pupils at the school. He had also founded two junior ones during his lifetime, so that musical girls might profit by the school's teaching. Jacynth's idea had originally been to enter for the Thérèse Lepattre Scholarship, which would have taken her to either Oxford or Cambridge, with an additional period at the Sorbonne if she wanted it, but it soon became apparent to everyone that her whole heart was in music. She was a steady worker in every way; but her music came first, and already she was outstandingly good with her 'cello, considering that she had done nothing till she had come to the Chalet School and met Gay, who was good for her age, and who, finding that home funds would run to no extras, had undertaken to teach her friend the beginnings. Jacynth had made such headway that the school's 'cello master had taken her on after two terms, and he had great hopes for her with the scholarships.

"You'll get your training, anyhow," Jo said, after a little silence. "If you don't win—though I rather expect you will —you needn't worry about that. Who's entered for the Thérèse Lepattre this year?"

"Me," Kathie said, "and Janet and Joan and Mollie. That was last week too, so it's out of the way now, and we mean to enjoy ourselves for the rest of the term. It's our last, worse luck!"

"Goodness me! You're eighteen all of you. You couldn't expect to stay at school *much* longer," Jo said mildly. Little though they knew it, this came strangely from a girl who had fought desperately against having to grow up. Jo cast a thought to those days and chuckled inwardly.

"I know that," Kathie said, cutting her thread, and beginning to fold up the frock she had been mending. "All the same, it's been a wizard time, and I'm sorry it's nearly over. Still, the University should be almost as much fun."

"What are you going to do—teach?"

Kathie shook her head. "Not me: I shouldn't have the patience. I'm going to read modern languages, and then I'd like a decent job somewhere as interpreter. Janet means to teach, though; and so does Mollie."

"And what are you going to do, Joan?" Jo turned to that quiet damsel.

"Farm. I'd like to get my degree in pure science, and then take a course at one of the Agricultural Colleges— Cirencester, for choice."

"And you three?" Jo looked at the last trio in the room, the rest being on duty with their Juniors.

"I want to be a curator in a museum," Nancy Canton told her unexpectedly. "I've been reading quite a lot about old ceramics lately. Daddy's mad on antiques, you know, and he's brought me up to know something about them. I'm specially keen on the very early periods—Egyptian, and Greek, and Cretan. I'm going to the School of Economics first, though. And later on, he and Mummy are taking me to Egypt and all the Levantine countries for practical observation. We're all saving madly for it, as it won't be exactly a cheap trip."

"Good for you! And now, Pamela and Mary; what about you?"

"I'm going to nurse. I go to St. Luke's in September to begin my training," Pamela replied. "Then, unless I change my mind, I want to take up work at the San, and go all out for T.B. cases."

Jo nodded, inwardly making up her mind to mention Pamela to Jack. She said nothing at the moment, though, but raised her eyebrows at Mary Ireson, who blushed before she spoke.

"I hope to enter a Community when I've had a year out of school, Mrs. Maynard. I've seen the Reverend Mother already, but she won't take me till I've had twelve months outside. I don't think I'll change, though."

Jo's face was grave as she replied quietly: "I'm glad. We've had other girls who became nuns, though not very recently. Have any of you heard of Luigia di Ferrara?"

"Isn't her name on the Honours Board at Plas Howell?" Gay asked.

Jo nodded. "It is. Did you ever look to see *why* it's there, though?"

No one had, so Jo enlightened them. "Luigia was at school with me. Actually, she was a year or two older, and a prefect when I was a Middle. She entered the Poor Clares a year or so after she left school, and was received as a novice about eighteen months later. She was transferred to a German convent, and—well, she died in a concentration camp."

Silence fell on the room. Jo watched the girls for a minute or two before she said: "You see, if you have a Call like that, you can't ignore it. Bless you, Mary! I hope you'll be as happy as Luigia was."

"Thank you," Mary replied in low tones.

Jo changed the subject then, and when the bell went at half-past ten they were laughing again. But she knew that they would not forget Luigia even though they might never speak of her among themselves.

Guides followed Elevenses, but the meeting was cut short to-day, as they were to have an early dinner, and set off for Brandon Mawr at half-past one. A motor-boat proprietor was to take them over, and they must be ready for him. One or two people had suggested during the morning that some of them might row over, but Hilary Burn, to whom the suggestion had been made, had squashed it at once.

"After one afternoon's practice—and only a short one for any of you at that! Do have a little sense!" she had said. "You'll have to be very much more in trim, and we'll have to know considerably more about the local currents than we do at the moment before you do that."

They had to rush to change from Guide uniform into the shirts and slacks they were to wear. There would be a good deal of scrambling about and slacks were the most sensible attire for it. Some of the younger mistresses also wore them; but their elders appeared in cotton frocks.

As Miss Annersley said: "Slacks are all very well for the slim and youthful; but they're no attire for middle-aged folk!"

They streamed down to the landing-stage where the big motor-boat was awaiting them, and were speedily aboard her. There were thirty-two of them all told. The rest of the school watched them go with envious eyes before they turned to their own amusements. Mary-Lou, especially, voiced her grievances to her own clan.

"I wish it could be us!" she grumbled. "I'm going to do as Father did when I grow up, and go in for foreign birds and insects and things, and I'm sure I ought to know something about English ones first."

"We'll have our turn later," Anne Webster told her consolingly. "Then it'll be them who'll want to be *us*. Come on, Mary-Lou! We're to get ready to go to tea with Cherry, and Mrs. Christy asked us to be early so we could have a nice long time together."

Thus reminded, Mary-Lou forgot her complaints, and ran to change into a clean frock before trotting off with the rest to spend a happy time at Wistaria House.

Meanwhile, the Sixths, with Jo, Hilary Burn, Ivy Norman, Gillian Linton, and Miss Wilson, were enjoying the swift run across the calm water of the sound to Brandon Mawr. They turned due west when they left the landing, and then swept round to the south, running at first along the north-west coast of St. Briavel's.

"Brandon Mawr is over there," Gay said, pointing westwards. "Why are we going this way?"

Dickie knew. "Because of the Callachs—those rocks low down in the water. There's quite a nasty swell there, no matter how calm the day is. Dad says the reef runs under the sea for a good distance, and that means a swell any time. We go between them and the Wreckers—those three things over there—and then run right round the island to get to the landing-place which is at the north. You'll see the cliffs on the west side. They're packed with birds, especially just now."

"Shall we go near enough to see them?" someone asked.

"No fear! There's a nasty current swirls round just there, and we'll keep outside of that. Shipwrecks may be fun in stories, but I shouldn't think they're much fun to *be* in. Besides, the cliffs fall sheer into the sea. We'd be in a rather sticky mess if we piled up anywhere round there."

"Thanks, Dickie! Since I'm in charge of you all, I'd rather be excused," Miss Wilson said, over-hearing this. "I've had *one* unpleasant thrill in my life, and I don't want another."

"*Only* one?" Jo queried, with a saucy grin. "I don't know if you're referring to our escape from Spärtz; but what price what came *after*?"

"I suppose I'd got more or less hardened to it by that time," answered Miss Wilson. "It never seemed as bad to me as that awful trek through the underground passage. In fact, after the first day or two, I remember very little about it. My foot hurt too much for me to care about anything else, I think. All the business of getting over the Alps into Switzerland has always been more like a bad dream than a reality."

"Did you really do all that—as it is in *Nancy Meets a Nazi*?" Dickie asked, in awed tones. "I always thought that part was just invented."

"Oh, it happened all right," Jo told her drily. Then she added characteristically, "I got *that* book out of it, anyhow."

The girls laughed. Then, as they altered course once more to pass between the terrible Wreckers, and the scarcely less terrible Callachs, they turned their attention to what they saw.

They could see the heave and swell that went on ceaselessly round the Callachs, low-lying, threatening-looking rocks, shiny under the sun with masses of seaweed. Closer at hand were the three Wreckers, tiny islets of granite, heaving lowering shoulders out of the water. Dickie said that nothing grew there, not even the coarse sand dune grass, for there was nothing in which it could gain rooting. The lower parts were covered with seaweeds; but the upper rose above them, bare and inhospitable, with ledges where the sea-birds shrieked and mewed and squabbled. There was a silvery glinting of powerful wings as seagulls swooped about their boat, on the look-out for scraps. No one had anything, though the birds flew close to them, mewing and scolding, almost the whole way round the island.

Brandon Mawr was much smaller than St. Briavel's, but to the west, at least, it was much more rugged. Huge cliffs fell sheer down to the water, the upper parts ledged, whereon colonies of gulls, mainly kittiwakes and herring gulls, nested. To-day, the water heaved restlessly and oilily against the base of the relentless rock-face, with only now and then a wave breaking with a roar into a thick froth of foam which flew high, to fall back again on itself. Dickie pointed to one or two darker shadows in the water-darkened rock, and explained that they were the openings to the caves where the grey seals had their calves, and where the babies lived till they were old enough to take to the water on their own account.

"Do they make—sort of nests there?" Gay wanted to know.

"Mr. Bellever says not. He says they only go there during the breeding season, and that it's only because man has driven them to it by his seal-hunts," Dickie explained. "In places where man doesn't go, the baby seals are born on the bare rocks. It's rather horrible, isn't it, to think that because of man's cruelty to them, the poor mites have to be born in those dark caves?"

"That queer kid, Fauna McDonald, told me that in the Hebrides there's a clan who believe they are descended from the seal-folk," Nancy Canton remarked. "I remember when we were all kids her telling us a story about an old woman who appeared every night at Haskeir where they had a grand annual hunt of seals. Fauna said she always came weeping and wailing and wringing her hands, crying over the loss of her family."

"That's a legend in the McCodrum family," Janet Scott put in. "I was at a school near Glasgow before I came here, and in my form there was a Jean McCodrum, and she told me that legend, too. She says the story is that they come from the People of the Sea, very far back."

"They surely didn't believe it, though—not in these days?" gasped Frances Coleman, open-mouthed.

Janet shrugged her shoulders. "I wouldn't know. Jean McCodrum pretended to think it was just a silly tale; but she wasn't very inclined to be friendly with people—we'd a few English girls from Northumberland and Lancashire—who laughed at it."

The cliffs swung back in an irregular curve to form a bay. The motor-boat kept wide of the two headlands that formed each end of the bay, for this was where the current known as the Wreckers' Race poured in a resistless stream round the island, swinging across from a mainland bay a few miles farther west. It swirled down on the southernmost point, to be broken into two forks by a great rock that stood about a quarter of a mile out from the island,

and to continue, much weaker in strength, in opposite directions, for one fork curved round the Wreckers, and the other swung out across the sea towards Ireland. It was easy enough to see from the boat, for some freak of the water made it look dark green against the Mediterranean blue of the sea.

"How do we get round it to the harbour?" Jacynth asked Dickie.

"We don't. We swing right across," Dickie replied. "You needn't worry, Jacynth. Mr. Parry's done it scores of times, and he knows just where to turn. There—see! We're clearing Fallin Bay. In a few minutes we'll turn at right angles, and cut across the Race."

She was right. The motor-boat went on a little farther. Then she swung sharply to the east, and they were driving across the Race with the throttle open. There were a few moments of thrills; then they were through, and passing round the North Point behind which lay the harbour of Brandon Mawr, an absolutely safe anchorage, since the great head sheltered it from the west gales, and the mainland was a protection to the north. They ran alongside a small stone quay where Kester Bellever was waiting for them, a nondescript-looking sheepdog beside him.

He welcomed them to the island as they disembarked, and then led the way up a sandy track which zigzagged in long ramps up the side of the cliff. This was a much more civilised-looking coast than the west, for the cliff sloped gently backwards from the sea, and here and there was pink with clumps of thrift where that sturdy plant had found root. Gay exclaimed with delight that she saw a rabbit. At the sound of her voice there was a flicker of white among the pink of the flowers as the startled beast whisked out of sight, and Kester Bellever laughed.

"Quite a common sight. You can often see them sunning themselves on ledges and shelves on this side. Not the other, of course. There's no footing there that the maddest of mountain goats could tackle. When I've gone over, as I have on occasion to study the birds' nests and their young, I've had to do it with ropes and a windlass. It's the only way."

By this time they had reached the top of the cliff, and were standing looking across the island from north to south. It seemed to slope upwards from a wide-mouthed bay to the great cliffs of the west coast. Most of it was rough pasturage, with bushes of gorse filling the air with the heady perfume of their rich gold. In a hollow, well protected by the dip in the ground from the relentless western gales, was a little stone house with a roof of deep thatch held safely by ropes slung across and across. A small garden in front was gay with nasturtiums, double daisies, love-in-a-mist and thrift, all flowers that will grow in sea air. To one side was a healthy-looking kitchen-garden, and Mr. Bellever announced proudly that last year he had grown all the potatoes he needed for the year, as well as various greens and roots. A heavily wired run sheltered some hens and half a dozen strutting cockerels, and he explained that his fowls always had to be protected so from the murderous black-backed gulls which take dreadful toll of all smaller birds.

"I thought gulls lived on fish," Kathie said, as she looked at the fowls, which seemed well-fed and fat.

"So they do. But they like a fine fat puffin or a shearwater as well. And as for baby gannets—well, a black-backed gull will hang about for a long time if he thinks that in the end he will have such a delicious titbit for his pains."

"Pigs!" said Gay indignantly. "How horrid nature can be!"

He laughed. "I dare say. But the black-backed gull is a hungry gentleman, intent on filling his tummy to the best advantage. He sees nothing lovely about baby birds. To him they are just so much fodder. So I keep my poultry well protected against him, as you see. Now," he turned and addressed Miss Wilson, "what would you like to do first?"

"I think we'll leave it to you," she answered promptly. "Show us just what you like. I know we'll enjoy it, whatever it may be."

"Well, then, suppose we make a round of the island? It

isn't a very long walk, really, and I can point out some interesting things to you."

"Oh, will you show us the places where you watch the birds from?" Gay asked. "Hides, aren't they called?"

"Yes; that's right. You'll see 'em as we go. Come along; we'll go this way." And he led them along the cliffs which here dipped lower and lower towards the water until, as they reached the south side, they were little more than forty feet high.

The girls followed eagerly, listening and watching keenly for what he had to show them. Suddenly Jacynth started. "Why, there's a crowing noise from over there," she exclaimed, "and it seemed to come from underground! "

He nodded. "We are just near the shear-water colony; and that's about all you'll hear of them at this time of day. Towards sunset, the crowing becomes more frequent; and after dark you get the full benefit of their voices. A most eerie sound it is, too, like the crying of lost souls."

"Ugh! How ghastly! " impressionable Gay shuddered. "How can you stay here with that horrid noise going on in the night?"

"Don't be a gubbins! " Dickie said swiftly. "It's only the birds, and Mr. Bellever knows it. What is there to be afraid of?"

"Well, you wouldn't catch me doing it," Gay declared.

"Oh, you'd soon get accustomed to it," he told her. "Now look over there. That's the shear-waters' burrows. The whole place is tunnelled by them. The rabbits occupy the burrows in the winter, but they have to turn out for the birds in the early spring. The same thing applies to the puffins, though we have only a very small colony of them. That big parrot-beak of Mr. Puffin can inflict a nasty bite, and bunny doesn't like it. He scuttles when they arrive. Now come to the cliff edge. It's quite safe, and I've something special to show you. Quietly, please! "

Tense with excitement, the girls moved quietly to the edge of the cliff to look down on a shingly beach. He pointed out to them some queer-looking objects standing among the shingle, heads tucked under one wing, stilt-like legs very stiff and straight.

"What are they—storks?" breathed Kathie, watching them eagerly.

"No; those are oyster-catchers. They don't inhabit the high cliffs, but prefer a shingle beach. They don't really live on oysters, either—or not our home-grown variety. Years ago they were called sea-pies; I suppose from their black and white uniforms which remind one of the magpie. You nearly always see them paired, though the pairs fly in great flocks, and when the flocks are broken up they utter their cry, 'Tu-lup! Tu-lup!'" He imitated the shrill, musical cry very softly. "Take a good look at them. They are among the wariest of birds, and very difficult to approach, even in the breeding season when most birds are a good deal bolder than normally."

"What sort of nest do they build?" Janet asked.

"Well, it starts off as a hollow in the ground, not far from the sea. A very slight hollow it is, and the hen lays three eggs there. As she broods them, the hollow deepens. Father may bring along some haulm to build round the edge, and so you get a very fair nest by the time the chicks arrive. I may say that it is the most difficult thing in the world to spot those chicks. If they haven't been hatched on shingle, Pa and Ma take them there as soon as possible, and as they are mottled in colour, it's very hard to pick them out. At the least fright, they squat down and remain perfectly still till the danger is past."

"What do they feed on if not oysters?" Jacynth asked.

"Oh, sea-worms—limpets—mussels. They are supposed to lay the head sideways, grip the limpet's shell close to the rock, and then use their mandibles like scissors to prise him from his hold."

"What are 'mandibles'?" Frances asked Dickie, in a whisper.

"Not the foggiest," Dickie raised her voice slightly. "Mr. Bellever, what do you mean by its mandibles?"

"The two parts of the beak, of course."

"Oh, thank you. We weren't sure. Oh, and do oyster-catchers live here all the year round, or do they migrate like other birds?"

"We-ell, that's rather a question. They can be *seen* all

the year round, but it's thought that our particular crowd migrate elsewhere, and those we have during the winter come from farther north. The oyster-catcher can be found from Iceland to the Red Sea, and as far south as the Falklands he has cousins. No one seems to know for certain, though."

"What are the eggs like?" someone wanted to know.

"Not very pretty as you might expect. They are clay-colour, splotched with black. The adult bird is very striking with his coral-coloured bill and carmine legs. Now, if you've seen enough of them, we'll go on."

He took them now to the south-west tip of the island where the cliffs began to rise steeply, and after bidding them lie down on their faces, pointed downwards to a narrow ledge.

"See that! That's a falcon's nest—the only one on the island. They are devils with the smaller birds, of course, but one can't help admiring a falcon. To see him hover against a blue sky, and then suddenly dive downwards with unerring aim on his prey, is to have seen something amazingly beautiful. Falconry has gone out very largely now; but one can feel the fascination it must have had for our fore-fathers."

"Aren't there still a few people here and there who run falconries?" asked Jo, who had left it to the girls to ask questions up to now.

"Here and there, yes. I shall never forget an experience I once had," he went on, as the girls wriggled back from the cliff edge at the command of Miss Wilson, who had felt excusably nervous about them. "I was walking down a country lane when I heard a silvery chime of bells above me. I knew what it was at once. Some falcon had either escaped or lost herself. Strange to relate, the female falcon is the best hunter—most easily tamed and trained. I was carrying a brace of grouse I had shot, so I used them as a lure, gave the falconer's cry, and, sure enough, she came straight for the grouse. I hadn't a glove with me, but I was wearing a shooting coat with leather elbows. I pulled it off, and twisted it over one arm while she fed—she was hungry, poor creature! —then I set her on it, and fastened her by

112

her broken jesses. She'd escaped from some falconry. After that, I marched on to the friends' house where I was staying. I shall never forget their faces when we arrived! "

"What did you do with her?" Jo asked, listening intently.

"Well, we contrived some sort of mount for her in a windowless shed, as my friends had no idea where she came from. We advertised her next day, and the morning after that her owner arrived, delighted to find her. He had been afraid she would be trapped or shot. He took her off home again after inviting us to visit him—which we did next day, and I got a good deal of information about training and hunting falcons from him."

"Why did you want a glove?" Dickie demanded, as he finished.

He grinned involuntarily. "My dear girl, if you'd ever seen a falcon's claws you wouldn't ask that. They grip when they perch, and they'd soon make mincemeat of your skin if you weren't well protected. The falconer wears a glove of very stout leather when he carries his bird."

"Oh, I see. I rather wondered. By the way, you said she had broken jesses. What *are* jesses?"

"Short straps which are fastened round a falcon's legs and which also carry the bells. When the falcon is carried for hunting, she is strapped to her falconer's wrists by the jesses, and is usually hooded. When she is sent after prey, the hood is removed from her eyes, the jesses loosed, and she is flung up. The bells, of course, are to help the hunter to find her in cover. This was a very pampered lady. Her bells were silver, and her jesses red leather. Shall we go on, now? I want to show you the gulls' cliff, and time's getting on."

They went on, taking a short cut across the rough pasturage, sweet with wild thyme and misty with the dancing blue of harebells. When they reached the great threatening cliffs they had passed in the motor-boat, once more they all lay down to peer at the narrow shelves and ledges closely crowded with the untidy nests of the kittiwakes and herring gulls. The noise which greeted their arrival nearly deafened them. The birds scolded vigorously, wheeling round and round overhead, loudly expressing their opinion of these intruders.

"What messy places! " Gay remarked.

"They're a good deal messier when you get close," he said. "And as for the smell——"

"Awful, I suppose?" Dickie grinned.

"You've said it! Stinking fish! They feed the young on fish, of course, and the refuse is just chucked about outside the nests."

"Then we won't ask to be lowered for a social call," Jo said cheerfully. "I like being friendly, but I draw the line at ancient and fish-like smells! Have you any gannets here, Mr. Bellever? I was reading such a wizard account of a gannetry the other day, and I thought I'd like to see one. Is there one here, by any chance?"

He shook his head. "Unfortunately, no. I don't know just where the nearest is at the moment. Of course you know that all the gannetries round these islands are known and numbered?"

"Yes; the book said so."

"What other birds do you get here?" Miss Wilson asked.

"Oh, ravens—swallows—swifts—martins—the usual lot. On Vendell, the other island for which I am responsible, we get a good many wild geese. It lies much lower than this, and at least half of it is marshy. I'd like you people to see it some day. It's quite different from this one, and we get quite a different type of bird."

He was taking them back to the house now, and the girls were scattering, examining the wild flowers, and calling to each other.

"I put a kettle on the hook before I met you," Mr. Bellever said. "I expect it's boiling by this time, and I'm sure you'd like a cup of tea."

"Oh, you shouldn't have bothered! " Miss Wilson exclaimed. "We've got milk and lemonade, and we could manage quite well. I hope you'll come and share our picnic baskets. By the way, what can you grow here in the way of fruit trees?"

"Well, nothing in the way of trees. The house is sheltered enough, but even the hardiest apple I've tried looks sick

114

and sorry before a couple of years are over. I've got rasp-
berry canes, and some gooseberry and currant bushes. The
goosegogs and the currants don't do badly, but the rasps
aren't up to much. I expect the soil doesn't feed them."

"We've a great basket of rasps," Bill told him. "You
must share them in return for the tea."

"Come in," he said, as they reached the door of the little
house.

They entered, Jo with all her instincts as a writer well
roused. It was a quaint little room into which he took them,
with a wood and peat fire burning on the great hearth slab,
over which hung a gigantic kettle, slung from a hook and
chain. The kettle was singing merrily, and the steam from
its spout gave promise of a cup of tea which made the hot
and weary Miss Wilson sigh with gratitude. A solid wooden
table stood under the window in the deep embrasure, and
a couple of chairs to match were set at either end of it. A
big armchair occupied one side of the hearth, and a wooden
settle with a bearskin flung across it the other. A huge
Welsh tridarn or dresser stood against the wall facing the
window, and was filled with a variety of things, including
books, china, ink, packets of seeds, a scrubbing-brush, and,
rather unexpectedly, a view of Fleet Street on a rainy day.
The only other article of furniture was a solemn-faced
grandfather clock with a slow, portentous tick, and a gleaming brass face. Miss Wilson eyed it as she turned from the
hearth, and she gave an exclamation of dismay.

"It's half-past six! Jo, for goodness' sake call those girls
for tea. The boat will be here in half an hour's time! I told
Parry not to be a minute later than seven, and they must be
famished!"

"They've been too excited to think of food, bless them,"
Jo said, in her most maternal tones. "All right, Bill. Don't
you worry. I'll fix them." And she went to the door, and
uttered a long, musical cry, "Yoo-hoo-oo!"

They came running at her call, and she explained to them
that they must get their baskets and start tea at once. "And
bring the basket of rasps to me first," she ordered. "We
want to give Mr. Bellever some."

The girls looked at each other. Then Jacynth spoke. "Do

115

you think Miss Wilson would mind awfully if we gave the lot to Mr. Bellever? It's been awfully decent of him to give us such a super afternoon, and he hasn't any canes in the garden. We know that, for we've just been looking."

"Bless you, my children! It's a wizard idea. By all means give them to him. You've any amount of eats without them, I know."

"Then we will. Kathie, you and Gay take the basket and do it."

"Why us?" Kathie demanded. "You're Head Girl, my child."

"Yes; but you've lots more sauce than I have. Go on, you two! "

"The less *you* say about sauce after that, the better! " Gay ejaculated. "Oh, all right! I don't mind doing it. Come on, Kath! "

Between them, they picked up the big basket of rosy fruit, carried it into the house, and offered it to the embarrassed Kester Bellever. He finally agreed to accept it on condition that if they had a calm day in the autumn they would come again and see his birds under autumn conditions. After that, it was a scramble to finish their tea and be ready when the motor-boat came.

Mr. Bellever walked down to the little quay to see them off. He said a few words to Parry, who nodded understandingly. Then the host turned to Bill, who was uttering her final thanks for their delightful afternoon.

"I've just been telling Parry to take you back the other way," he said. "It won't make you much later, and you'll see the mainland coastline, and get a good view of St. Bride's. Goodbye! I hope you'll come again next term."

He waved good-bye to them, and then, as the boat drew out from the little harbour, turned and ran swiftly up the sandy path to the top of the low cliff, where he stood waving to them as they were carried across towards the Welsh coast. Then, as they turned to run eastwards to round St. Bride's, he gave a final wave, and vanished.

"This," said Gay, "has been a bonza afternoon. If I weren't going in for music, I wouldn't mind being a birdwatcher myself. Only," she added prudently, "I wouldn't want to be absolutely on my own. That would be a lot too lonesome for me. Still, with a pal to help, I should think it would be quite a decent life."

"In summer," Bill told her. "I doubt if you'd enjoy it at all in the winter."

"Oh, well!" Gay was insouciant as usual. "It was just an idea. All the same, I've enjoyed it awfully, and I know a lot more about birds than I ever did before."

And the entire party agreed with her in that.

CHAPTER TEN

A Letter for Annis

"THE only crab I have about this place is that you don't get your letters till midday, and when they've got to come from Edinburgh, it makes it a jolly long time between letters." Thus spoke Kathie Roberston the following Saturday afternoon in the Tin Hut where they were disporting themselves, since a silvery curtain of rain had stopped all outdoor amusements.

The Seniors and the Senior Middles were together, and they had been dancing. Now dancing had stopped, and they were sitting about in groups, chatting, reading, or otherwise employing themselves. Jacynth and Gay were on duty with the Juniors, having volunteered to take charge for the afternoon to relieve the mistresses. Incidentally, they had plans of their own which they wanted to work out, and had got permission to take the party over to the old coach-house, which had been turned into a geography room, on condition that they would be responsible for any damage done by their charges. They had agreed cheerfully to this.

As Gay said *sotto voce* to Jacynth as they went to round up the younger girls, "They won't get one solitary chance to make little mooks of themselves, even if they want to —and I don't think they do somehow."

"It's a nuisance," Nancy Canton agreed in reply to Kathie's remark. "All the same, it's the only weak spot in the whole outfit, so I'm not grumbling."

Tom Gay, sitting astride a chair nearby, her firm chin resting on its back, joined in the conversation. "It doesn't make much odds as a rule," she said, "but it's a bit of a curse if there's anything worrying going on at home."

"You worried about something, Tom?" Kathie asked, in a friendly way.

Tom shook her head. "Not me! Far's I know, everything's o-kay at home. But young Annis is expecting a letter which hasn't come, so she's got to wait till Monday now, and she's gone off into one of her moods."

Since Annis had recovered from the last trouble, Tom and her own particular chums had kept a kindly eye on their firebrand. Annis had made no special friend in the school, though she was friendly with two or three in her own form. Tom and Co, as they were largely called by most of the school, had their own interests, but they contrived to draw Annis into the one or two that mattered less to them than the others, saw that she had plenty of partners for tennis and dancing, and generally played sheepdog to her. That they had been able so far to do it without her realising what they were after spoke well for their tact, though it must be confessed that Tom, at any rate, was not over-gifted with that virtue.

The prefects also gave an eye to Annis. No one wanted a repetition of the trouble at the beginning of term. However, if she had, as Tom said, gone off in 'a mood', it needed care. Kathie pulled up a chair and sat down, an example followed by Nancy. Bride Bettany and Anne Webster squatted on the floor beside them. The rest of the room were too busy with their own concerns to watch the little group beside the far window, so they were, to all intents and purposes, alone.

"I wish you'd sit properly, Tom," Nancy remarked. "After all, you're nearly sixteen. You might remember you're not a boy, whatever you may wish. It's an awful example for the kids."

Tom stood up, reversed her chair, and sat down again,

one leg slung over the other in gentlemanly style, and hugged her knees. "There aren't any kids here—just our own crowd," she remarked. "However, anything to oblige! Now—about Annis! She's been looking black as night ever since the letters were given out after Guides, and I know she was expecting one because she was fed to the teeth when it didn't come yesterday. She's fedder to-day. A blind monkey's grandson could see that!"

"Any idea why?" Kathie asked.

"Blob!" said Tom laconically. "All I know is she was just the same this morning—oh, a little down as she hadn't got her letter yesterday, but nothing to write home about. She was all right at Guides, wasn't she, you people?" to Bride and Anne, who both nodded. "Then, when we went into the dining-room for letters and there weren't any for her, she growled something—I didn't hear what—and went off. She wouldn't come down here this afternoon, either. She's stuck in the common-room with a book, though I'll bet you what you like she's not *reading*. We tossed up for it to see who'd better keep an eye on her, and Rosalie got it. So she's there, too, scribbling at that everlasting story she's writing." Tom suddenly went off at a tangent. "You know, you people, it wouldn't surprise me a lot if young Rosalie didn't become the school's second authoress. That yarn of hers isn't too dusty."

"You stick to Annis and never mind Rosalie," Kathie said severely. "I want to know what *sort* of a mood Annis is in. Is she mad, or miserable, or what? Buck up and tell us. Annis gave us a doing a few weeks ago, and we had enough then. If she's likely to go off the deep end now, I want to know about it. We can't exactly stop her, I suppose; but we might be able to do something with her before she gets to that pitch."

"*I* think she's miserable," Bride said, as she sat hugging her knees on the floor. "I'm certain she was just about howling when Bill handed out the last letter and there wasn't a thing for her."

"*I* thought she was feeling pretty mad myself." Anne took a hand. "She looked it, anyhow, with those black eyes of hers flashing. As for what she said, Tom, she said, 'Oh, *curse* Aunt Margaret! Lousy as usual! ' I didn't say anything; I thought it better not. And don't you prees take it up, either," she added hurriedly. "That bit's off the record."

"O-kay; you needn't worry. This whole chat's off the record," Kathie replied amiably. "Later on, we must see about reforming the language of this school. Some people use a lot more slang than is good for them! "

"Meaning me?" Tom asked, with a grin.

"Oh, you're not the only one. And I *will* say for you you avoid some words—like 'lousy', for instance. What a little gubbins Annis is! She knows the Staff are definitely down on things like that, and she'd get a double fine if they caught her using it. Why can't she show some sense?"

"Hasn't any to show, *I* think! " Bride retorted.

"It's time she found some, then! Tom—or any of you! Have you the least idea why she's so keen on a letter from her aunt? There isn't illness or anything like that at her home, is there?"

"I don't think so." Tom spoke thoughtfully. "You know, Kathie, Annis has had a raw deal in some ways."

"Oh? I hadn't heard about that. How do you know, by the way?"

"Pater's brother lives in the same place—he's the doctor there—and he knows Mrs. Bain—that's Annis's aunt. He told Pater about it when he came for Easter week-end. Annis has no mater, and her pa was in the Merchant Navy. His ship was lost off the Horn with all hands. Anyhow, no one has ever heard anything of her or them for the last two years. Captain Lovell had sent Annis to a quite decent day-school in the place where they lived. She boarded with friends of her mother's, and went to school with the girls who were her chums. When they decided that Captain Lovell was gone, they found that Mrs. Bain was her guardian, only she hadn't seen much of her. Mrs. Bain lives round in hotels and boarding-houses, you see."

"That would be a pretty poor life for a kid," Nancy said gravely.

"Well, Mrs. Bain was awfully fed up. She's Captain Bain's cousin, really, and she'd only agreed to be Annis's guardian because she never expected to have to do anything about it. Anyhow," pursued Tom, warming to her story, "she went to see the kid, and took a dislike to the folk Annis was with. She said they were slangy and rude and impudent. She took Annis away, and carted her off to Hodley —that's the place where she lives. It's a seaside resort, and there's dozens of hotels and boarding-houses there. Uncle Bill said Mrs. Bain stayed in one till she had a row with whoever kept it, and then moved on to another. She was in a boarding-house just then, and she kept Annis with her, and sent her to a footy little day-school there. Annis loathed it, and she made things hot for her aunt. So at last the old lady decided to send the kid here and be rid of her for the term, at any rate. Annis was raging. She wanted to go back to the folk she'd been with, but Mrs. Bain wouldn't hear of it, though *I* think she was an awful mook not to allow it. She'd have been rid of the kid more or less for keeps then. Anyhow, that's the story, so far as Uncle Bill knows it. So you see if Mrs. Bain is ill, I don't suppose it 'ud worry Annis much. No; *I* think she wants to go and spend the hols with the Maples—that's the people she was living with—and she's waiting to hear if her aunt will let her. After all, it's past half-term now, and I dare say they'll want to know so that they can make arrangements. If you ask me, that's why Annis goes mad sometimes."

"Tom told us when she was in that row at the beginning of term." Bride took up the tale. "We felt jolly sorry for the kid, and thought when it was all over we'd do what we could to save her other rows. After all, if she's miserable anyhow, there's no point in her being *more* miserable because she's in a fearful row here. Besides, it makes the Staff love *us* less, and we get the backwash of the whole thing."

"I see—six for Annis and half a dozen for yourselves," Nancy began.

Kathie interrupted her. "Rot! It isn't that at all, Nance, and you're a gubbins if you think that! You folk have been decent to the kid, Bride and Tom. I hope she isn't going to break out again. It won't do her any good with that aunt or cousin of hers, or whatever she is, if the Heads

121

decide they won't keep her. And if she goes on having outsizes in rows, that's what's going to happen—definitely!"

Tom pulled a long face. "I say! D'you really think that?"

"Oh, they surely wouldn't do that?" Bride added distressfully.

"Well, what would *you* do in their place?" Kathie asked reasonably. "They can't go on keeping a girl who breaks out with cheek and that sort of thing. I don't suppose they know what's really at the bottom of it."

"Jolly sure they don't." Tom was definite about this. She came to a sudden stop, and glanced round the group. "You know, what I think is that inside her Annis feels that the way her blinking aunt has behaved—taking her away from the Maples, and saying all she *has* said about them to Annis and outsiders, too—makes the kid feel that Mrs. Bain is sort of criticising her father. Annis is a complete ass, but she thinks a lot of her father, and that sort of thing makes her see red. I don't blame her, either. I'd see red myself if anyone did that to me."

"So'd I!" Anne suddenly spoke up. "Of course, she's a fearful idiot not to see that the school is a jolly good one as schools go. Anyhow, from what she says, it's a long sight better than the place her aunt sent her to first go off. If only we could get her to see that, I honestly think she'd be better. But she seems to feel that she's got to stick to the place where her father sent her, and so—and so—" Anne ran down, being unable to express her ideas clearly.

Kathie did it for her. "I see! A case of mistaken loyalty! Well, it definitely is hard lines on her if she feels like that; but she can't be allowed to muck things up here for herself and everyone else for that reason. Only I don't see just what *we* can do about it—unless someone goes to the Heads and tells them all this."

Tom jumped to her feet. "You can't! We told you in confidence. You *said* this chat was off the record! You can't go and split now, Kathie!"

"If you do, none of us will trust you again," Bride warned her.

Kathie saw their point. The difficulty was that her sense of duty told her that someone in authority ought to know what was at the bottom of Annis's conduct, and unless the Fifth Formers would agree to their being told, it was hard to see how they were to know about it.

"Sit down, Tom," she said. "Of course we aren't going to say anything that you told us was off the record—*unless* you'll agree to it. I quite see how you folk feel about it. At the same time, don't you see that if the Heads haven't any good reason for the sort of thing the little ass does and says, there's going to be a most unholy row? Annis was in pretty bad trouble for cheek last term, and she's had another lot this. If that sort of thing goes on, I don't see how they can keep her. I mean, she'll get the name for being utterly incorrigible. It wouldn't matter quite so much if it was only in front of you lot, or us; but she doesn't seem to care if it's that way or before all the kids. No school is going to keep a girl who makes a habit of saucing mistresses before juniors. It couldn't be done. All discipline would go haywire. Look at the row those little idiots Mary-Lou and Co had a few weeks ago! "

"That had nothing to do with Annis," Tom said sturdily. "She wasn't there, and she knew nothing about it, any more than most of us did until it was all over. You can't blame her because Lower Thirds lost their idiot heads and had a free fight! "

"I know that—I'm not crackers! " Kathie argued. "But can't you *see* that an example like Annis's sets the kids thinking they can get away with the same sort of thing? Oh, I know they didn't sauce anyone—I will say for that lot that most of them have more sense. But they did go for each other like little wild-cats. It—it makes a kind of lax feeling in the school. Can't you *understand*?" she added despairingly.

"I see what you mean—at least I think I do," Bride said, "but we told you a lot of private stuff about one of ourselves in confidence, and I don't see how we can let you go spilling it to the Heads. Annis would be mad in real earnest then, and when she gets really mad, she doesn't seem to care two hoots what she does. All the same," she

123

went on, "if that letter doesn't come soon, there's going to be trouble."

"Let's hope it comes on Monday, then," Nancy observed. "As for Annis's home troubles, I'm as sorry for her as the rest of you, but I don't see how *we* can help them. Be as jolly with her as you can to-night and to-morrow, and try to cheer her up. That's the only thing I can think of."

"Oh, we'll do that, all right. The bother is she doesn't want to be cheered up," Tom informed the prefects. "She acts as if every blinking creature was against her. It's mad —but it's Annis!"

Ursula came over to their party and called Kathie and Nancy off for some private business in the Sixth, and the Fifth Formers were left alone."

"I vote we go up and see what's happening," Bride suggested. "It's rather mingy to leave it all to Rosalie, even if it does give her a chance to get on with that yarn of hers. D'you think it'll ever be published, any of you? She let me read the first three chapters, and I thought it wasn't half bad. I told Auntie Jo when she was here, and she said if Rosalie would let her, she'd read it and advise her when it was finished."

"Rather her than me!" Tom said, with great lack of grammar. "Young Rosalie's writing is like a spider track gone crackers. She'd better copy it in script before she lets you have it to send—not that her script's much better," she added, as they pulled on their hooded cloaks and left the Tin Hut. "It's all curls and squiggles."

"She's sending it home to be typed," Bride said. "She asked her dad if someone in his office could do it, and he agreed. I believe the first lot's gone off already."

"Well, come on and see what's happening." Tom led the way to the cloakroom, where they hung up their cloaks and pulled off their goloshes before they ran upstairs to the common-room. There they found Annis sitting on one of the window seats, staring out at the rain, while Rosalie, at a table nearby, was scribbling for dear life. Both looked up as the three girls entered. Rosalie smiled dreamily at them, and bent her head again over her paper. Tom doubted if she had really grasped who they were. Rosalie, busy with her writing, was apt to be painfully vague at times. Annis simply looked at them and scowled.

Tom marched up to the table, and picked up a handful of finished sheets. "It's time we had a dekko at this masterpiece of yours!" she said calmly. "Can't let you send rot out for anyone else to see, you know."

This woke Rosalie up, and she protested, "It's only the rough! You're not going to read it, Tom! Wait till I get a fair copy done."

Tom grinned, holding the sheets well out of Rosalie's reach. "Not on your life! You're one of us, and we aren't going to let you send out any sort of muck for other people to giggle over, I can tell you!"

"Oh, Tom you are a pig!" But Rosalie subsided, placated by being claimed as 'one of us'.

Her friendship with Tom and the others dated from her first term at the school to which she had come, being put into an indignant Tom's charge at York station by an over-anxious mother. The first days of their association had been stormy, for Tom, boyish, matter-of-fact, and utterly without sentiment, was the direct antithesis of Rosalie, who was, to quote Bride at the time, 'a perfect *mush* of slop'. Rosalie had developed a fond admiration for the girl who was so unlike herself; and Tom, at thirteen, had not quite known what to do about it. There had been sundry storms before they finally settled down; and even now, Rosalie had fits of wondering if Tom cared for her as she cared for Tom, though she had gained enough sense by this time to keep such things to herself. Therefore, however shy she might feel about this first-born of her imagination, Tom's remark had settled their right to censor her work.

"Come on, you folk!" Tom squatted down on a pouffe nearby. "We're all in on this. You, too, Annis; you're Fifth Form as well as us. Come and help us veto any rot Rosalie may have written."

"I'm not interested." Annis spoke briefly, and then turned her back.

"O-kay; just as you like. All the same, we must see that this book is all right. Can't have young Rosalie wasting her time over tosh!" quoth Tom austerely, while Rosalie

125

flushed, and cast an indignant glance at Annis, who didn't see it, and wouldn't have cared if she had.

However, there was to be no reading for them just then. Tom was puckering up her brows over her friend's scrawl when the tea-bell rang, and as punctuality was considered one of the virtues at the Chalet School, there was nothing for it but to hand the pages back to Rosalie to put away in her case, and then hurry off to wash their hands and go to the dining-room. Nor was there any time after tea, for they must change their frocks in readiness for the evening's dancing and games. So Rosalie escaped for the time being, much to her relief.

Sunday passed as most of the school Sundays did. The Protestant members of the school went to morning service, while one of the monks from the Community on St. Bride's rowed over to say Mass for the Catholics. In the afternoon, which was fine, they went for a ramble about the island, and in the evening they came together for reading and hymns, after which they had supper. Then the younger girls went to bed while their elders sat about quietly, reading or writing letters.

Monday came in with a summer mist which only cleared off slowly, but it had vanished by eleven. At the end of morning school, when the letters were given out, those members of the Fifth concerned were thankful to see that Annis had her long-looked-for letter. There was rarely time to read correspondence before Mittagessen, so she slipped it into her blazer pocket. But when they settled down on the drive and paths for their usual half-hour's rest in deck chairs, she ignored Bride's friendly invitation to 'come on and sit with us', and carried her chair to the far end of the drive where she could be comparatively alone. There she pulled the thick envelope, addressed in Mrs. Bain's firm black script, out of her pocket, ripped it open with fingers that shook with eagerness, and pulled out the four or five sheets, closely written over. Now she would know whether she could go to spend the summer holidays with Helen and Elizabeth as she hoped!

"My dear Annis," her aunt had written, "I was glad to have your letter and hear that you are quite well. I am afraid I am not so pleased to hear that you are only ninth in your form for the half-term. I see by the report that there are seventeen girls in your form, so that means that you have only managed to reach the middle of the list. For a girl with your brains, I hardly think this is good enough. Indeed, all things considered, it strikes me as very bad. You are not stupid, and you can do well when you choose. Evidently you have *not* chosen this term.

"Now, Annis, mediocre work will get you nowhere, and I should not do my duty if I did not point this out to you very firmly. Also, I feel I must explain matters to you, though I had hoped to be able to leave things until you were a little older, and therefore better able to appreciate the position. Please read what follows very carefully, and give it your most earnest thought, for it deals with your future.

"As you know, your father was a comparatively young man when he died, and though he had saved, what he left for you is not a large sum. It is sufficient to keep you at your present school until you are eighteen, and there will be enough left to take you to one of the smaller universities if you wish to take a degree; or, better still, to one of the Government Training Colleges, where the fees are lower and the course lasts only two years. I understand that a degree course takes three.

"If you decided on the Training College, it would mean that there would be two or three hundred pounds left to help you through your first year or so of teaching. I feel you should know that once your training is over you can look to me for no further help than an occasional present. I have undertaken to provide your clothes and holidays until you are of age, and though this means that I have to sacrifice many little pleasures and luxuries I should like, I am very pleased to do so much for you. But once your training ends, *you must stand on you own feet*. You cannot expect me to support you any longer.

"I am telling you all this to impress on you the fact that you *must* work hard while at school, or you will get nowhere. If you leave the school with a good record, and gain either a good degree or a good diploma when you finish your course, you will be able to command a good post in a school, and therefore a good salary, from which you should try to save at least ten per cent every year. Then, if you should not wish to continue teaching till you are old enough for a pension, you will have investments which, if you are careful, ought to give you a sufficient income to live in quiet comfort. This is many years ahead, of course, and one cannot say what will happen before that time. But I must warn you that, apart from a little jewellery and personal possessions, you can expect nothing from me, as *all* my income comes from annuities and will, therefore, cease at my death. Owing to my many and unforeseen expenses, I have been unable to save.

"Now I have explained the situation fully to you, and I *expect* that you will have a much better report and be far higher in your form at the end of the term, and that next term you will do still better. I am sure that you can, for, as I said before, you have an excellent brain.

"I shall hope to see you in five weeks' time when your holidays begin at my present address,

         "Until then, I am,

            "Yours affectionately,

              "Margaret F. Bain.

"P.S.—I see I have forgotten to reply to your request. Even if you deserved to have it granted, which, in view of your low form position, I cannot think to be the case, I should certainly not agree to allowing you to have anything more to do with those unpleasant girls Helen and Elizabeth Maples so long as I am in charge of you, so please say no more about it. It will be waste of time and stamps."

Annis finished reading this cruel letter. When she had reached the last words, she gave a smothered exclamation, and crumpled it violently in her hands. Perhaps Mrs. Bain, who was an insensitive person, had no intention of being deliberately unkind, but to sixteen-year-old Annis her father's cousin seemed at that moment a heartless monster. She knew very well that her low place in form for the first half of the term was the result of the trouble she had been in. Had it not been for that, she would probably have been among the first four, for Mrs. Bain was right when she said the girl had a good brain. That the letter had been partly called forth by her own obstinacy and silliness never struck her. What hurt her most was the implied slur on her father's memory. Annis had known comparatively little of him, but they had loved each other dearly, and she had suffered badly when she was told by motherly Mrs. Maples that it was feared he and his ship had gone down in the bitter waters off Cape Horn. She had said little, and she never mentioned him if she could help it; but she brooded on the change his loss had made in her life, and this had helped to warp a character always difficult. Now, as the thoughts of her wrongs came rushing over her, she felt rage surging up within her, and her dark, gipsy face became very unpleasant. She could make no decision yet as to what she should do; but spend the seven weeks of the summer holidays with Aunt Margaret after all that she had said, she would *not*! She would rather go out and do scrubbing! She would not go back to Hodley, no matter what was said. But then, where could she go? The Maples would take her in, but she knew that Aunt Margaret would think of them at once, and wire to Mrs. Maples to send her unless she descended on them herself to claim her charge. That would be worse than all.

"No; I must just write to Mrs. Maples and tell her Aunt Margaret won't let me come to them," she thought, as she sat clutching the crumpled pages of the letter in hands that were icy cold, though the sun was blazing down on the lawn now, and even here, in the shade of the trees, it was warm. "I must slip off somehow—somehow——"

The school bell rang, and she had to go to take her chair to the shed and then join the rest of her form for a boating lesson. Well, there was a month and more to think what she would do. Aunt Margaret said she was clever, did she? She would just show her *how* clever she could be.

"It'll be queer if I can't hide from her somehow!" she thought, as she pulled on her shady hat before joining the others. "The thing will be to get away. Once I've done that, I can manage. And luckily I must have over thirty shillings in the bank. I'll manage somehow!"

129

E

Then she left the cloakroom and went to join up with Tom Gay who was waiting for her. Annis's face was so lowering that even the tactless Tom hurriedly revised her intention of asking if her letter had been the one she wanted, talking busily about school matters the whole way to the boathouse instead.

CHAPTER ELEVEN

A Fallen Castle

THE hard work of the afternoon gave no one any chance for meditation. Miss Burn believed in making the most of what time they had, and she worked the three Fifths relentlessly, aided by Dickie Christy. The Sixth had art on Monday afternoons, and Dickie had no gift that way. Therefore she had coaxed her father into asking Miss Annersley if she need take it. That lady had agreed at once, since she had memories of a Jo Bettany who had also been very poor, and whose work had been so consistently appalling that on one occasion the irritable art master, Herr Laubach, had lost control of himself and flung paper and pencils at her. Herr Laubach still took the senior five forms, and no one wanted that particular incident repeated. Usually Dickie went for extra French to Mlle de Lachenais, but on this afternoon Mlle had succumbed to an attack of migraine as happened on rare occasions, so Dickie was free, and had been joyfully claimed by Hilary Burn as her aide for the afternoon. Commander Christy had seen to it that Dickie should do him credit with boats, and she could handle them as well as other girls handle a needle or a pencil. Miss Burn sent her off with a load consisting of Bride Bettany, Tom Gay, Annis Lovell, Anne Webster, and Elfie Woodward, while she herself concentrated on the others.

Of Dickie's five, Tom, who had lived by the sea all her life, was a fair oar. Bride Bettany's parents had returned from India a year or two previously, and made their home in an old family house, the Quadrant, which stood not very far from Bideford. Bride had known nothing about boats up till then, and the Quadrant stood on a high cliff where boating was not very safe for amateurs, thanks to tricky currents; but she had been out with her father and elder brothers a few times during the summer holidays, and had some idea of it. Annis, too, had been out on the bay at her old home occasionally, so was not *quite* a tyro. The other two had known nothing at all about it until the boats had arrived, but were keen. Dickie made a good coach. Her father had seen to it that she knew the why of everything he taught her, and she passed on her knowledge in clear, crisp remarks. She chaffed Tom and Bride unmercifully for faults in style, and was ruthlessly plain-spoken with Anne and Elfie, who seemed to be under the impression that the farther you dug the blades of your oars into the water the faster you would go, but she was very gentle with Annis, correcting her mistakes quietly, and yet contriving to make the girl feel that the Sixth Former was really anxious that she should do well for her own sake.

Despite herself, this treatment and the hard work combined with the fresh breeze that they met on the water soothed the pain her Aunt Margaret's unkind letter had given her. When Miss Burn's whistle blew for their return, she felt considerably calmer than she had done.

"You went out pretty far, Dickie," said the mistress, as they helped to haul the boats up. "I know there's not much current about here, but be careful, won't you? We don't want to have to get a man to come and salvage you, so to speak."

"I should think not! Dad *would* lead me a life of it if I let us in for that," Dickie laughed. "It was all right, Miss Burn. I had my eye on the water, and you can see the current if you know how to spot it. We weren't within twenty yards of it at any time."

Hilary Burn nodded. "Very well; I can trust you, I know. I expect you have the whole chart of this area in your head by this time."

"Not quite," Dickie answered modestly. "I know a lot of it, but not like Dad, of course. I'll be careful, Miss Burn."

"Good! Well, the tide's going out still, and won't turn till six, so we can leave the boats here. Upper Fourth are coming out to-night."

"Miss Burn, do you think we could have inter-house races before the term ends?" Bride asked, as they left the sandy shore and scrambled up to the roadway. "Peggy had a letter from Auntie Jo, and she said if we could, the inter-house cup they used to have in Tirol is at the Round House, and she'd get it and bring it on the day. What do you think?"

"The Inter-house Rowing Cup! I haven't thought of it for years!" Hilary's eyes became dreamy. "*I* stroked St. Clare's when it was last won—by St. Clare's, too. We got it by about a third of a length. St. Thérèse gave us a gruelling race of it! We rowed level practically the whole way and I didn't really believe we'd got it until we heard the judges' decision. It was the most thrilling race I ever took part in."

"What about St. Scholastika's?" asked Elfie, who was an ornament of that House.

Hilary considered as she waited for the girls to form line. "I rather think they came fourth," she said at last. "They got the Tennis Cup, though, that year. They had Winnie Silk, and she could take on any two other players at the school and give them a stiff game. What became of her, Bride? I haven't any idea, I'm afraid. We lost sight of each other, and I've heard nothing of her for years now. Married, probably. She was very pretty, and very charming. No brains to speak of, but a really nice girl! And, as I've said, a demon with a racquet. We've never had anyone to touch her at the school since."

"Daisy's jolly good," Bride said, speaking of her grown-up cousin who was an Old Girl of the school, and at present at a big London hospital where she was "walking the wards" with the intention of taking up work among sick children later on.

"Oh yes—for an amateur. Winnie was good enough for a professional." Hilary spoke with great briskness. "Let me see: didn't we have a Junior Cup, too? No; I don't think we did. Well, you people, I'll bring it up at the next

Staff meeting, but I can't say more till after that. In the meantime, you must try to get some polish on your style. Some of you dig your oars in as if you were gardening; and more of you bring them out with the most awful jerks. Remember that style as well as pace count. In fact," Hilary went on, warming to her subject, "good or bad style makes all the difference between good and bad pace. I know you can't expect to get the style for skiff rowing. These broad boats don't give you much chance of it. But you can be a neat oarsman just as well in them as in a skiff. If ever we get the chance of skiffs, you'll have a good solid foundation if you'll only put your backs into it now."

After these words of wisdom, she marched them forward, and they set off up the winding road, chattering eagerly about the new idea. Even Annis was drawn into the talk, for Tom and Bride had had time for a hasty word or two before they entered the boat, and had decided that, to judge by her face when they went down to the shore, her letter had not been what she wanted. How much more was in it than that, they could have no idea; but they carried out Nancy's advice on the Saturday, and continually drew her into their chatter.

It was not until they were all safely in bed that Annis had a chance to think deeply on what Mrs. Bain had written in her letter. Then, curled up against her pillow, she pondered over the matter.

She was a sensitive girl, with a touchy pride that made her feel that she would rather go shabby than be dressed at her aunt's expense after what she had said. The great difficulty was that she could not see how she was to avoid it. Annis had very little idea of money matters, but she guessed that no one would allow her to control what her father had left her until she came of age.

"But I'm not going to have her flinging it in my face that she's got to do without her precious luxuries just because of me!" she thought hotly. "And I won't have a university training—nor a training college, either. I don't want to teach—I loathe the very idea! That doesn't seem to have occurred to Aunt Margaret. I suppose she thinks that all that matters is a decent screw and holidays. Well,

I can have a go at the screw in another way; but I *won't* teach! That's definite. And if I'm not going to teach, then there's no need for me to stay at school a minute longer than the end of this term. I'll be sixteen then—quite old enough to begin to earn my own living. I'm not going to be beholden to her for another ha'penny more than I can help! I'll tell her so, too, when I write." Having settled so much to her satisfaction, she lay down, and giving way to the drowsiness that she had been fighting while she thought, dropped off to sleep at once.

Next day, she went to Miss Annersley before school, and asked permission to write to her aunt instead of waiting till the end of the week.

"Is it really necessary?" the Head asked.

"Yes; I think so, Miss Annersley. It—it's about business, really."

With an inward smile—what "business" could this youngster want to discuss?—Miss Annersley nodded. "Very well, dear. Write your letter and take it to Miss Dene. She has to go over to Carnbach later this morning, so she will post it there for you, and it will go sooner." She glanced at her watch. "You may be excused from the walk for once so that you can write it." She turned to her desk and scribbled a few lines of excuse which she handed to Annis. "There you are. Give it to whoever is on duty, and bring your letter to Miss Dene before Prayers. Run along now, or you won't have time to do it."

Annis bobbed her curtsy with a quiet "Thank you!" and departed, leaving the Head to wonder to herself what was wrong. She was a busy woman, however, so she let it go, and turned to the lists she was preparing for her secretary. By the time that young lady was crossing in the ferry, the whole thing had passed out of her mind, and did not recur for some time.

Meanwhile, Annis went off to find Miss Burnett, who was on duty for their walk, handed her the excuse note, and then skipped off to her form-room to sit down and write her letter, leaving Bride, Tom, and Co in a state of wild curiosity as to *why* Annis Lovell should have been excused the walk. They discussed it among themselves,

134

but could find no reason, and when Bride asked on their return, the only reply she got was that Annis had had some business to see to.

"Snubs to me!" Bride said sadly, when she reported to the others. "Anyhow," and she cheered up considerably, "she isn't in a row, so that's *some*thing to be thankful for!"

Indeed, Annis had no intention of getting into further "rows". Mrs. Bain's remarks had done so much good. The girl was determined to have a good report for the last, as she thought, she was likely to get from the Chalet School. With this in mind, she set to work on her letter at once, in order to have a few minutes afterwards in which to look over her history again.

"Dear Aunt," she wrote, "I have had your letter. I am sorry you should feel obliged to give up your luxuries for me. I am sure my father never meant you to do such a thing, and I know I do not. However, there will be no need after this. I am sixteen at the beginning of July, and I shall be old enough to leave school then. In any case, I could not teach, so I shall not be going to either a university or a training college. I want to be——" This was where Annis stuck. She had no idea what she wanted to be. In point of fact, she had given very little thought to it, unlike a good many of the others. Bride, for instance, *did* want to teach. Tom meant to go in for science with a view to becoming a dispenser. Elfie Woodward had, from the very first, set her heart on becoming a Physical Training mistress. Rosalie had decided to be a writer. Most of the others had definite ideas about their future. Annis, more childish in many ways than her contemporaries, as she was older in others, had given very little thought to the matter. She sat, sucking the end of her pen, and wondering what she should put. The sound of the clock chiming the half-hour set her to writing the first thing that came into her head. "——a nurse," she wrote. "In that way, I can begin to earn my living at once. That will save the rest of the money my father left me to pay for my clothes for the present."

Annis had no idea what a probationer was paid, nor how long the training would last, but she thought she would earn enough to pay for any holidays she might have. Anyway, if she were earning her own living she could always go to the Maples, who had been so good to her. Aunt Margaret would not be able to interfere then. With a triumphant feeling that she was going to win in this battle—Aunt Margaret would be only too glad to agree and be spared the need for buying her clothes!—Annis wound up her letter with a prim message of thanks for what Mrs. Bain had done for her, and a promise that as soon as it was possible she should be repaid in full. She signed her name with a flourish, put the letter into its envelope, which she had addressed and stamped already, and ran along to the office with it with the pleasant feeling that she had at least a quarter of an hour in which to look over that history again.

Miss Dene took the letter, glanced at the address, and nodded. "Very well, Annis. That will be all right."

"Thank you for bothering," Annis said, giving the secretary such a pleasant smile that Miss Dene, who was rather more accustomed to receiving glowers and scowls from her, was startled. Then Miss Annersley's bell rang, and she went off to get her orders while Annis hurried back to the form-room, and devoted the rest of her time to her history with such good effect that she gained full marks for it, and a commending, "Good, Annis! I'm very pleased with your work!" from Miss Burnett.

This pleasant state of affairs lasted for the rest of the week. The letter, posted from Carnbach on the Tuesday, did not reach Hodley until the first post on Thursday, and Mrs. Bain's reply did not come until the Saturday. During all that time, Annis was pleasant to the others, polite to the mistresses, and worked her hardest, proving, if proof had been needed, that Aunt Margaret was right in saying that she had a good brain.

She received her aunt's reply carelessly. She felt very sure what it would say. Alas for Annis! When she was able to open it and read it, all her airy castles fell to the ground. Mrs. Bain wrote to say that the girl had shocked her by her lack of gratitude for all that was being done for her.

136

"You will certainly *not* leave school until you are eighteen," she wrote. "To begin with, no hospital of standing would take you before that age. I believe that some hospitals refuse probationers until they are eighteen and a half. If you really wish to be a nurse, I can have no objection; but if you do, you will go to a good hospital and have a good training. As for the money your father has left you, neither Mr. Morgan, his solicitor who is a co-trustee with me, nor I will consent to your touching it until you are of age. So please do not mention the matter to me again. I can have no other answer for you.

"As for leaving school at the end of this term, do you not realise that a term's notice must be given before that? No notice has been sent to Miss Annersley, and I have no intention of sending it. Unless you behave so badly that the school refuses to keep you, you will stay where you are for the next two years. Of course, if you are expelled, you can scarcely hope to become a nurse. A nurse must be trustworthy. I do not imagine that hospitals have vacancies for a girl who has been expelled from school for bad behaviour or laziness in work.

"Now, Annis, I have said all I mean to say on the subject. I shall not speak of this again, nor allow you to do so, so please do not try. When you come home for your holidays, I hope to see you show your gratitude for all I am doing for you by being pleasant, obliging, and helpful. In that case, we may hope for a happy time together. I am not very well just now, and should be glad of help in many ways. Of course, if you behave as you have done during the past year, you cannot expect me to be pleased with you, nor to show pleasure in having you with me.

"Now, I hope I have said the last I need to say about all this. Make up your mind to accept the fact that you have two more years of school. Do your best, and bring home a good report. Then, perhaps, I may be able to forget the shocking ingratitude your letter shows.

"Believe me,
"Your affectionate aunt,
"M. Bain.

"P.S.—I am not certain that I shall stay on here, so do

137

not write until I let you know my plans. If I leave, it will be very shortly."

Annis let the letter drop into her lap, and sat staring across the sunny lawn with eyes that saw nothing. It was at an end, all her lovely plans! After all, she was not to be free of Aunt Margaret at once. She was to stay at school for two years more, doing lessons, and being dependent on her guardian for her clothes, though she felt sure that lady grudged every sixpence spent on her. Worst of all, there would be no seeing the Maples soon as she had hoped. It would just be the same old thing over again—being at school—a school she *hated*! And in the holidays she would be expected to run round after Aunt Margaret, never having a moment to call her own unless her aunt was resting—and even then, there was no relying on her resting for more than an hour at a time.

If she had been alone, there is no doubt that at this point Annis would have given way and cried whole-heartedly. But there was no chance of that with all the others sitting round. It was rather a pity in one way. If she could have relieved herself with a good cry, the chances are that what was to follow would never have happened, so that several people would have been saved a great deal of worry and anxiety, and Annis herself a nasty experience. As it was, however, she forced herself to take up that hateful letter, fold it neatly, and slip it back into the envelope.

That done, Annis glanced round at her immediate circle. She was sitting with the usual crowd, and all had letters with which they were busy, so no one had seen the change in her face as she read hers. She slipped it into her blazer pocket, stretched out her legs and arms, and yawned.

"Had a decent letter?" Bride asked kindly, looking up from a lengthy epistle from Jo.

"Oh, so-so! Yours all right?" Annis returned the question.

"Oh, smashing! It's from Auntie Jo. The new book's been accepted, and should be out next year. She and Uncle Jack and the boys are going to spend the next week-end with Mummy as Daddy has to go to London on business, and she says just *p'raps* they may come to see us. Won't that be wizard?"

"You're lucky to have an aunt like that," Annis said, as lightly as she could.

"I know it! You can't tell me anything about Auntie Jo!" Bride returned to her letter, and Annis lay quietly, watching the rest as they read, and then put their letters with sighs of satisfaction into their pockets.

Annis had often envied the Maple girls their jolly, chummy mother, but it had never occurred to her till that moment that others were just as fortunate. A very bitter feeling took hold of her as she watched them. Why should she be the only one to be without father or mother, and to have only someone like Aunt Margaret who was so unpleasant? There was something very unfair about it!

Her gaze wandered on to a group of the prefects. Jacynth Hardy was among them, and everyone knew that Jacynth was an orphan with no relations left at all; but she had Gay Lambert and Gay's sister who had practically adopted her. The letter she was reading was probably from Mrs. Lambert. Annis had heard that she wrote to Jacynth as regularly as she wrote to Gay. As a matter of fact, the letter was from Bride's cousin, Daisy Venables, but Annis could not know that. *She* could have had a jolly home, too, if only Aunt Margaret had let her stay with the Maples. She knew they had wanted to keep her. Mr. Maples had done his best; but Aunt Margaret had taken a dislike to Helen and Elizabeth with their hail-fellow-well-met ways, saying they were impertinent and badly brought up, and she had refused to hear of it.

"I don't know why she acted like that," Annis thought resentfully. "She can't pretend to *love* me, and I'm an awful nuisance to her, and cost her no end, to judge by what she says. The Maples would never have made a fuss about buying my clothes because they had sent me to an expensive school. I'd have stayed at the High School, and the money could have bought all I needed then, and I shouldn't be depending on anyone's charity!" The bitter word filled her mind with self-pity. Then the bell rang, and they had to put their chairs away and go to get their hats and baskets for the picnic they were to have. The cricket team were playing an away match, so Tom was with them. So were Elfie and Anne Webster, who were also in the Eleven. She and Bride would go off together, she supposed, since Bride and that crowd had been so chummy to her lately.

She was quite right. Bride somehow felt that something had gone wrong with Annis, though why she should feel like that, she had no idea. However, it meant that they must be together. Bride grabbed Rosalie as she ran past to get her hat, and they both closed up round Annis, talking hard. Annis never got a moment to herself all the rest of that day.

The picnic was to take place on St. Bride's by invitation of the Superior of the small Community of Dominicans there. He had sent a note to Miss Wilson whom he had met, by the friar who had come over on the previous Sunday. They would be delighted to welcome the school and let the girls ramble about the island, but they were unable to provide them—so many of them—with a meal, though they could give them goats' milk in plenty, for the Community had several goats.

Miss Annersley, who had sent back the reply, since Miss Wilson happened to be over on the mainland at Howells, had said they would be delighted to come, and would certainly bring their own food. The Community's big boat was to come to fetch off as many as it would hold, and Hilary Burn considered that those of the girls accustomed to boating could manage to row the comparatively short distance as well, so even the Juniors might go. The Kindergarten babies were to have a visit to Carnbach, and picnic on the shore there with their own mistresses in charge of them. Hilary Burn had gone with the Eleven, but most of the mistresses could pull an oar, and all could swim. If the weather was fine, it should be safe enough.

Laden with their baskets, the school marched down to the ferry-landing where the big, clumsy-looking boat belonging to St. Bride's was waiting for them, two of the friars in their rough white flannel robes, with leather belts girdling the waists, in charge. The girls had seen their

140

particular friar in his black cowl before this, so there were startled looks exchanged. Dickie was on the boat already, beaming at them, even as she chatted with the Brothers in her usual insouciant way. She jumped out as the long train came down the road, and made for the other side of the little jetty where the Christy dinghy was tied up.

"Dad said I could bring *Silver Wings*, Miss Wilson," she cried, "so long as we don't try to use the sail. I've un-stepped the mast, and left it in the boathouse, so that's all safe. May some of the others come with me, please? We'll be awfully careful."

Miss Wilson, who was leading them, laughed. "That'll be all right, Dickie; who do you want? Take Seniors for choice, please."

"Oh, then, will you come, Jacynth? And Bride and Rosalie and Annis?" Dickie asked, choosing those nearest at hand. "We can squeeze in two more, I think. Lesley Pitt, what about you? And—oh, Frances! I didn't see you before. Come along in! May we get off, Miss Wilson?"

Miss Annersley had come up now, and the two Heads laughed as they looked down at the throng of girls in the little boat.

"Yes, I think you'd better," Miss Wilson agreed. "Be careful, won't you, Dickie? We don't want to turn this picnic into a rescue party!"

"O-kay—I mean, that'll be all right." Dickie went red. "Bride and I can row, and the rest have only to sit still. I can take a few of those baskets," she added. "They'll tuck under the seats."

The baskets were handed down and tucked away, and then Dickie untied her sailor-like knot, pushed off, and they were drifting out on the water which was as smooth as a mill pond.

"You seem jolly bucked with life, Dick," Jacynth said, as Dickie and Bride settled down to a steady pace with the oars. "Been left a fortune?"

Dickie laughed. "Better than that, my dear! You know Dad took Cherry to London on Monday for examination? Well, we had a letter this morning to tell us that the hospital folk say she's making wonderful progress. They hope that she'll be able to do without her crutches by this time next year, and just need a stick for support. *And*," Dickie became very impressive, "they also say that by the time she is grown-up she ought to be absolutely all right! Isn't that better than any fortune?"

"Rather! Dick, what wizard news!" Jacynth exclaimed.

"And I've something else to tell you. Dad says that Cherry told him that she had made up her mind to come to school next term."

"I say! That's an advance!" Jacynth exclaimed.

"Yes; isn't it? You know, we had an awful time with her when we first knew the school was coming to the Big House. Dad said she and I must both go, of course. I was bucked, all right; but Cherry nearly had a fit at the bare idea. She just howled one night when Mother Carey was trying to coax her into it, and said if we tried to make her, she'd run away. She'd get a boat, and go off to America where we couldn't find her, and never come back again. Poor kid! She didn't mean to be naughty, but she's been so shy and queer ever since that beastly illness. Mother Carey nearly cried when she read what Dad had to say this morning. You can just imagine that we all feel pretty whoops-a-daisy over it!"

Annis had listened to this in silence. Now she spoke. "I'm glad about Cherry," she said abruptly. "She's had a rotten deal, poor kid!"

Dickie gave her a glance. "Yes; it's been tough luck on Cherry," she agreed. "Give that starboard rope a pull, Jacynth, will you? We're getting a bit too far out. All the same, Annis, though it's been hard for her, in some ways I think it's been worse for Mother Carey. I mean," as the others exclaimed at this, "Cherry's had to bear it for herself; but Mother Carey had to bear it for Cherry. I think that's worse. You can stand your own troubles by yourself if you dig your toes in and keep your chin up; but it's awfully sticky for the people who care anything for you. You can understand that."

The others murmured that they could; but Annis was silent. She had no one to care for. Dickie saw it, and her eyes widened. However, she said nothing about it. They were nearing the island, and she gave her attention to bringing the boat round and running her alongside the tiny quay where two more Brothers awaited them, ready to help. They were quickly there, and while the men steadied the boat, the girls climbed out, and jumped ashore. Then Dickie, guided by one of the Brothers, moved her dinghy round to the other side where there were rings driven into the stonework. After tying up *Silver Wings*, she joined the others. They waited by the quay until the other boats had all arrived, and, led by the Superior who had now joined them, and the two Heads, set off to visit the chapel, and the gardens. After that, they rambled about the island, admiring the potato field, the goats, some of them with adorable little kids at heel, and the beautiful collie which guarded them. They had tea with mugfuls of rich goats' milk which some of them tasted rather dubiously, though most of them drank it without thought. Finally, all those who wished went to the chapel to join in Benediction before they piled into the boats once more, and pulled back to St. Briavel's. Dickie unloaded her cargo, then left them with a wave of the hand to row round to the little beach below Wistaria House.

Bride and Rosalie had kept with Annis most of the time, and Bride was inclined to think that the girl had got over her upset, whatever it had been. Anyhow, the Eleven had come back, bathed in glory, having beaten their opponents by an innings and two runs. Bride let everything else go, and joined in the rejoicing at such a magnificent victory. But that night, as she lay, wakeful, in bed, Annis thought hard about what Dickie had said of Cherry's distress over coming to school.

"That might be a way out," she thought. "Well, I can't do anything yet. It must wait till the end of term. *Then*——"

She turned over for the last time, and fell asleep.

CHAPTER TWELVE

School Regatta

"Mary-Lou! Mary-Lou! Go to it, Mary-Lou!"

"To-o-om! To-o-om! You're gaining! Keep it up!"

"Mary-Lou—Lower Thi-ird! Go it the Lower Third!"

The yells drifted across the quiet bay from the ferry decks, which were crowded with excited girls, and from some of the small boats floating lazily on the surface of the glassy waters. They came even from the Willoughby yacht where those of the Staff not otherwise engaged were clustered at the rail. With them were Mrs. Willoughby, mother of Blossom and Judy Willoughby who were members of the school, Joey Maynard, and her three closest friends, Frieda von Ahlen, Marie von un zu Wertheimer, come to England for a brief holiday from the wonderful old castle in Tirol where her home was, and Simone de Bersac who now lived in France. It had been decided to arrange a regatta for the end of term entertainment, and as many parents as could come had been accommodated with chairs along the ferry landing, while the school used its boats and the ferry which had been hired for the purpose. Luckily, the day had turned out a hot, still one. No breeze stirred, even on the water, and the people in the boats wore their big shady hats which, as Jo remarked, looked comic in the extreme when they were in swimming suits.

Jo turned to Mary-Lou's mother, Mrs. Trelawney, who was also on the *Sea Witch*. "Mary-Lou is a born sea-baby, Doris! Just look at her! Oh, I know she had a jolly good start; but her arms are going like little pistons. It won't surprise me if she wins this, though she *is* the youngest of them all! She's a grand little swimmer!"

Doris Trelawney, a slight, rather sad-looking woman, smiled. "I don't expect her to win. Tom Gay is overhauling her now, and Tom has the extra strength and length which ought to give her the race. Still, I don't mind owning to you, Jo, that I feel proud of her."

"I should jolly well hope you did!" Jo retorted. "I only wish that mine will be as good when they're her age." Then she leaned over the rail again to shout encouragement. "Go it, Mary-Lou! You're beating her! Keep it up! Hurrah—hurrah!"

To Mary-Lou, forging her way through the still water with almost every ounce in her, that encouraging call came as a stimulant. She could just see ahead the boats where the judges sat, though the rope drawn between them was beyond her sight. She had remembered what Clem Barnes had said to her just before the start, and was still moving well within herself. Was it time for the final spurt? She had no means of knowing. Then a well-known shriek from one of the boats near at hand warned her and she quickened her stroke, much to the surprise of Tom Gay who, starting from scratch, had been steadily overhauling this persistent Junior, and who had been expecting a comparatively easy win on the whole, since she had passed all the others.

In the boat, Clem, who had stood up to watch more easily, gave a wild skip of joy, and promptly overbalanced and fell in with a splash and a yell that outdid anything she had uttered so far. Mary-Lou, grimly determined to win that race or die in the attempt, paid no heed. Tom, less concentrated, glanced across, and lost a yard. That did it. With a final effort, Mary-Lou drove forward, to grab the rope a bare five seconds before the Senior, who had recovered herself almost at once, and put her back well into the last twenty yards.

Jack Maynard, seated well forward, leaned out, and flung an arm about the dripping little figure, drawing her up to the judges' boat. Mary-Lou's face was nearly purple; her eyes were half shut, and her breath was coming in great gasps, for that last spurt had taken everything out of her. But she had won! She knew it, even before the wild yells of the others told her, or "Uncle Jack", setting her down on the bottom of the boat so that she could sit leaning against him until she had got her breath back, said abruptly: "You've won! Sit there, and don't speak till I say so! Cherry, pass that water, please."

A swallow or two of water helped the victor to recover. By the time Miss Burn in her waiting boat had scooped up Tom Gay and the next three people who had kept it up to the end, Mary-Lou was breathing more easily and the stitch in her side was almost gone. Hilary Burn rowed over to claim her and congratulate her, amid the shouts of her boatload. She was handed over by Jack Maynard, who then sat down with a very rueful glance down at what had been spotless flannels when he went aboard that morning.

"That's the last race this morning," Commander Christy, who was one of the judges, said consolingly. "Just listen to those kids howling! I should think they must be heard all over Carnbach! I'll bet those birds of yours get a good old scare, Kester!"

Kester Bellever chuckled. "Won't hurt 'em. Well, we'd best pull in, now, I suppose. Mind out of the way, Cherry. Can't use any sails this weather." He sat down and took an oar as he spoke. Then, as the Commander hauled up the small anchor, coiling the light chain down neatly as he did so, the Bird Man, as the school now called him, added: "You know, I shouldn't be surprised if it didn't end in a mist. Days like this very often do. You ready, Tom? Oke! Here we go!" And he bent to the oar.

The school had all come in by the time the light dinghy had reached the ferry landing, and most of the guests had disappeared up the road to the Big House where they were to have lunch on the lawn. Only Joey and Mother Carey were there, Doris Trelawney having gone off with Mary-Lou.

Jo cast a horrified glance at her husband, and exclaimed: "Jack Maynard! I sent you out speckless, and just look at you now!"

"It was when he pulled Mary-Lou out, Mrs. Maynard!" Cherry burst in, eager to defend this new friend. "She sat against him till she got her breath, and she made him all wet. He couldn't help it."

Jo chuckled. "I suppose not. All the same, you've got the boat-racing to judge this afternoon, and for a judge, I must say you look simply awful! What are you going to do about it?"

"Borrow some of my things," Commander Christy told them. "Look here, Mrs. Maynard, you and Carey take Bellever and go on to the Big House. I'll borrow that little runabout over there to take Jack along to our place, and give him something to change into. We'll follow after you."

"Okey-doke! That seems the best thing to do. Come on, Mrs. Christy, and Mr. Bellever. Where's your young Gaynor, by the way?" Jo stopped short. Gaynor had been with her mother during the swimming races, and now she was missing.

Mother Carey smiled. "Dickie went off with her. She was wild to be with the school. Tom, help Cherry into her chair, and we'll go up to the Big House. Mind you and Dr. Maynard aren't too late."

"I'll speak to Hilda and get her to put some of the best eats aside for you," Jo promised, as Cherry was helped into her chair, and Kester Bellever took the handles. "Jack, wasn't it great Mary-Lou beating even Tom Gay like that?"

"Ye-es; but I hope she'll be kept quiet for the rest of the day. Her heart was going like a trip-hammer when I picked her up. I don't think I approve of kids like that competing in open races. However, she's a sturdy youngster, so I don't suppose it'll do her any harm if she isn't allowed to rush about this afternoon, and goes to bed early to-night."

"It's early bed for the whole school—Nell Wilson told me so," Joey called over her shoulder, as she and Mrs. Christy set out on either side of the chair. "She's staying with Doris this afternoon, so she won't have much chance to go ramping around."

The last words floated over the hedge as the three turned a curve in the road.

Twenty minutes later, Dr. Maynard and Commander Christy strolled on to the lawn where big trestle tables had been set up, and where a mixed company, waited on by those girls who were neither swimming nor rowing in the races, were having lunch. Jo waved, and they came to find that seats had been kept for them. Frances Coleman hurried off, to return with two plates of chicken and salad,

147

while Joan Wentworth filled their glasses with lemon squash.

"Where are the kids feeding?" Jack asked, when he had cleared his plate.

"In the dining-room, of course," Jo replied. "You didn't expect to have your daughters dancing round you when you're a judge at a regatta, did you? Anyhow, they're coming home on Tuesday, so you'll see plenty of them then. Finished? Here comes Frances with your fruit salad. When do the boat races begin?"

"Not till half-past two," Miss Annersley replied, from her seat at the other side of the table. "The girls will go up to their dormitories as soon as they've finished, and lie down for half an hour. Then those who are not racing may join their parents—or such of them as *have* parents here; and the rest will be in the boats or on the ferry. Have some more fruit salad, Mr. Bellever?" She signed to Joan, and the talk changed to another subject.

When the meal was over, people sat about in groups and talked. Jo went off with some of the Staff, and Jack Maynard had a few words with the Heads, in which he stressed his opinion that the open race was too much for such small girls as Mary-Lou.

"Well, I was doubtful when she entered," Miss Wilson acknowledged, "but she's a good little swimmer, and she had a big lead to start with. Besides, if you really want to know, none of us expected her to keep up till the end as she did. I don't think it's hurt her. Matey grabbed her the first chance she had, and gave her a quick overhaul, and she says she seems all right. They'll go to bed at seven, and to-morrow's Sunday, so they'll have a very quiet day. If Mary-Lou seems at all overdone, Matey will keep her lying down most of the day in one of the hammocks. But it really was just at the last that she went all out. I was watching her carefully from the guard-boat, and I could see she was well within herself until then. Matey says the monkey told her that Clem Barras had warned her to go on quietly till she heard a yell from Clem herself, and then she was to spurt like mad—which she certainly did."

"All the same, I think you're right," Miss Annersley put

in. "Another year if we're still here, as we seem likely to be, no girl under fourteen shall enter for the open race."

Miss Wilson suddenly began to laugh.

"What's biting you, Nell?" the doctor demanded.

"Just Clem's little exploit. Did you see what happened? No; I suppose not. Well, when she saw the way Mary-Lou spurted, she was so excited, she began a war dance in the boat, and went clean over the side. That, by the way, is what gave Mary-Lou her advantage—or so Tom tells me. She says she herself heard the fuss and glanced across to see what was happening. She says she's glad Mary-Lou won, for she deserved to as she kept her head, and never bothered about anything but the race. Tom, I believe, is ready to kick herself for being so silly. As for Clem, she's heard any amount from the others about making an idiot of herself! Well, I can hear the girls coming down, so we'd better push off."

"O-kay. I'll take a look at Mary-Lou before we leave this evening. I don't suppose it's really hurt her, but we'll make sure." And with this, he departed to seek his fellow judges and make for the dinghy, which they had to row out to the big buoy to which it would be tied for the boat races.

The first race was the Junior single-oars, and was won after a hard tussle by Elfie Woodward. The Senior single-oar went to Annis, who had her own peculiar reasons for wanting to win. She started off at a great pace which she kept up the whole way, so that none of the others came anywhere near her, Kathie, who was second, being three lengths behind.

"Goodness, Annis!" Gay observed, after the race when they were congratulating her. "You went at it as if your life hung on it! No one had a chance with you! Jolly well rowed, my girl!"

Annis flushed at the praise. "I'm glad," she murmured.

"I should just think so," Kathie laughed. "If you go to a university when you've finished with school, I should think you'd be a gift from the gods to them—if they go in for rowing," she added.

"I don't think I'm going to a university," Annis said.

149

Then Tom and Bride came racing to slap her on the back, and chaff her about pitching in at her rowing for all she was worth. The prefects moved off in a body to watch the next race, which was Junior pair-oars, won by two excited people from Lower Fourth.

Senior pair-oars, which followed, was won by Kathie and Janet Scott, both Edinburgh girls. When they returned, they were greeted with a terrific hail of "Hooch ayes! — Scotland forever! " from the others. Gay, for no very clear reason, began to sing, "Wi' a Hundred Pipers"—a song that was hushed sternly by Miss Burn, who glared them into silence before she demanded freezingly: "Do you happen to remember that we have an *audience* to-day?"

After that came the inter-house races. Junior inter-house was, on the whole, a rather tame affair. The younger girls rowed pretty well, but it was plain from the first that St. Agnes' would win. They drew away at the start, and, pulling steadily, finished the course with the others paddling after them—"just like a string of ducklings! " Gay observed.

Senior inter-house was a very different affair. For one thing, the crews were very much more evenly matched. For another, the elder girls were, as crews, very much better together than the Junior crews had been; this made it a very open race. As Jo said after watching the first minute of the start, *any*one might win. Bride Bettany stroked the St. Thérèse boat, and she had profited by her lessons as she showed, for she set a steady stroke which her crew followed well. In St. Agnes', they had four girls who could all row before ever the boats had come to the school; and two others who had proved the best of the tyros. The result was not *quite* so good as St. Thérèse's, and Jo, watching from the *Sea Witch*, was moved to murmur to her next-door neighbour, Miss Denny: "All the crew rowed fast, but Stroke was fastest! "

"What in heaven's name are you talking about?" Miss Denny demanded.

Jo gave her an infectious grin. "Don't you know that quote? It comes from one of 'Ouida's' novels. She didn't know much about rowing, did she?"

"Evidently not. How on earth did you come to read any of those outdated things?" Miss Denny returned, with a chuckle.

"I didn't. It was a magazine article on 'Writer's Howlers'. It was all priceless; but I thought that quite the most priceless of the lot, and it stuck. I say," went on Jo, returning to the race, "St. Scholastika's are coming along very nicely, aren't they? If St. Thérèse's don't look out, they'll wipe their eyes completely! Audrey Simpson is setting a good steady stroke, and she's got her crew exactly where she wants them."

The St. Thérèse cox—one Wendy Robson—saw it, too, and she said a warning word to Bride, who nodded. "Tell 'em—to quicken!" she gasped.

Wendy nodded back, and then raised her shrill voice to warn the crew. "One—two—three—four—Bow, you're late. Oh, good!" The last word was a screech as Bow, who was Annis, settled grimly to the stroke.

It was an exciting race, for St. Scholastika's strove tooth and nail to gain on St. Thérèse, and the other two boats also did their best. But though the experts worked hard, they found their two beginners a heavy liability, for when Kathie tried to quicken, it was too much, and Primrose Day disgraced herself, eternally, to her own mind, by catching a magnificent crab and sprawling full length, completely dislocating the rowing of the others. This so alarmed the St. Clare crew, that though they continued with their first steady stroke, they made no effort to quicken, and were well among the also-rans, to quote Jo.

Finally, St. Thérèse, with a handsome effort, contrived to draw ahead, and just won by half a length; but it had been a near thing. The girls rested on their oars, breathless and crimson with their work. The audience clapped them vociferously when they managed to pull themselves sufficiently together to paddle slowly back to the ferry landing, where they were greeted with cheers and clapping.

The final race was a frankly funny one. The boats were all beached, and various pairs of girls appeared, carrying paddles, and lugging wash-tubs between them. The judges' boat, duly warned, came much closer in, and Miss Burn,

151

in her light pair-oar, rowed over to a big red buoy not far from the land, where she tied up, while the guard-boats formed round it in a big semi-circle, the base of which was the shore.

Jack Maynard rose with the speaking-trumpet he had been wielding with much joy during the day. "This is a tub race!" he bellowed through it. "When the pistol goes, each pair will launch their tub, climb in, and then paddle round the buoy, and back home. The first pair safely in will be the winners. Starter, please!"

The Starter was the doctor from the mainland. The mistresses had seen that the pairs, each swinging their tub between them by its handles, paddles set ready inside, toed a mark. They were all in swimming kit, and only good swimmers had been allowed to enter.

"Are you ready?" chanted the doctor. "Get ready!" Then, "Crash", came the shot, and the pairs floundered into the water, wading till they were up to their waists. Then the tubs were launched and the fun began.

The whole secret of climbing in without over-balancing the things is for both rowers to be exactly opposite, and to get in at the same moment, so that the tubs trim. The audience joyfully watched the girls struggling wildly to keep those tubs erect and get into them, time and again failing, so that tubs and girls were well ducked, while the island rang with shouts of laughter. Jo leaned up against Miss Denny weakly, and mopped her streaming eyes, while Miss Denny moaned between her bursts of laughter, "Oh my side."

"Ow! I'm aching!" sobbed Jo. Then she doubled up again as Nancy Canton, with a wildly contorted movement, contrived to get into the tub, and plump down on her knees, throwing her weight over to her side to make it balance. Gay Lambert, vainly attempting to imitate her, hung on to the side when she lost her footing, and swung the tub under, spilling the shrieking Nancy with a terrific splash into the sea. Then Janet Scott and Ursula Nicholls tried a different method. Each, holding one handle of the tub—opposite handles—made a long leg, and got one foot firmly in it. But then came the attempt to raise the other leg without capsizing the thing. They hopped about for a moment or so, hanging on to the tub. Then they suddenly leapt, landed in, and banged their heads together! At this point, Jo hooked a nearby deck-chair and collapsed into it, moaning feebly.

At long last, Leslie Pitt and Molly MacNab contrived to get into theirs and set to work with their paddles to urge the thing across the smooth water. Unfortunately, they had got in facing each other, and as one drove her paddle one way, the other did the same thing in the opposite direction. The tub bobbed uneasily round and round, and the two paddlers fought to get it to move on in vain. Then Daphne Russell and Peggy Bettany did manage to get under way, and paddle off, looking almost unbearably smug. Pride went before a fall, however. *Some* one made an unwary movement, and one side of the tub dipped under, tossing Peggy out. Daphne was left screaming wildly as the tub righted itself, while Peggy, coming to the surface, cleared her eyes hurriedly, looked round for her paddle, and saw it gaily disporting itself half a dozen yards away. She swam after it, and then turned to the tub; but if it was difficult to climb in before, it was much harder now. She was up to her shoulders in water, and how she was to get over the side without upsetting the thing again was more than she could see.

Two or three more tubs with their crews were paddled past them as Peggy consulted with Daphne as to how they were to manage. Not that any of these even reached the buoy without incident; something generally happened to send *one* side under. Julie Lucy and Margaret Benn crowned everything, for when their tub lurched to one side, spilling Margaret, Julie, with a terrified yell, flung all her weight against the other, with the very natural result of driving it under the water in its turn. She followed Margaret into the sea, and the tub, having gained a little impetus, floated merrily off, so that they had to swim after it.

It was good fun, and there was no danger, for the girls were all good swimmers, and the water was nowhere deeper than their shoulders. Finally Leslie and Molly contrived,

153

in some way that even they could not explain later on, to sit side by side, and paddle very warily. Counting aloud at the tops of their voices to keep their strokes even, they went round the buoy, where Miss Burn was whooping almost hysterically in her boat, certainly not troubling to keep an eye on the paddlers. At last they reached the landing-stage again, where they bumped into one of the posts, and reached land ignominiously on all fours. However, as none of the others got anywhere near them, they were judged the winners, and an audience that was gurgling, mopping its faces, and holding its sides hurriedly brought itself to order for the giving of the prizes.

This was done on the landing-stage so that the villagers, who had all been delighted to lend their wash-tubs for the last event, might share in it. They could not have done so if the ceremony had been held at the Big House, where there would not have been room.

Clapping and cheering greeted the winners, and Mary-Lou, not a penny the worse for her gruelling race, received a special ovation when she went forward to take the big silver cup with its equally big stand already crowded with shields bearing the names of former winners. A fresh round had been added to the base, and a very new shield had been fastened on it, ready to be engraved with Mary-Lou's name.

Annis also got an ovation for her exploit, which made her cheeks glow, and her eyes sparkle. Only Dickie Christy saw the light fade out as she returned to her place among the other girls, and wondered what it meant.

Leslie and Molly were greeted with shouts when they marched up to receive the big boxes of chocolates which they had won, and a small silvery voice was raised to say, with stunning distinctness: "Good old crabs!"

Clem Barras hushed the voice's owner with a shocked: "Verity-Ann Carey! You be quiet! You couldn't have done it yourself, I'll bet!" but by that time the audience had collapsed once more.

Finally, the Staff brought the hilarious proceedings to an end by striking up 'God save the King'. It was properly in keeping with the riot which had preceded it that Miss

Cochrane pitched it two tones too high, so that some people were squeaking, while the majority descended abruptly to a deep growl half-way through. All in all, it was about the funniest Summer Term entertainment that even Jo Maynard, that veteran of the Chalet School, could remember.

The ferry now resumed its proper function, and finally fussed off, laden with visitors, who kept breaking into giggles as they recalled various extra funny events. The school was marched up to the Big House where supper awaited it, and after supper came Prayers, then bed for everyone under sixteen. For once, no one made any objection. Between the hard work they had done, and their hurricane of laughter over the tub race, everyone was tired out. Matey, going the rounds an hour later, found the dormitories full of girls so soundly asleep, that even when she accidentally let one door bang, not one of them stirred. The Seniors followed shortly after. Last of all, the aching and weary Staff climbed the stairs. By ten o'clock all the lights were out, even in the room of Miss Wilson, who was famed for being a late bird, and the Big House was sunk in sleep.

CHAPTER THIRTEEN

Lonesome Adventure

"WHAT a funny, still night it is!" The watcher at the window gave a little shiver. Then she turned away, and moving very cautiously, began to dress. She rejected her gingham frock, and pulled on her slacks and a short-sleeved woollen jumper. She had a small attaché case laid on the bed, and she rolled her frock up tightly, and tucked it in with a pair of stockings, her comb, toothbrush and paste, and a cake of soap. Some handkerchiefs followed; then she stood looking round irresolutely. A sob suddenly rose in her throat, and she dashed the back of her hand across her eyes. Then she turned back to her drawers, added her purse and a packet of chocolate to the contents of the case, and snapped it shut. The noise the catches made startled her, and she stood stock still, listening anxiously. There was no other sound, however, but the regular breathing of the others in the room, and an occasional cry from Bride Bettany, who was given to talking in her sleep.

Annis gave a soft sigh of relief, and turned to the task of closing her drawers as noiselessly as possible. That done, she glanced round again. Now that it had come to the point, she felt a sudden passionate love for her little curtained cubicle. She very nearly gave up her idea, pushed the case under a chair, undressed, and returned to the bed she had made so neatly. But if she did that, then she must make up her mind to remain a kind of pensioner on Aunt Margaret's grudging bounty, and that was more than her pride would allow. She set her lips firmly, picked up a big woollen scarf lying on the bed, and tied the case over her shoulders. Then she went to the open window again, and looked out.

It was a very still night, and the sky was overcast. Not a star, not a glimmer of moonlight was to be seen; but it was light enough for all that, with a curious, greyish light. Annis swung herself up on the window-sill, and swivelled round until she was sitting with her legs dangling outside. An old pear-tree grew under the window, and some of the branches swept up very close to the house. She stretched up and caught one. Then she swung out, for a moment, before she could get her feet on a lower bough. After that, it was easy enough to climb down, though some of the small, slowly-swelling pears were swept off by her passage down the tree. At last she reached the lowest branch, hung for a moment or two by her hands, then dropped to the thick soft grass beneath. For a minute or two she stood, breathing quickly, and recovering herself. She listened carefully, but heard nothing except the sudden hooting of an owl which made her jump and glance nervously over her shoulder. Then she turned, and keeping carefully in the shadows, tiptoed round the house to the back, where she struck off down a narrow path. It led through the orchard, where she crept from one to another of the little bush apple-trees which filled it. At length she reached the bottom, climbed over the little gate which was locked at night, and dropped down into the lane. Along this she ran, once slipping in a deep rut, and nearly falling. She turned her ankle slightly, but she set her teeth against the sharp pain that shot through it, and went on, limping a little.

At the head of the lane, she turned sharply left, and went down the path which led to the cliffs and Kittiwake Cove. The boats had been left there when they came home after a last picnic—mainly organised to get them out of the way for the afternoon—and the silly girl had decided to get across to the mainland, and then make for Liverpool. There she had some idea of offering her services as a nurse-maid for the voyage in return for her passage to America. Once in that country, she felt sure she would be able to find some way of keeping herself until she was of age. Then she meant to come back, face Aunt Margaret, repay her out of her savings, and be her own mistress for the future. It was almost as silly a scheme as even Cherry could have planned, but Annis was so absorbed in her own self-pity and misery that she never realised that it was most unlikely that any of it would come off. She simply felt that she must get away somehow, and this seemed to her the best way.

She arrived on the beach safely, and looked over the boats which had been left tied up to the rings in the little quay, since there was no likelihood of a storm that night. Annis was thankful for this. If they had been drawn up on the beach, she had no idea that she could hope to move one of them. That would be unnecessary now. She looked them over quickly, decided on St. Hild, slipped her case off her shoulders, and dropped it into the bottom of the boat. Then she bent her energies to untying the knot. It had to be done by feeling only, for the light was not sufficient for her to see; but it was quickly done, and Annis, sitting down on the centre seat, set her oars on the row-locks. She began to pull with a quiet, short stroke, till she was clear of the other boats, for she had no wish to foul them.

When at last she was clear, the falling tide carried her

157

out farther than she had intended. Her plan had been to row to the mainland, keeping well within the sweep of the Wreckers' Race, but the tide and her own lack of proper knowledge drove her almost directly on to its fringe, and before she knew where she was, she was being swept down by its irresistible force much farther towards the Bristol Channel than she had meant.

At first she did not realise this, though she was agreeably surprised at the headway she was making. Then it struck her that she was getting rather far out, and she essayed a stroke or two with the port oar to turn farther towards the land. To her horror, she found herself unable to do it. Further, a thin mist was creeping up, blotting out what light there had been, and wetting and chilling her through her clothes. Suddenly it flashed over her what had happened, and for a moment she almost panicked. Then pluckily she set herself to a grim struggle with the Race. She had no idea where it was likely to take her; but she did know that the cliffs along the coast were steep in parts, and the memory of the awe-inspiring cliffs of Brandon Mawr came back to her, filling her with an icy fear which urged her on with her fight.

She was burning hot, and wet with sweat as she fought, with so much concentration that she never saw how the mist was thickening. All at once she realised that she was walled about with white, moving walls where every sound was deadened, except the sound of the relentless water swirling her along with it. Still she attempted to give battle, but she was tiring quickly now, and her arms and shoulders were aching as they had never ached before.

Then catastrophe came! A great lump of wreckage hove up from nowhere, just as she dipped her oars in with dogged force, and the blow cracked the oar. The blade vanished, and she was left with only the stem and one good oar!

Annis nearly gave up then—nearly; but not quite. She knew that she must discontinue her struggle with the Race now. Sooner or later the boat must pile up somewhere, for she could not prevent it. If it was to be at the foot of a cliff like those of Brandon Mawr, or the western tip of St.

Briavel's, then she had no chance at all. But there was just a faint hope that there might be some uncovered rocks, and she could get on to them, and shout, and just *perhaps* someone might hear her and save her before the tide came up again. She had no knowledge of the tide save that it must be getting near the turn. If only the awful mist would lift so that she could *see*! But far from lifting, the mist seemed to be thickening. How could she know where the boat was going?

A sudden horrible thought came into her head—"Listen for the surf! Listen for the surf!"

Annis did lose her nerve then, for just one moment. Overcome by the ghastliness of it all, she uttered a bitter cry for help—help that seemed to be nowhere near at hand. There were only those gliding white walls, and the black, swiftly-running water which was hurrying the boat along —whither? She had no idea.

"But I can't die—I *can't* die yet!" she thought wildly. "I'm too young! I haven't *had* any life yet!" Letting go her useless single oar, she clasped her hands together so tightly that the nails dented the flesh, and prayed: "Oh, God, please help me! Please save me—somehow!" Then she glanced down, and found her oar gone. There was only the stump of the other, and she grabbed it fiercely. It was no use for rowing, but perhaps if she could avoid being crashed on the rocks she could swim for it.

Far away, she fancied she heard the mournful sound of a fog-horn, reaching her with muffled eeriness through the thick, clammy mists. If it was a fog-horn, then she must be either in the route of the steamers, or nearing some point on the mainland. Either way disaster might lie ahead of her. Freeing the stump from the rowlock, she knelt on one knee, ready to leap if the boat reached anywhere where she could find foothold, and waited, every sense strained almost to breaking-point.

Then she realised that the smooth passage of the boat was changing. She was beginning to heave a little, and— Annis strained her ears—yes; there was the sound of surf breaking on rock! So it was coming near! She got carefully to her feet, swaying to the heaving of the boat, which

159

seemed suddenly to be moving faster and faster. The sound of breaking waves came nearer, assuming to her terrified mind a positive roar. There came a bump, and the bow of the boat swerved. She seemed to be rubbing along a rocky ledge, for the terrified girl could feel the grazing. Annis put out a hand, and cried out, as it buried itself deep in a clump of seaweed which cut her fingers with its sharp edges as she went past in the boat. She could not hold it —it was much too slippery; but a faint hope came into her heart. With the stump of the oar, she prodded, and met rock. She must risk it. Gathering together every atom of strength she had left, Annis drew a long breath, and with an inarticulate prayer for help, sprang, to land on all fours on a rocky edge. The boat, freed of her weight, bobbed gaily off into the white curtain which was beginning to look brighter somehow. At the same moment, there rang out a sound that helped the girl to recover her sanity. A cock crowed shrilly from not very far off. The dawn was at hand!

Annis scrambled to her feet. She had not the faintest idea where she was, and, as long as the mist held, she felt it would be wiser to stay put. If the tide came up, she must risk moving, of course. The rock here was thick in sea-weed, and she knew that meant that at high tide it would be covered. But surely the mist could not last all that time. Day was near at hand, and it would clear with the coming of the sun. In the meantime, she was not very sure what to do. She was wet and cold now that her strenuous work at the oars was over. Her black hair was curling tightly over her head. Some of it had tumbled over her eyes—she had lost her slide somehow—and she could see the beads of mist hanging on it. She put up her hand, and pushed it back. Then she jumped, for her fingers were bleeding. She fumbled in the pockets of her slacks, and found a handker-chief which she contrived to tie round them with one hand and her teeth. It took a little time, and when it was done and she looked up, she gave a gasp of relief. The light was gleaming through the mists, and in a few minutes more it became clearer. She could see much farther back and she realised that she was on a reef. Seaweed lay before her and behind her, so those rocks would be covered at full tide if not sooner; but full tide was a few hours away. Meantime, she must try to scramble somewhere safer.

"And if ever I get safely out of this," she muttered to herself, "I'll go back to school, take my medicine, and make the best of Aunt Margaret until I'm of age. I will—as sure as my name's Annis Jane Lovell!"

She went farther back with due caution, prodding the rock in front of her with the stump of the oar which she still carried. The seaweed was very thick, and she had no wish to break anything by stepping off into a hole anywhere. However, beyond the usual little dips, there seemed to be no holes. Once or twice she slid on the slippery weed, and once she went down on her back; but she was up again in a moment, bruised and shaken, but otherwise none the worse, though the ankle she had turned in the lane was beginning to throb unpleasantly. And then she reached the farther end of the rock, and found herself up against the cliff wall.

The mists had thinned a little, but they still remained down, though the light was growing stronger. Annis peered up through them, and thought she could see a little ledge just above her head. If she could get up there, it would be something, anyhow. The question was how was she to do it?

Tucking her oar-stump between her knees, she felt the face of the cliff with her hands, and found that there were tiny niches here and there. She thought that with an effort she might contrive to get up by them. The first thing to do was to take off her plimsolls. She plumped down where she stood, still clutching her stump, and uttered a startled "Ow!" She had sat squarely into a shallow pool which was hidden by the seaweed. Well, it was a nuisance, but goodness knew she was damp enough already. A little more couldn't make so much difference to her. Anyhow, sea-water was said never to give you a cold. She untied her laces, knotted the shoes together, and slung them round her neck. The stump was the next difficulty. She did not want to leave it behind, but she could not see how she was to hold it and climb. It would take all her fingers

161

and toes to get her up to that ledge. She stood up, and
dabbled her swollen ankle in the pool into which she had
sat. The cold water eased the pain a little, and she considered what she had better do. The only thing she could
think of was to tuck the stump into her slacks at the back.
It would make it harder to climb, but she might be able
to manage that way. It took a little time to fix, but at
length it was done. Annis gave a little giggle as she thought
what she would look like to anyone who might see her
with the ragged end sticking out well above her head. Then
she turned to her task, the pain in her ankle subdued for
the moment.

Months later—next term, to be exact, someone said to
her: "How *did* you get up that cliff?" and Annis replied
truthfully: "I couldn't tell you if you offered me a fortune!
And I *know* I couldn't do it again!"

Clinging with toes and fingers, she slowly and painfully
hoisted herself inch by inch up the wall, which, mercifully,
sloped backwards slightly. Halfway up, she began to think
she could never do it. Her arms and shoulders ached vilely,
and as for the ankle, it was a red-hot torture. Then there
came a little 'Wop!', and glancing down, she could see,
faintly, a tiny froth of foam leaping up over the place
where she had been standing. The tide had turned, and
was coming in.

It gave her the needed spur. For the next few minutes,
she concentrated on getting to her ledge so fiercely that
even the pain was forgotten. At long last she was there.
Her fingers, stretching out, clutched a jut of rock which
gave her more purchase than she had had before. With a
final effort, she got one knee on to the shelf, and then to
bring the other up beside it was child's play after all she
had gone through. She sank down, panting with her
struggle, and lay where she had fallen for a good ten
minutes before she was able to sit up and take stock of her
surroundings. She realised at once that she was not safe,
even yet, for seaweed was here, too, though only scantily.
She guessed that the sea just washed this part, but she knew
that in her present state of weariness there was always the
risk that she might fall asleep, and then she might just as

well have waited down below. Her ankle was *awful*, but she must go on if it were possible.

Getting on to her knees, Annis lifted herself slowly to her feet, gripping that friendly jut of rock which had been her final help to the ledge, and hanging on to a big clump of seaweed nearby. Then she stared upward hopefully. The next moment, she gave a gasp of relief, for here hung a ladder—or *part* of a ladder, anyway. Rungs were missing here and there, and the chances were that it was rotten and quite unsafe; but at least it would be a help.

"It's pretty rusty, but I'm not fearfully heavy, thank goodness! " she said aloud. "If I can get up it, there's probably another ledge or something like that where I'll be safe for the present. It may even go right to the top. Now then, Annis my girl! Pull yourself together, and get cracking! If you stay here, you've had it—definitely! "

Whrissh! A larger wave than any other must have come and broken over the rocks below. Annis could not see it; but she had heard the sound of it breaking, and then dripping back into the sea. Again it acted as a spur and she stretched up, grasped the bottom rung with both hands, and heaved, wondering to herself if her weight would break the rung and she would be thrown down on to the rocks. She knew that if that happened, nothing could save her. The rung held, however, and she got one knee on it, and was able to stretch an arm to the next, raising herself till she was standing on the bottom rung. So far, so good!

Another crash from below warned her to waste as little time as possible. Seaweed clung here and there to the face of the cliff, and she could not count herself safe until she was well above that danger sign.

She mounted, slowly and painfully, till at last she was above any seaweed, and there was only the bare rock about her. Ordinarily she would never have dreamed of tackling such a ladder, for the missing rungs every here and there made horrid gaps and uncomfortable stretches which she found hard to tackle. But by this time her whole being was set on climbing as far up as she could. She ignored danger, weariness, and the torment of her damaged foot, and struggled on valiantly, till the end of the ladder came with a shelf which held a gay clump of sea-pinks on the edge. Annis knew she had done it, and she was safe at last, for the shelf was a couple of feet broad here, and looked as if it might be broader still if she could only follow it along the cliff. That was beyond her, however. She did get over the edge with a final effort; but then she dropped. The knowledge that she was safe ended her resistance to pain and aching limbs. In the reaction, Annis fainted.

How long she remained unconscious, she had no idea; but when she roused up at last, it was to find the mists about her vanished, though below her they still hung, close and mysterious, to the surface of the sea. A glorious sun was beating down on her, warming her comfortably, and her wet clothes were merely rather clammy now. For a minute or two she lay where she was, scarcely conscious of all that had happened. The realisation came, and very cautiously she sat up. At once a red-hot pain shot through her ankle, and she gave a wild cry. Luckily, she did not move much as she reached down and clutched the swollen leg. Even more luckily, once she was still, the pain subsided into a dull, steady ache which was at least bearable, and she was able to consider where she was, and how she was to go on.

Up above her was the grassy edge of the top of the cliff, cutting a clean line against a blue, cloudless sky. Below lay the mist, and from out of its veils she could hear the crash of waves breaking on rocks, and realised that the water was probably over her reef by this time. If she had still been there—thought stopped short at this, and Annis shuddered violently. She must have been swept off by the force of the water and drowned. She knew well enough that, good swimmer as she was, she could never have hoped to swim to safety in that rough sea.

Suddenly, another sound rang out—the musical "Honk —honk—honk!" of wild geese. Next moment, the blue of the sky was cut by a skein of beating wings, and she saw one of the loveliest things on earth—the flight of wild geese, with the sunshine turning their wings and bodies silvery as they flew out to sea to fish for their living.

Unbidden, the words of the Benedicite which they had

sung in church two days before came to her mind: "Oh, all ye works of the Lord, bless ye the Lord!" In a sudden rush of gratitude for her almost miraculous escape from death, Annis clasped her hands together as she squatted there, and said: "Oh, God—thank You! Thank You most awfully!"

That done, she turned her mind at once to the problem of how she was to finish her journey. She tried to get up, but the movement again sent that awful pain through her foot, and she screamed with the agony. For a minute she sat where she was, the tears pouring down her cheeks, sobbing aloud, so that she never heard footsteps above her until a man's voice exclaimed: "A kid *here*! Well, I'll be——" He stopped, as Annis lifted her head and stared upwards, showing him her white and grimy face, with the tears dripping down it, her mouth twisted with her efforts to stop sobbing.

Above her, his eyes looking ready to drop out, his mouth wide open in his amazement, was Kester Bellever!

"Then—have I got to Brandon Mawr?" she asked feebly.

"Brandon Mawr? Thank God, no! This is Vendell," he said. "You stay where you are. I'll be with you in two minutes."

He moved away as he spoke, and Annis lay back, still crying quietly, but now from relief that the worst was over. She felt sure that he would help her over the last bit somehow, and at least she was no longer *alone*. She realised that awful as it had been, by far the worst part had been the loneliness of it all. That was ended, anyhow. Then his shadow fell across her, and he was kneeling down beside her, raising her in his arms, and wiping her face with his handkerchief.

"You poor kid! How in heaven's name did you get here? What are you doing on Vendell at this hour, anyhow? Are you hurt anywhere?"

"My—my ankle!" It was all Annis could say for the moment.

He ran a big gentle hand over the poor ankle. "I see! A sprain or a twist, I think. Don't cry, kid. I'll get you to the hut—though goodness knows there's not much there. But I can lash up that ankle and that will relieve the pain. And I can brew you a cup of tea, and then you'll feel better. Now set your teeth a bit. I'll carry you to the hut, but I must fix this ankle first, or you'll be fainting on my hands when I lift you." He laid her gently down on the ground, and fumbled in his pockets. "Here you are—a strip of cotton. Lucky I generally carry some about with me in case of accidents. Now keep your chin up. This will hurt."

"I'm not a baby!" Annis retorted indignantly, though she still choked a little. "Carry on; I can stick it."

All the same, it took her all her time not to scream again when he tied up the ankle. He was gentle and quick, but just then Annis felt that if that foot were moved again, she would *die*! It was over after a minute or two that seemed eternal, and then he was raising her. He set her down almost at once.

"What on earth have you got down your back?" he gasped.

Annis gave a tearful giggle. "It's what's left of my oar. It broke, you know, and the other got swept away, so then I knew it was hopeless; I must just jump when I reached the rocks, and hope for the best. But I stuck to the oar in case I needed it."

"Well, you won't—not now. I'll get it out. There!" He drew the stump out, and laid it down. Annis grabbed it. "What's that for? Want it?"

"Yes; to remind me." But she said no more.

He gave her a look. She was nearer fainting than he liked, so he made no more bones about it, but lifted her in strong arms as if she had been no bigger than Cherry, and turned back the way he had come. Annis lay in his arms contentedly. His bandaging had relieved the worst of the pain and she could bear the nagging ache of her foot. She lay with her head against his shoulder, watching half dreamily as he carried her along the ledge which turned upwards in a gentle slope to the top of the cliff. Then he strode over the grass, going steadily downwards till at last a small stone cabin came into sight. He carried her into it, and laid her down on the wooden bunk which ran along

166

one side. Annis pulled at its covering, and looked at it for a moment.

"Patchwork quilt," she observed feebly. Then she really did faint.

CHAPTER FOURTEEN

On Vendell

"ANNIS! Are you waking up now?"

Annis turned her head lazily, and looked up into a pair of saucer-like dark-grey eyes set in a face that seemed vaguely familiar, though at first she could not place it. Then, as the drowsiness swept from her, she exclaimed, "Cherry Christy!"

To her surprise, Cherry made no attempt to answer her. Instead, she turned on her crutches, swung off to a door opposite the bed, and called out: "Uncle Kester! It's all right! She's awake, and she knows me! Come along with that broth!"

It was beyond Annis; but she felt so warm and comfortable, that she made no attempt to move or even to solve the puzzle. Instead, she snuggled down under the blankets that were tucked in from chin to toes, and sighed happily. She had an idea that she had been having dreadful dreams of wet mists and a terrible climb that went on and *on* and never seemed to come to an end. Somehow, she was in a strange place, but at present she was not properly awake, and she was content to let things drift. It was no shock to her when Cherry limped back to the bedside, followed by Mr. Bellever, who was carrying a bowl full of something that steamed, and smelt delicious. The smell woke Annis up to the fact that she was desperately hungry, and brought full consciousness. She began to sit up, but fell back again with a little gasp at the pain that shot through her foot when she tried to draw it up.

Mr. Bellever set his bowl down on a small table nearby, and came to her.

"Steady on," he said. "No need for you to move by yourself at all. I'll lift you." He bent and lifted her carefully into a sitting position, doubling a thick blanket behind her back as a support. Then he brought the broth which was in a wooden bowl, and held a spoonful to her lips, saying: "Put this where it'll do most good! "

Annis took it, and several more. When the bowl was empty, he set it aside, and offered her a handkerchief to wipe her mouth. That done, he sat down beside her, and pulled Cherry down on to his knees.

"Now," he said, "how do you feel?"

"Except for my silly foot, quite all right," Annis replied.

"No aches anywhere? No pains? Head all right?"

"I'm a bit stiff. I expect that's with the rowing—and the climbing! "

"Good! Then we'd better have some sort of explanation. I want to know how on earth you got here, first."

Annis went scarlet, and her long lashes drooped over her eyes. "I—I was—running away," she faltered at last, seeing that he was waiting for an answer and meant to have it.

"I rather guessed that. Now why on earth? I should have said from all young Dickie tells me that as schools go yours isn't too bad."

"Oh, it wasn't the school—or not exactly."

"Then what was it?"

"My Aunt Margaret?"

He gave her a quick look. Then he set Cherry down. "Cherry, you said you'd go and see if there were any eggs in the nests. Off you go and look. You shall hear Annis's story later on; but I want those eggs for supper. Get cracking! And ask Mr. Amberley to go with you."

Cherry made no demur. She picked up her crutches, and hopped out of the room, calling: "I'll hear it later, Annis."

Annis paid no heed to her. She looked up at Mr. Bellever. "*Supper!*" she exclaimed. "Why—whatever time is it now?"

He glanced at his watch. "Close on seven. You've slept all day, you know. Or since half-past six this morning, anyhow. You fainted when I got you here, Annis, and

168

when you came to, you just slid off into a deep sleep, and as it was the best thing you could do, we left you to have it out. You've slept for about twelve and a half hours without stirring, and I should think you needed it after all you must have gone through."

Annis gave a little shudder. Memory had come back while he was feeding her, and it seemed to her that much of what she *had* gone through was nearer a frightful nightmare than reality. He watched her closely.

"You'd better tell me the whole thing," he remarked. "If you don't, it may come back to haunt your dreams. If you can manage to tell me, the chances are you'll get clear of it. It doesn't do to bottle things up too much. Just give me the whole tale as far as you can, and I'll guarantee you a peaceful night's sleep, after which, apart from your foot, you ought to be all right again. Can you do it, Annis?"

She flushed. "I'll try. But, Mr. Bellever——"

"Well—what?" he asked; for she had stopped suddenly.

"What about school? I mean—they'll have found that a boat has gone. I never thought of it at the time; but I expect Miss Annersley and Miss Wilson will be nearly crackers, thinking I'm drowned."

He nodded. "That's all right. Like me to explain it before you begin? Very well, then. I had to give a talk on sea-birds for the Children's Hour at the B.B.C. I brought Cherry over to ask the proper questions; and, of course, they sent an engineer with us to rig up the doings, and see to the mechanics of it for us. That's Mr. Amberley. After I'd got you safely parked in bed, I broke in on an interval —I'll hear about it later from the Corporation, I expect! and broadcast the news that Annis Lovell, missing from her boarding-school, was safely on Vendell Island, and as soon as the mists lifted, I would return her. Someone would be sure to hear it and relay it to the school—after all, it's the only boarding-school near at hand—so I'm certain they know all about it, and aren't worrying over your whereabouts since twelve o'clock. It was the only thing we could do, seeing there's no means of communication here, either with St. Briavel's or the mainland."

Annis heaved a sigh of relief. "Thank goodness! It

169

never dawned on me at the time; but since I woke up I've been worrying about it."

"Yes; so I should imagine. It would be the only thing you could do if you were any way decent. Well, now for your story, since that matter's settled. Why did you run away?"

Annis told him. He made no comment as she proceeded, but his lips tightened when he heard even the watered-down version of Mrs. Bain's letter which she gave him. Then she told how she had felt that it was impossible to go on being a pensioner on someone's begrudged bounty like that, so she had decided to run away. Something she had heard gave her the idea of rowing across to the mainland, and she had meant to go to America and try to get a job there.

"Cherry! " he said unexpectedly, as she paused.

Annis jumped. "How do you mean?"

"That was Cherry's idea when they tried to make her go to the school. It was just a small kid's idea, of course, and she didn't think what might happen after, poor bairn! You, being older, did."

Annis's cheeks burned. "I—I suppose you think I ought to have had more sense?" she said, in a very small voice.

He frowned judicially. "I can see your point of view. It was a—well, let's say a *young* thing to try to do. Still, after that letter, I expect you were too mad to think straight. It happens to most of us once or twice in our lives. Well—so you got out of the window at midnight? What happened next?"

Annis swallowed rather painfully, but she went on, helped by occasional questions from him. By the time Cherry returned with five eggs and an air of great triumph, he knew the whole tale. Mr. Amberley was with her, a dark, stocky young man, who spoke little, though he looked kindly at the castaway, and hoped—between grunts —that she was feeling O.K. now. Kester Bellever made no further comments on what Annis told him. He took the eggs, told Cherry to wash her hands and then come to sit with Annis until supper was ready, and removed himself and his inarticulate friend to the outer room, where he gave

Mr. Amberley the gist of Annis's story. Mr. Amberley waited till the end. Then he said explosively: "Brute of a woman! I'd like to wring her neck for her!"

"Or else set *her* to climbing that cliff with a rising tide behind her," Mr. Bellever amended. "She needs a stiff lesson."

When Cherry came, she found Annis admiring the patchwork quilt on which she had remarked when she was first laid down on it. Cherry, under orders from Kester Bellever not to worry Annis with questions about her adventures until the morrow, sat down on the chair, and beamed at the girl in the bed—or rather bunk.

"You've not to talk about what you've been doing," she began. "Anyhow, not till to-morrow. You'll tell me then, won't you?"

"Some of it, perhaps," Annis replied, with a tiny shudder. She felt a great deal better for having unburdened herself to Kester Bellever, but it would be long enough before she could bear to talk much about it to anyone else.

Cherry saw her whiten, and decided to obey orders. "Do you know what?" she said importantly. "We've been broadcasting for the Children's Hour. I had to call Mr. Bellever Uncle Kester, and he says I can always, and so can Dickie and Gaynor if they like. I had to ask him questions about the birds—they were all typed out for me, you know—and he answered them. They were things like, 'Where do wild geese build their nests?' and 'How many eggs does the goose lay at a time?' and things like that. I loved doing it. It really is fun."

"It must be," Annis agreed. She looked round. "Is this where I came first? I thought, somehow, there was a fireplace."

Cherry gave a chuckle. "Uncle Kester brought you, and laid you down in the outer room," she explained. "I was asleep in here, you see—it was fearfully early, of course. We crossed yesterday so that Mr. Amberley could—could arrange the things for the broadcast. I don't know how you call it properly, but you know what I mean. Then we had the broadcast, and when it was over, we all played Rummy till supper-time, and after that I went to be in here. Mr. Amberley had a camp-bed in the other room, but Uncle Kester went to the hide in the middle of the night—at least, it was about four o'clock. He wanted to watch the geese for some special reason or other. I wanted to go, too, but he wouldn't let me. He was up there when he heard you. He brought you back, so he'll have to do the watching to-night instead. He laid you on his own bunk—that's what they are; wooden bunks, fastened to the wall —and when I got up, he brought you in here. And 'cos you'd said something about the quilt, he brought it, too, so that you'd have something you knew when you woke up. This is really his bedroom, and the bunk in the outer room is a sofa or something. It's quite a small hut, you know. There's just this bunk in here, and the chair and the table, and a mirror hanging on *that* wall with a shelf below for things. There's more in the other room—a big table, and two or three stools, and an oil stove so that he can cook a meal when he's over here. And there's a big dresser-thing, too, with plates and the wooden bowls, and the lamps stand there as well."

"It sounds awfully interesting," Annis said languidly. She was still tired, and only half listening to Cherry's chatter.

"What have you done to your foot?" the younger girl asked.

"Twisted my ankle in a rut. It doesn't really hurt—not much. Anyhow, it doesn't hurt so long as I keep still." Annis turned and looked at Cherry. "And that's the worst of it. I do feel so restless! "

"Uncle Kester will move you when he comes back," said Cherry soothingly. "Or shall I ask Mr. Amberley to come and do it?"

Annis shook her head. "No; I can wait."

"You aren't hurt anywhere else, are you?" the small nurse asked.

Annis laughed forlornly. "If you really want to know, Cherry, I feel just as if someone had taken a stick and hit me all over with it. I'm stiff, of course. And I did get a knock or two when I——"

"Hush! " said Cherry imperatively. "Uncle Kester said

you weren't to talk about it any more to-night, and what he says jolly well has to go! I say! D'you know what you've got on for a nighty?"

So far, her attire had not bothered Annis much. She realised that she was wearing some kind of loose garment, but what it was, she had no idea. Cherry kindly told her. "It's one of Uncle Kester's shirts. He keeps two spare ones here in case of accidents, and it was all he could think of. He carried you in here, and pulled the shirt over your head, and then I pulled off your other clothes before he tucked you up in the blankets. He hasn't any sheets, you know."

Annis laughed. "Blankets are jolly cosy and warm."

The door opened, and Kester Bellever came in with two plates heaped with scrambled eggs. "Here you are," he said, planking them down on the table. "We're just going to get ours, too. I'll bring you some cocoa and bread and butter. When you've finished, Cherry, you must get off to bed. It's eight o'clock now."

"But where will Cherry sleep?" Annis cried, suddenly realising that she had Cherry's bed, and the bunk was very narrow.

He gave her a humorous twinkle. "What's the matter with lying heads and tails? You couldn't lie side by side, but we could pack you in like sardines all right. You'll have to keep your feet still, though; I don't suppose either of you would like a mouthful of toes through the night!"

"Ooh! Scrummy!" Cherry gave a gurgle. "I won't hurt you, Annis, 'cos I don't wear my irons in bed. Uncle Kester, could you lift Annis a bit? It hurts her to move herself."

He nodded. "Just wait till I bring the rest of your eats, and then we'll see to it," he said, vanishing again to re-appear with a plate of bread and butter in one hand, a jug of cocoa in the other, and two mugs dangling from his fingers. Knives and forks came from his pockets, and then he lifted Annis to a sitting position, and left the girls to get on with their meal while he and Mr. Amberley disposed of theirs in the outer room.

When it was over, he carried the dishes off to wash them,

and Cherry slowly undressed and pulled on her nightgown. She was ready to be lifted into her place in the bunk when he tapped again. Then he lowered Annis to a comfortable position, and left them to go to sleep, while he and his friend smoked a silent pipe outside before turning in. He glanced in at the girls before that, and found them both sound asleep, and Annis recovering her normal colour. Apart from the foot and some stiffness, she had evidently taken no physical harm. He expected that having got her to tell him the whole story almost at once, the experience would have done no harm to her mind either. No doubt if she had a nightmare at some later date it might return vaguely; but he didn't think it would haunt her as it very well might have done.

Annis and Cherry slept through the night quite peacefully. Indeed, they never woke up until Mr. Bellever came to the door of their room, calling to them that it was eight o'clock, and high time for breakfast. Annis sat up with a jerk, while Cherry rolled over, rubbing her eyes, and gazing sleepily round her.

"It's a grand morning," their host said. "The mist's gone at last. Here are your clothes, Annis. I've dried 'em, but I couldn't do anything else about 'em. However, you'll be able to get into fresh ones as soon as you're back at school. How's the foot this morning?"

"It aches a bit; not much," Annis said, moving it cautiously. "I can get about though, I think. I can hop all right."

"O-kay! Then suppose you get up, you two, and dress, while Amberley and I see about breakfast? I'll rebandage your ankle properly after that, Annis, and then I expect it'll be fairly comfortable." He vanished, to reappear with an enamelled bowl and a big jug of water. "There's your washing kit. Cherry has soap and a towel, and you'll have to share. Your mother told me to remind you to wash the back of your neck and your ears, Cherry!"

With this, he departed, leaving Cherry wildly indignant. The two girls got out of bed carefully, Cherry because this had become a habit, and Annis because, though her ankle was much better after the rest, it still ached, and sudden

174

movements gave her twinges that were sharp reminders that it was damaged. By the time they were dressed, and had gone into the outer room, four bowls of porridge were smoking on the big table. There were four mugs of coffee, and a platterful of oatcakes. Everyone was hungry, and they cleared the board. Then the blankets had to be folded and stored in a big chest lined with zinc against the damp. The odds and ends of food were scattered outside, where watchful birds swooped on them, and disposed of them in short order. Everything was reduced to shining cleanliness, while Mr. Amberley saw to the final fastening up of his cases. Finally they left the little stone house, Kester Bellever locking the stout door behind him.

"This way," he said, leading the way down a gentle slope by the side of a trickling stream that meandered down to spread itself among marshy ground at the foot of the hill. He had Annis leaning on one arm, and carried a basket on the other, while Cherry hopped on ahead on her crutches with Mr. Amberley. "It's easy going, so you won't find it too bad, Annis. Hang on to my arm firmly. I can take your weight all right."

"My ankle feels heaps better now you've tied it up so firmly," Annis said as she limped slowly down the path. "Is Vendell a bird sanctuary too, Mr. Bellever?"

"Yes; the geese like the marshy ground. Some day I'm hoping your Heads will bring you girls over to see all this," he said. "Then I can tell you more about it. At the moment, I'm rather anxious to return you both safely. Hi! Cherry! Turn off to the left! Never mind those flowers. You can come and get some another day."

"I wanted to take them back to Mummy," Cherry explained, as she and her escort turned left in obedience to the call.

"You shall come another day and pick all you want," he promised. "Come along, now."

At length they reached the shingle beach where, moored to a buoy close in, was a little white and gold motor-boat. Annis had been looking rather apprehensive as they neared the shore, but when she saw the boat, her face cleared.

Kester Bellever saw it—there was little that escaped his watchful eyes—and he nodded.

"I use the motor-boat because I'm bound to cross the Wreckers' Race somewhere when I go back to Brandon Mawr," he explained, as he rolled up his trousers, preparatory to picking up Cherry and carrying her to the boat. "We'll go by the back of Vendell to get to St. Briavel's, so you needn't worry. Now then, Cherry; *hup* you go!" And he swung her to his shoulder, and waded in with her. Then he came back for Annis; Mr. Amberley followed; and in less than twenty minutes the little vessel was chuff-chuffing importantly along, skirting what he called 'the back of Vendell'.

There were no high cliffs here, for Vendell sloped down steadily from the high cliff on the south-west to the salt marshes where the geese had a colony on the landward side. Annis was thankful to be spared any sight of the scene of her struggles the day before. It would be a long time before she could look at any cliffs with pleasure. They rounded the point of the marshy shore, and then shot off across the bay to St. Briavel's, where they fetched up alongside the little quay that led to the ferry-landing just as the church clock chimed twelve. Mr. Bellever moored his little craft, lifted Cherry and her crutches to the quay, helped Annis out, and then followed them, leaving Mr. Amberley in the boat with his belongings. When the girls had been handed over, the latter was to be taken across to Carnbach to catch his train back to Cardiff.

There came the sound of a motor, and then the Christy runabout drew up at the end of the quay, driven by Commander Christy. His face brightened as he saw the trio on the quayside, and he hailed them with a shout.

"Hi, you people! Come along! I've got the car here to take you home." He left the car, slamming the door behind him, and came to join them. "Well, Cherry!" He bent to kiss her, and then turned to shamefaced Annis, who was standing a little to one side, not very sure what to do. "Annis, I'm not saying anything to you, child, except that I'm glad to see you safe. You'll hear all you want up at the Big House, I know."

Annis's head couldn't go lower, nor her cheeks grow redder. She mumbled: "I'm most awfully sorry I did it."

"Well," he said, "that's about all you can do. I'm only going to say this, Annis—and it applies to you, too, Cherry. In future, never shirk your fences, no matter how high or how difficult they may seem. Face up to them, and you'll generally find they're a lot easier than you thought. Now come along, and I'll run you back. Bellever, you're coming too, aren't you? We'll hand Annis over, and then pick up Dickie who's waiting for us, and bring you back, as I know you have to make Carnbach for the train."

Annis gave a gasp. "Oh!" she exclaimed. "This is breaking-up day, and I'd forgotten all about the show!"

"What show?" Kester Bellever demanded, eyeing her as if he thought she had gone off her head. "What are you talking about?"

Cherry butted in. "I know! You were to give Miss Linton and Miss Burnett their wedding presents after Prayers this morning. Oh, Annis! You will have missed all the fun! What *mingy* luck!"

"*Missed* it? *Spoilt* it, you mean!" Annis wrung her hands. "Oh, what can I ever do? No one will forgive me for this!"

"Don't be such a little moke!" Commander Christy spoke sharply.

"They won't—they won't!" Annis wailed. "I've spoilt the whole show, and—oh, why didn't I *think*!"

"Probably because you're a good deal of an ass," he told her. "Anyhow, wailing about it isn't going to do any good. I don't suppose the others *will* be too pleased with you, but you've got to face that. Come on! Get into the car, and get ready to take your medicine. You've asked for it."

More nearly in tears than she had been during the best part of the whole adventure, Annis clambered into the car, helped by Kester Bellever, and subsided into a corner to think things over. They ran up the white road, turned into the drive with its walls of holly hedge, and so arrived at the door of the Big House, where Miss Annersley, hearing the humming of the motor, had come out to receive them.

Behind her were most of the Staff, including Matron, and at the sight, Annis shrank farther into her corner. Only now was she realising in full what she had done.

Miss Annersley swept forward, her face eager. "You've got her safe?" she asked. Then, as she saw the guilty-looking person huddled up at the back of the car, she came round and opened the door. "Annis! Oh, my dear girl, how thankful I am to see you again! Are you all right, child?"

Annis lifted incredulous eyes to her face. "You—you can't *mean* it!" she faltered.

Miss Annersley looked puzzled. "Can't mean what? Come along out and let us see for ourselves that you are all right!" She drew Annis from the car with a firm but gentle hand, and helped her down. "Oh, you *silly* child! Why couldn't you have come to one of us? But never mind that——"

Someone else burst into the little crowd standing by the car—someone at sight of whom Annis's bewilderment became complete. How in the name of all that was true did Joey Maynard happen to be here now?

"Have you told her?" demanded that lady excitedly. "Has anyone said anything yet? What have you said?"

"No one's said anything—*much*," Matron retorted, her very crispest self. "We all knew it was as much as our lives were worth when *you* were anywhere round. Suppose we go in instead of standing here, making shows of ourselves for all and sundry to see. Annis, when you've heard what Miss Annersley has to say, I'll have a look at you. Limping? What have you done to your foot?"

"It's only a simple twist," Kester Bellever explained, seeing that Annis stood there, turning from red to white, and opening and shutting her mouth rather like a stranded cod. "I tied it up, but I expect it will need your care, Matron."

"I see. Well—oh, here comes Dickie!" That young lady descended the stairs like a whirlwind. "Is that the way to come downstairs, may I ask?"

Dickie jumped, and looked as guilty as Annis. As Hilary Linton said later, Matron could make the most elderly person feel like a naughty small child when she looked a certain way, and there was a certain tone in her voice. Having reduced the sinner to a suitable state of confusion, Matron hustled them all into the house, down the hall, and into Miss Annersley's study, where Annis was put into a chair. Jo, kneeling beside her, took the chilly hands in her own warm ones, and said in the golden voice that was one of her greatest charms: "Annis, if anyone gave you just *one* wish, what would you wish for most?"

Annis was dumb. She had pictured herself arriving in deepest disgrace, being severely lectured, even, perhaps, told that she must leave the school; and whatever her intentions at the beginning of term, she knew now that she would hate such a thing to happen. To find herself welcomed almost with open arms was so overwhelming, that she could think of nothing to say.

"Come along!" Jo coaxed. "Tell us, Annis! What is your greatest wish?"

Annis swallowed. Then the words came. "To have Father back again."

Miss Annersley took a hand now. "I'll tell her, Jo. You're bewildering her with your exuberance. Annis dear, listen! News has come of your father and the men who were with him. They were found on a small island near Kerguelen Land. He is on his way home now, and may be expected here almost any time. Do you understand, dear?"

She might well ask! Annis looked positively dazed. She sat silent for a moment, staring at the Head. Then she said: "It's really *true*?"

"Absolutely true." It was Jo who spoke.

"Then—then Aunt Margaret—she won't need to do anything more for me? And I *needn't* be a teacher?"

"Oh, it's not such a bad thing to be," Miss Wilson assured her with a laugh. "But if you don't want to be, I don't see why you should. As for Mrs. Bain," her lips twisted in a curl, "I feel sure she will never again be asked to do anything more for you."

"Well," Matron said, "I think that's enough. She looks tired out, and no wonder after everything that's happened.

I'm taking her off to bed for the rest of the day. Come along, Annis, and don't keep me waiting."

Annis went meekly. She felt too stunned to do anything else. Jo waited until the door had shut behind them. Then she turned to the rest of the company.

"I should like," she said solemnly, "to be there when Captain Lovell sees that precious Mrs. Bain, and gives her his unbiased opinion of her doings. And I should like—oh, *how* I should like! —to be able to give her my own."

"I don't doubt you'd make her curl up like a caterpillar," Miss Wilson told her. "I imagine your language would do it, never to speak of what your opinion may be! However, it's not likely you'll get either wish. Now I for one have heaps to do before Mittagessen, so I'm going. Mr. Bellever, we all hope very much that you and Commander and Mrs. Christy will come over to-night and tell us what you know of the story. Most of us will be going off to-morrow, and even thoughts of their approaching nuptials won't put it out of the heads of Gillian and Mary, I know." She cast a teasing grin at the two blushing brides-to-be.

"We'll come," the Commander promised. "Now, I think, I'll collect what Matron has left of my graceless daughter, and we'll get home."

Kester Bellever faced Miss Annersley with his shy smile. "I see it's not necessary to ask you to be gentle with that poor kid," he said. "I'm glad the school's got such a Head."

Then he fled after Commander Christy, and a moment or two later, the car had turned and was going down the drive again, while the excited Staff tried to calm down and go to their packing. Jo went off to join her two small daughters and bring them in to wash in readiness for the journey home that afternoon.

CHAPTER FIFTEEN

Joey Tells the Story

IT was the first week in September. Summer holidays were coming to an end, and Len and Con Maynard were already talking mournfully about having to go back to school. Dickie Christy laughed at them, and told them that Cherry was looking forward to it, and Gaynor was worrying every day to be allowed to go too. The Maynards had been staying on the Cornish coast during August, and had broken their journey to Plas Gwyn in order to spend a week with the Christys.

When the invitation had come, Jo had laughed and demanded to know how they were all to be fitted into little Wistaria House. Jack informed her that the Christys had left there, renting it to an elderly couple, and taken possession of Llanywyn, which had been vacated by its former occupants when they went to join a married son in Rhodesia. Llanywyn, was a large house than Wistaria, and there was plenty of room for them all.

"So you'll be able to see the Christys and tell them the end of the Annis story in your own way," he wound up.

"Super!" Jo remarked cheerfully. "I liked little Mrs. Christy and I'm interested in Cherry. As for Dickie, she's earmarked for a prefectship this coming term, seeing that Gay and Jacynth and Co have all left. Oh dear! I wish we didn't live so far away! There are changes impending in the school, and I want to be there to share in them. It'll be the first time I haven't done so." Whereupon Jack chuckled and held his peace, while she continued: "And I do so hate having the girls away from me so soon. They're not much more than babies yet, and I'd have liked to keep them at home till they were fourteen, anyhow."

"We may be thankful," her husband told her, "that the school was able to get so good a place as the Big House. And I wouldn't begin moaning till I had something to

181

moan about if I were you. Wait and see what happens. You may be able to be there when term begins after all."

"What do you mean?"

He looked provoking. "Nothing—as yet. You'll have to wait till I really have something to tell you." And despite all her teasing, further than that he would not go.

Now they had arrived at the new home, and while Dickie had taken charge of the four elder children, Jo, escorted by Mother Carey, had carried Michael off upstairs, fed and washed him, and laid him on Gaynor's old cot which had been brought into her bedroom for the occasion.

"What a lovely lad he is!" Mother Carey murmured, as she bent over the big fellow who lay looking at them with opaquely sleepy eyes. "But he's not in the least like the others, Mrs. Maynard—he's so fair."

"He's like Margot, the missing Triplet," Jo explained, as she left him and went to the dressing-table to make herself tidy. "She's as fair as he is. And while I remember, I don't see how you can 'Mrs. Maynard' me for a whole week. Make it 'Jo', won't you?"

Mother Carey laughed. "I'd love it! And my name's Carey. It's Caroline really; but I've always been called 'Carey', and when I married again, Dickie promptly made 'Mother Carey' of it. Tom liked it, and so did I."

"Carey's a dear little name, and just fits you. Dickie was a clever girl. By the way, how much better Cherry looks! She's gone ahead since the first time I saw her—at that lecture of Kester Bellever's."

"Yes; she's progressing," Mother Carey agreed. "This boy is off now. If you're ready, shall we go downstairs?"

Jo laid down her comb and came to look at Michael, who was sound asleep. "Yes; I think he'll be safe for the next hour or two. Thank goodness he had no trouble with his last tooth! Jack says he thinks the worst is probably over now. But we've had a doing with him, poor little man! Still," she added, as they left the room and crossed the sunny landing, "it might have been worse. If it hadn't been for that, Jack would never have insisted that we went to a Guest-house for our holiday so that I should have a proper rest after a week of badly broken nights. Usually, you know, we go to a house the family shares between them on the Yorkshire moors. But that husband of mine wouldn't hear of it this year. So we went to a lovely place overlooking a little bay in Cornwall, where they took children without a murmur. Most places of that kind look askance at the mention of a family; but this nice place *caters* for families. They have a private beach where the kiddies play with such a nice girl in charge, and a children's dining-room where they feed apart from the grown-ups. For the first week or so, I did nothing but sleep —or not much. After that, I felt fit enough, and Michael has behaved beautifully, so it's been a glorious holiday, and I'm as well as ever I was."

"Where is it?" Mother Carey demanded. When she heard, she nodded. "I thought so! The proprietor married an old schoolfellow of mine. He was captain on one of the Union Castle liners, and she was a school matron. When he lost his leg owing to an accident, they decided to pool their savings in this Guest-house. I've stayed there with the children, and I know just how restful it is. Edith Browne told me that after the first two years, when they had a struggle, it paid hand over fist from every point of view. You couldn't have gone to a better place to rest."

"What's that?" Commander Christy asked, as he and Jack Maynard joined them at the door of the drawing-room. Then, when he heard, "Oh, rather! Penny Rest was certainly the place for a tired mother."

Dickie arrived with tea, and assurances that she would look after the children, and left the elders to settle down to a leisurely tea.

"You know," said Jo, as she received her second cup, "Penny Rest also granted a wish of mine."

"What was that?" asked her host curiously.

Jack laughed. "A most unregenerate wish," he declared. "I can't say I'm sorry it was granted, though. We had a good deal of quiet fun out of it."

"Tell!" his friend insisted.

"Jo can; it's her story really. Get cracking, Joey!"

Jo gulped down the rest of her tea, set the cup down, and smiled complacently. "O.K. You shall have it. Dickie
183

will see to the kids, and Michael should be good for another hour or so of peace. Well, Carey, you know about the awful fright everyone got over Annis Lovell last term when the little ass cleared off—thanks to that toad of a woman Mrs. Bain?"

Carey Christy nodded. "I should think I do! Poor Miss Wilson sounded nearly frantic when she rang Tom up at seven o'clock that morning to ask what he thought they could do. It was an awful position for them."

Jo looked serious for a moment. "The mist made it all so ghastly," she agreed. "I'd got to Carnbach the night before, meaning to cross over next morning—I was coming to school for the last day or two so as to be present when Gillian and Mary were given their wedding presents from the school. But there wasn't a chance of crossing all that day. I heard about Annis when I rang up the Big House to explain that we'd have to wait till the mist lifted. I felt somewhat sick myself, I don't mind telling you! Especially," she added, "when Nell Wilson told me about that *disgusting* letter of Mrs. Bain's which they'd come across when they were looking through Annis's things to see if they could get any clue as to where she was likely to go. I could have *scragged* the woman!"

"Do you know what Captain Lovell has done about it?" Carey asked.

"Do I *know*? My dear, I was in the thick of it all at Penny Rest!" Jo bubbled with excitement. "That's the story I have to tell you, so just sit back, and lend me your ears, and I'll—I'll give you a real earful!"

Commander Christy distributed cigarettes, and they all lit up. Then Jo began her tale.

"Going to Penny Rest was Jack's idea. He fixed it all up, and then calmly told me that we weren't going to the moors this summer, but to Cornwall, where he'd found a marvellous place that catered for tired-out mammas of families. I didn't argue about it. I really did feel like a wet rag. Michael's had an awful time ever since March with his teeth, and he'd ended up with a week of wailing nights and howling days, so that I was just all in by the time that wretched tooth came through.

"Well, it sounded all right to me, so I said: 'Any blessed thing you like. I'm too whacked to fuss.' But I *did* sit up when he proceeded to inform me that we were off next day. Bless you! He'd told Anna to do the packing, and sent the kids to Doris Trevellyan for the day, and taken me and Michael off in the car for a run into Wales, just so that I shouldn't interfere! Next day, he piled us all in, tied the boxes and cases to the carrier, and off we went. and arrived at Penny Rest about teatime. I hadn't been given a chance to say yea or nay!

"Well, the Brownes walked the family off, and I saw no more of them till bed-time when I went to hear their prayers. Michael was sleeping, and I was packed off to bed myself as soon as I'd had some tea."

"Not before time, either!" Jack broke in. "You were done to the wide, Jo, and if it hadn't been for my bright idea, you'd have spent last month with a sticky bout of illness, let me tell you. *I* saw which way you were heading, all right! Luckily, Penny Rest came in the nick of time."

Jo made a face at him. "Want a new hat, old boy? Your present affairs won't go anywhere near your head at this rate! Never mind him, you two. It isn't often the poor thing gets a brain waggle. When he does, he's all over himself about it. If he had a tail to wag, he'd wag it off! Which reminds me, I hope you don't mind our bringing Rufus with us? But I never stir without him now. He's getting so old, and we were separated at one time in our lives for so long, and he frets if we aren't with him."

"Rufus is more than welcome," her hostess said, with a glance out of the window at the big chestnut tree under which Dickie was presiding at tea with all the children, while old Rufus, Jo's adored St. Bernard, lay between Len and Con. "He's a beautiful fellow, and we all love dogs."

Jo sighed. "He's seventeen now, and that's a good age for a dog. But he's very well, and we take all the care we can of him."

"He's all right," Jack said. "You go on with your story, or we'll have the kids swarming round before you've finished."

"O.K. Well, they kept me more or less in bed for the
185

next day or two. The kids were allowed to come up at stated intervals—Jack had to get back to the San once he'd settled us in—and, as I said before, I just slept and slept. I don't think I've ever been so tired in my life! By the third day, I was feeling a little more alive, and I got up after lunch, and dressed, and went downstairs to sit in the garden.

"I had tea with the other visitors, and began to make acquaintances. Most of them were mothers of families like myself; but there was one lady—so called!—there, who seemed to be by herself. She wasn't what I'd call of the matey kind, and she took no notice of *me*. There were two or three other nice people I chummed up with, so I just didn't bother about her. I didn't even find out her name—wasn't interested.

"Then, one morning, when we were all reading our letters at breakfast, I happened to look up from a Canadian epistle from my sister, and saw that she was looking—well, rather as if someone had told her that the cat had eaten her pet canary and she couldn't get another because the canary breed had all died out!" Jo said graphically.

"Well?" Carey Christy demanded, for her guest had paused.

"Well—perhaps you've heard from someone that I'm considered the butter-in of the family? I couldn't see anyone looking like that without asking if there was anything I could do. My table was next to hers, so I leaned across to her and asked as kindly as I could: 'I say, I hope there's nothing wrong? Can I do anything to help?'

"You should have seen her face! She glared at me as if I was a—a—a wireworm of the most unpleasant kind," gabbled Jo. "Then she said icily, 'Thank you, there is nothing wrong, and I am in no need of help!' With that she screwed up her letter, pushed back her chair, and sailed out of the room, looking like an offended duchess. I was left to say: 'Squash for you, Joey, my girl! Why can't you mind your own business?' Not that it worried me in the least. Please don't think that. I went on with my brekker, *and* Madge's letter, quite happily. If she didn't *want* my help, she didn't have to have it!"

186

The other three chuckled. Then they looked eagerly at the story-teller. This was a good yarn. They had all guessed who the offended lady was, of course. What was coming next, the Christys wondered? Jack knew.

"After brekker, and when I'd seen the family," Jo continued, throwing away the cigarette, which had gone out, "I decided to answer Madge's letter, as she'd asked two or three questions that would be all the better for a prompt reply. Carey, you know the second lounge at Penny Rest? The one where they keep all the papers and magazines?"

Mrs. Christy nodded. "Yes; of course. What about it?"

"Well, do you chance to remember that there's a kind of alcove at one corner—just a little place with a chair and a writing-table under the window that makes the back of it? There's a curtain over it, so that you can be quite private if you like. I went there. The sun just blazes in in the morning, and I love the sun at any time. I'd better say, by the way," Jo interrupted herself, "that by the time I got there, it was well after ten, and the family had gone off to the shore. Most of the other visitors had gone too. I saw them through the window while I was re-reading Madge's letter. I thought I more or less had the place to myself, so I pulled the curtain over, and settled down to write, quite cheerfully.

"I must have been writing for about twenty minutes, when I suddenly heard a voice saying: 'Well, Margaret? I've come to have it out with you.'

"And *there*," Jo said dramatically, "was a nice situation for me if you like! A row in the making, and evidently the worst kind of row. Me, stuck in that silly alcove, with no chance of getting away unseen—the window doesn't open except for an odd pane or two, you may remember, Carey —or able to do much about it. *And* someone called 'Margaret' who was plainly going to get it in the neck!"

"Puzzle: What does A do?" Jack interjected, with a teasing grin at her.

"You hold your tongue! You weren't there, so you really know nothing about it, except what I've told you myself," his wife rebuked him. "But really, Carey, what *would* you have done?"

Carey looked puzzled. "It was a problem, wasn't it? I don't see what you *could* do but cover up your ears. If you'd burst in on them, the chances are it would have made things very much more awkward for everyone."

"Precisely! That's just what *I* thought, and just what I did, once I'd realised the situation. I dropped my pen, stuffed my ears with my fingers, and lay low, hoping that the row, whatever it might be, would be over in short order."

"And was it?" inquired Commander Christy, who had been listening with deep interest.

"*Was* it? I should think it jolly well *wasn't*!" retorted Jo, with emphasis. "Incidentally, neither of the two seemed to think there was the faintest chance of anyone but themselves being around. I stuffed my ears for all I was worth, but it didn't help much. *He* spoke in a quarter-deck voice; and she, when she was fully roused, went up in wild squeaks which got through most piercingly. I shouldn't like," she added, with an impish grin, "to be on the phone to that lady if she was in a tearing rage!"

Carey Christy burst into laughter, and for a moment the narrator was held up. But she soon went on.

"When I found that whatever I did I couldn't help hearing, I very nearly walked out on them. Then I heard something and—well," she smiled disarmingly at them, "it just made me forget that I'm supposed to be a lady. When we got Annis safely back at school, I *said* I'd like to hear what Captain Lovell had to say to her guardian. I also added that I'd like to tell her what I thought of her myself. Bill told me that it wasn't likely I'd get either wish. As it turned out, I got them both. What I heard was 'Margaret' saying, 'Have it out with me, Eric? I'm afraid I do not understand in the least. But I must say,' and this was where she squeaked, 'I consider Annis is the most ungrateful, ill-conditioned girl I have ever heard of! If you do your duty, you will punish her severely for her rudeness and ingratitude to me, and for running away as she did, and giving everyone concerned such a terribly anxious time. When I received Miss Annersley's wire, I was quite ill with worry. Personally, I considered it a pity that she is too old to be

188

whipped!'" Jo paused. Then she asked dramatically: "What would *you* have done in my place?"

"What you did," Carey Christy said promptly.

"Yes; well, I've never eavesdropped before in my life, but I did it then. I tell you, my ears positively *waggled*," Jo replied unashamedly. "I can't tell you everything that was said. I did keep my fingers in my ears, but between *his* roaring and *her* squeaking, I simply couldn't help myself —short of butting in on the scene. And I'd had enough of butting in where she was concerned at brekker. So I stayed put." Jo stopped short, and began to giggle. "In all my life I've never heard anyone give such an appalling ticking-off to anyone as Captain Lovell gave to Mrs. Bain. He told her that she wasn't fit to have charge of a *penguin*, let alone a sensitive girl like Annis. He said that when he had asked her to be Annis's guardian he had hoped that if it was necessary for her to act, she would treat the poor kid decently. He must have seen that lovely letter of hers, for he told her that any woman who could write like that to a girl who was still suffering from the shock of thinking her father dead wasn't fit to associate with decent people. And then the really uncomfortable part of it began, and I must say I wished to goodness I could either clear out, or else deafen myself adequately. By that time, of course, I'd realised I couldn't do the last thing, so I had to do the first. I don't know what I *looked* like, but I felt a lovely puce!"

"But I don't understand." Mrs. Christy looked bewildered. "If you'd heard so much, why should you suddenly appear on the scene then?"

Jo blushed. "Well, you see, he started in on money matters."

"Money matters? But I thought we all knew what had happened about them!" Jack Maynard exclaimed. "Nell Wilson told me about that letter, and I understood that Mrs. Bain's reason for treating Annis as she did about her school and so on was that Captain Lovell left a comparatively small amount, and it was decided to use what there was to give her a good education and training for some job or other. I didn't quarrel with that idea. It was the rotten way she told the kid."

"I know." Jo looked round them. "Look here; if I tell you three, you must swear you'll never repeat this to anyone. You see, Mrs. Bain hasn't a particularly large income of her own, and Captain Lovell had been sending her a hundred a year to help her out. Well, when she thought he was gone, that fiend of a woman produced some letter or other of his in which he had said that he would allow her that as long as she lived. His will, so far as I could understand it, put the money into her hands to spend or otherwise to the best advantage for Annis, and the first thing she did was to invest enough in her own name in an annuity to give her something even if it wasn't quite a hundred!"

"What?" Jack Maynard bounced up off his chair. "Didn't the silly idiot realise the risk she ran in doing a thing like that? Where was the lawyer that he allowed it? He ought to be struck off the Rolls!"

"I don't think he could prevent it. The money was entirely in her hands," Jo said. "But you can quite see that that was the point where I simply had to emerge—so I did!"

"What happened?" Carey Christy asked eagerly.

"Well, I went out, feeling an awful fool, and looking worse, I don't doubt," Jo explained. "They were standing with their backs to me, and were both so mad that if the alcove had only been near the door, I believe I could have slid out without their seeing me. But as it's at the far end of the room, that just wasn't possible. So I said, 'I beg your pardon, but I'm afraid I can't avoid hearing you, though I *have* tried. As you seem to be about to discuss a very private matter, I felt it best to let you know I was here. Captain Lovell, when you have finished your business with Mrs. Bain, I should like a word with you. I shall be on the terrace.' Then," finished Jo, "I simply swept through the room to the door; but he was after me. 'Who are you?' he asked. 'How do you know me?' 'Annis is a pupil of my sister's school,' I said. 'I know all about Annis and why she ran away, poor child, and I should like to discuss the matter with you when you are at liberty.' You would have *loved* to see me, Jack, I was so grand and duchessy! As for Mrs. Bain, she was literally green—oh, not because of me. I don't suppose I mattered. But because she had been well and truly found out. Anyhow, I departed, and left them to it. Later on, he came and joined me on the terrace, and explained a few things, including the will business. He also said that he'd heard of me from young Annis. He's rather nice, you know, and I quite see his point. He was off on these long voyages—sometimes he's been out of England for the best part of two years—and he had no other relation with whom to trust Annis. He evidently thought that his cousin would do her best for the girl because he'd tried to do his best for *her.* He certainly never imagined she would try to feather her nest at the kid's expense."

"That woman ought to be shown up!" said Commander Carey, who had listened in silence for the most part. "However, as she's a relation, I suppose he won't want to wash dirty linen in public, so she'll get away with it."

"I wouldn't know," Jo returned. "There's one thing I *do* know, though. Apparently, apart from this annuity business, there's a sum which was left to him to administer for her. After they thought he was dead, she tried to sell out whatever it was invested in to add it to the annuity. She couldn't do it, as when she and Captain Lovell die, it comes to Annis. One of her ideas had been to try to persuade him to let her have half outright. He won't agree, of course. What's more, he says he's made a new will now, and she can't touch a thing. So *that's* all right!"

"And how did you get your second wish?" Carey inquired.

"Oh—that!" Jo's eyes were pools of wicked laughter. "Well, you see, when he had gone, and I went back to finish my letter—I'd left my pen and everything else in the alcove in the excitement—she came to me. I suppose she wanted to try to make things look nicer for herself. Anyhow, she began a long rigmarole about how she'd only done what she had done because she'd felt sure her cousin wouldn't wish her to go without her little comforts. I cut right across it, and spent a most enjoyable three minutes in giving her my unvarnished opinion of her. I could have gone on quite a while longer, but she suddenly glared at me, burst into tears, and rushed from the room. I may add that she left Penny Rest within the hour. So that was that. Annis will finish her schooldays at the Chalet School, but she's spending any holidays when her father's away at sea with those friends of theirs—the Maples, aren't they? That's what she wanted more or less, so let's hope she settles down to ordinary school ways after this. Hello! Tea out there seems to be at an end, and the entire crowd is heading this way! Stand by to repel boarders—isn't that what you say, Commander Christy?—and then I must go up and take a dekko at young Michael."

The juvenile party, headed by long-legged Len, came tearing across the lawn, just as a yell from upstairs told them that Michael was wide awake, and felt he wanted to be the centre of admiration. Jo waved her hands at the throng, exclaimed: "I'll leave you three to deal with them!" and ran upstairs, like a schoolgirl herself, to console her youngest son.

"Just the same," she said later to Jack, "though it's been tough on Annis, I hope that all this will turn out for her good. She's learnt, anyhow, that doing mad things generally means very sticky consequences. As for her general behaviour, we can safely leave the School to settle that. I shouldn't wonder if later on she didn't become quite a credit to it—like me, for instance!"

"Oh, you!" he said, with affectionate scorn. "You think the school couldn't get on without you! You're a wife and a proud mamma, but in a good many ways, Jo, you're still nothing but a schoolgirl."

"You've missed out the chief part of it," she said. "I'm still, in part of me, what I shall always be—a Chalet School girl."

THE END